Critical acclaim for *The Family Markowitz*

"*THE FAMILY MARKOWITZ* has great consistency and charm."

—Claire Messud, *The New York Times Book Review*

"*THE FAMILY MARKOWITZ* sparkles with life. . . . With dazzling authority and copious amounts of wit and goodwill, Goodman tweaks the Markowitzes into life. She has a treasure in this fictional family. Let's hope she continues to mine it, because these are memorable characters—at times whiny and self-absorbed, at others goofy and endearing. In other words, they are bundles of contradictions, utterly human and familiar."

—Alicia Metcalf Miller, *The Plain Dealer* (Cleveland)

"A highly skillful collection of stories . . . wonderful, engrossing fiction. We're lucky Allegra Goodman is young; we get to read her for years and years to come."

—Bethany Schneider, *Elle*

"Poignant and funny."

—Eugenia Peretz, *Time Out New York*

"Goodman. . .leads a new generation of Jewish-American writers."

—Emily Benedek, *Harper's Bazaar*

"A bona fide wunderkind. . . .She has a keen eye and an ear for folly and writes always with intelligence. . . ."

—Mark Shechner, *The Buffalo News*

"Readers of *Total Immersion* knew that Allegra Goodman was a young writer to reckon with. *THE FAMILY MARKOWITZ* merely confirms this happy fact."

—Sanford Pinsker, *Hadassah Magazine*

"Rich, complicated humor. . . . Ms. Goodman is highly skilled in capturing the way, in small tugs and huge yanks, the Markowitzes pull on each other's strings, creating a hopelessly tangled web full of love and misunderstandings."

—Rachel Stoll, *Forward*

"Goodman's voice is fresh and distinctive as she limns a wry, funny, touching portrait of an American Jewish family in a brilliantly observed, lovingly rendered novel composed of interlocking stories."

—*Publishers Weekly*

"With wit, panache, and genuine affection for her characters, Goodman . . . offers a saga of an archetypal Jewish-American family."

—*Kirkus Reviews*

"Elegant writing and affectionate insight into the intertwined personalities. . . ."

—Stuart Schoffman, *The Jerusalem Report*

"Funny, charming and insightful."

—Donna Seaman, *Booklist*

"Goodman has mastered the art of melding pathos with humor in the best style of Jewish storytelling."

—Molly Abramowitz, *Library Journal*

"Goodman fulfills the promise of her debut with *THE FAMILY MARKOWITZ,* a smartly funny collection of interwoven stories. . . . She succeeds with straightforward mastery of the basics. She is a storyteller in the classic Jewish tradition . . . writing with an assured grace that would make many older writers envious. . . . Deeply insightful and accomplished. . . ."

—Michael Lowenthal, *Boston Phoenix Literary Section*

"I think I saw Rose Markowitz in line at Fairway."

—Sandee Brawarsky, *Jewish Week*

WINNER OF THE *SALON MAGAZINE*
1997 FIRST ANNUAL BOOK AWARD FOR FICTION

Praise for Allegra Goodman's *Total Immersion*

"Allegra Goodman is brilliant, funny, knowing, alive: A marvel. *All* the muse-fairies were present at her birth!"

—Cynthia Ozick

"Allegra Goodman is a remarkably gifted young writer, with a penchant for getting swiftly to the truth of things."

—Chaim Potok

"Allegra Goodman has observed as deeply as many writers can hope to do in a lifetime."

—Francine Prose

Also by Allegra Goodman

Total Immersion: Stories

The Family Markowitz

Allegra Goodman

WASHINGTON SQUARE PRESS
PUBLISHED BY POCKET BOOKS

New York London Toronto Sydney Singapore

A Washington Square Press Publication of
POCKET BOOKS, a division of Simon & Schuster, Inc.
1230 Avenue of the Americas, New York, NY 10020

Published by arrangement with Farrar Straus & Giroux, Inc.

ISBN: 0-671-01388-2

First Washington Square Press trade paperback printing October 1997

10 9 8 7

Cover design by Michael Kaye
Cover photo by Melissa Hayden

Printed in the U.S.A.

The author gratefully acknowledges *The New Yorker*, in whose pages "The Wedding of Henry Markowitz," "Mosquitoes," "Fantasy Rose," and "Sarah" first appeared, and *Commentary*, where "The Art Biz," "Oral History," "The Persians," "One Down," and "The Four Questions" first appeared.

For David

Contents

The Family Markowitz

Fannie Mae

"Esther," Rose calls through her neighbor's closed door, with its blistering paint and the new steel plate around the knob.

"Who is it?" Esther's muffled voice floats back.

"It's Rose."

"Who?"

"Rose Markowitz." The door opens, and they fall into each other's arms. "How are you dear?" Rose asks. "I thought I heard you last night on the stairs, but I couldn't leave him. Now the woman from the service is here. What business do you have taking a cab so late?"

"Come in, come in," Esther says. "My nephew met me."

"Who? Arthur?"

"Come in, Rose."

"No, I can't stay."

"Just for a minute. Let me get you some coffee. I've made it already."

"But I really can't stay," Rose says as she walks into Esther's apartment. "I was just going downstairs for the mail." They sit together at the kitchen table and sip coffee from Esther's china teacups. They have lived in the building for twelve years, and their apartments are mirror images of each other.

"I'm speaking Hebrew," Esther tells Rose. *"Ani midaberet ivrit."*

"You took those Hadassah classes?" Rose asks.

"I went on ulpan," Esther says, as if to say she went on safari. Rose thinks that anyone in the room would notice the contrast between Esther, full of energy after six weeks in Miami, and herself, wan and exhausted from staying here in the city all winter with Maury ill and no one to help. Having to do things when she didn't have the strength. Esther is tall, and big in hip and shoulder, her brown hair puffy, although thinning a little in the middle. Rose, who has always been petite, has lost weight—although she is still not thin. Her hair is short, once black and now iron gray. She no longer has time for herself or the beauty parlor. "And who do you think I met on the first day?" Esther asks. "Dr. Mednik's sister."

"He and I," says Rose, "are not on speaking terms."

"No, you are not," Esther agrees. "But it was strange to see the sister there. She looks nothing like him—it only came out later."

Rose stares at the place where Esther's oven should be, except that the apartment is a mirror image.

"And then right after, just a couple of days later, I went to the kids' hotel, where Dougie had his bankers' convention, and I was sitting by the pool and there out of the blue came Beatrice Schwartz with him; he's had surgery—he speaks artificially, you know, with a voice box—but she's still walking around with her fingernails out to here painted white, and the white slacks with the pleats, the knife-edge pleats. They weren't even the only people I saw. I could go on and on. It was just, you know, one small world after another. But I was worried about you, Rose."

"Well," says Rose, "he's very ill."

"But he's in good spirits?"

"Happy as a lark."

"I hope I have such a happy disposition at his age," Esther says. Rose's husband, Maury, is eighty-three, ten years older than Rose, fifteen years older than Esther.

"Now, on top of everything, today his daughter is coming."

"From Israel?"

"We haven't seen her in years, and now she decides to come."

"I can talk to her in Hebrew," Esther says.

"And she's staying with us," Rose tells Esther. "Here in the apartment."

"For how long?"

"She wouldn't say." Rose lowers her voice to a whisper. "She has an open ticket, and I think that she is determined to stay until, God forbid, the end."

Esther shakes her head.

"What else could she mean by coming now? She has never ever come before."

In the lobby, Rose pries the mail out of her small aluminum mailbox, number 5. There are bills, there are statements from the insurance, and there's a calendar from the Girls' Orphanage in Jerusalem, full of halftone pictures of the girls' laughing faces, their great big eyes and curly hair, their uniforms. She leafs through the calendar as she climbs the stairs. Rose loves the Girls' Orphanage and gives a little to them every year. She had always wanted to have a little girl of her own, but she and her first husband, Ben, had two sons. She would not have traded Henry and Edward, never. But she always wanted a little girl. She would have dressed her up in the summer in crisp white dresses with smocking; in the winter she would have sewn dresses with velvet sashes. There would have been tea parties and doll clothes; she would have trimmed doll hats. She has two granddaughters, it is true, but they are far away, almost too old for dolls, almost wild. Her eyesight is no longer good enough to sew small pieces. The Girls' Orphanage teaches sewing and the arts; the girls, it says on the calendar, "are instructed strictly according to the precepts of the Torah." Rose's small gifts support the schools, the woodworking shop and sewing classes, the dowry fund for brides—"to help them build a Jewish home."

When she walks into her own apartment she feels how stuffy it is; the air is so hot and close. On the sofa the woman from the service reads her magazines, and Maury is sleeping in his chair. His large-print library books are stacked at his feet, his plaid blanket spread over his knees as he dozes away. He is so sick he gets all the pills he wants. For Rose, Mednik won't prescribe a thing. She has come to him and begged for some relief from her pain. Nothing. The sun through the window warms Maury's upturned face, and he seems to be dreaming he is lounging on the deck of an ocean liner. How she would love to do that. To sail away with him out of Washington Heights over the slush and the ice and out onto the Hudson, and then across the Atlantic, far, far away. If he weren't ill. If they could leave the apartment. She bends over him and says, "Maury, I don't know what to do. Where are we going to put her? On the sofa in the study? Is that where she should sleep?"

Rose doesn't even know Maury's daughter, Dorothy. She's only met her once. Maury and his first wife divorced in 1950, when Dorothy was a child, and all she knows is that Dorothy lived here and she lived there and then ran away to Palestine. She simply grew up in greenhouses, raising tomatoes. She just grew and grew until she became a great lump of a woman, big and heavy, with thick, cropped black hair and down on her lip. Rose dreads having her in the house. He has been sick before and she's never come, but now Dorothy is visiting herself upon them. What will she do with her in the house? She will feel eyes on her all the time. She will have to cook for the angel of death. She cannot bear it. If Maury were well, it would be one thing. She would be happy to serve anyone at her table.

She and the woman wake him for his pills. They bring him lunch on a tray that clips onto his chair and try to get him to eat it. He pushes the food around on his plate. "Eat a few bites," Rose urges.

"I'll tell you what," he tells Rose in a light, dry voice; he weighs almost nothing. "You get this young lady to go down to 160th Street. I want a number 11 on light rye, extra lean, a side order of onion rings, and a cherry Coke."

"You aren't going to eat all that."

"I was going to share the onion rings with you," he says gallantly.

"But you aren't going to finish all that," Rose tells him. They send the young lady down to 160th Street all the time. Rose tells him the food is bad for his digestion, and he makes a face.

"What'll be?" he says. "Am I going to die from one corned beef and tongue on rye?"

"Don't talk that way," Rose snaps. She hates hearing him talk like that, because he is joking not only about his own condition but about her predicament, too.

He seems to be laughing at her, his eyes sparkling, magnified by the lenses of his glasses. "Aw, don't worry, kid," he tells her.

Dorothy is forty-five, and she sleeps and sleeps. She snores in the study on Rose's green silk nonconvertible sofa, her face against the bolster and all the antimacassars in a pile on the floor. She wears jogging suits but she never goes jogging, and in the mornings she uses up all the hot water in her shower. Emerging from the bathroom, she just shakes the water out of her cropped hair like a great black bear. Then, day in and day out, she sits and watches her father sleep, waits for him to wake up. The minute he wakes, she pounces, asking him questions. How is his heart, why this medication or that. She wants to know about the doctor. Then she starts asking him about his life. What he did in the union, how he did piecework, cutting the fabric. But it's all a ruse, as Rose can clearly see. As soon as Dorothy starts asking Maury about his life, she starts talking about her own. And then she starts in *schrei-ing* at him. "Father." She says it in deep voice—not just deep but lugubrious, and with an Israeli accent so dark and smoky you would have thought she was a native. "I have come here to be with you."

"What did she say?" Maury asks Rose.

"Because I am your only child," Dorothy continues, "and so I have come here to be with you, even though I never had the chance to know you. I have wanted to come and talk to you, so that you and I would know each other just once. I have wanted to tell you about my life, what I have done—"

"I can't hear you, dear," says Maury.

"What I have done," Dorothy tells him loudly.

"Yes, what have you done?" Maury asks.

"I have asked myself this question: What I have done to deserve this silence from you? You forgetting me, your daughter."

"Listen," Maury explains, "this was long ago. Needless to say, your mother and I were not on the best of terms. She threw me out. We had a divorce."

"But there was me also."

"So you went with her, too. Your mother said I wasn't fit to raise her child. All right, fine. I wasn't going to argue with the woman."

He is falling asleep; in his state, talking wears him out. Rose tries to shoo Dorothy away. Big, heavy tears fill Dorothy's eyes. It's horrible, as if, God forbid, Dorothy is starting up a funeral in the apartment. If she had come to bring some good cheer, it would be one thing. If she had come to help. But weeping and complaining is all she does. And she snoops, Rose is sure of it. She has heard her twice in the night, walking around the apartment. She thinks she heard her try to open the secretary where Rose keeps her Venetian glasses, the acorn tea set, the crystal she bought when she worked at Tiffany. At night she imagines she can hear her opening the glass doors. Then, during the day, she realizes it cannot be so, because Dorothy has no interest in the things in the secretary. Dorothy has probably never even heard of such a place as Tiffany, where Rose once stood behind the long glass counters and brushed with royalty in the form of the Duke of Windsor and his men browsing through the silver and the jewelry. Dorothy would not understand such things.

Then, early in the morning, Rose catches her. She walks into the study and finds Dorothy bending over, peering into the drawers of the desk. "That's Ben's desk," Rose exclaims. It is her dear late husband's desk. Maury has never used it. No one touches it. Its surface is clear, except for the R. C. Allen typewriter and the leather-trimmed blotter.

Dorothy looks back at Rose, mute.

"What are you looking at?" asks Rose.

"This," says Dorothy. She has opened a box of typewriter paper and is looking down into it.

"The Dissertation," Rose gasps. Quickly she puts the cover onto the box and shuts the drawer. Everyone in the family calls it The Dissertation. It is the thesis her dear husband Ben was writing when he was a doctoral student in Vienna in 1926. Of course, he could not finish it, because of the wars and the family, his immigration to America, and his job teaching high-school French and German. He taught all year, and in the summers he was a ghostwriter for a French textbook. The senior teacher at the school, his department head, was the official author, and Ben was the writer. He never breathed a word about it. He did not want to lose the job. Not in the middle of the Depression. No one in the family has read the dissertation; the children do not read German. Rose reads German well, but when she looks at the blue-black typescript it only makes her cry. And she does not care for works of history and literary criticism. The dissertation is a study of the works of Thomas Mann.

Rose is glaring at Dorothy; she does not tell her any of this. Dorothy just looks back at her, confused and baleful but unwilling to back down.

"She is driving me to distraction," Rose tells Esther that afternoon on Esther's gold sofa. Esther shakes her head. "She's like a bloodhound. A hound sniffing blood. Did we ever hear from her or see her before? Once, twice. Now, when he's sick, she comes for one week, two weeks—"

"It's been just a week," Esther says.

"I have never been a superstitious person," Rose tells Esther.

"No, of course not."

"But anyone can see that to come like this, to an elderly man's bedside, to come when your father is sick, and to keep going over the past. Over and over. It's terrible. Just terrible. If she would move into a hotel at least. I've tried to talk to her, to hint to her—she sits and she sits. She doesn't notice anything; she makes herself at home. She spreads out all over the study. Do you know what she does? She listens to the news on the radio all day and all night. The traffic reports. Do you know why? She loves catastrophes. This is what she does; she sits and sheds gloom."

Esther asks, "And how does he like it?"

"He? He's happy as can be."

"Then it's good for him that his daughter is here."

"Good for him? She's exhausting him, wearing him out."

"What does she do?"

"She sits and looks at him; she talks to him. He pretends he can't hear her. What do you think she's doing, going through the desk like that?"

"Rose," Esther says, "you're beside yourself. I'm sure it was just innocent curiosity."

"She was standing there with her great big hands all over Ben's dissertation, getting her fingerprints all over it. What do you think she meant by that?"

"Well, I think maybe she was looking for old pictures or letters Maury wrote when he was young."

"His pictures are in the albums in the chifforobe," Rose says.

"But she couldn't know that."

"If she wants to see pictures, she should ask for pictures; she shouldn't go snooping like a—a common thief."

"But she's his daughter," Esther says again.

Rose throws up her hands. "And that's why I don't say anything. Even if I did say something, where would she go? She has no money for a hotel. She's come here with no money; she's come here to sit."

"I imagine she's had a hard life," Esther says. Rose's eyes widen. "Because, you know, she was the child of a broken home, and she ran away when she was so young, and had to make her way."

"I was seven years old when I came to England, and I was all alone with no one in the world to look after me," Rose says heatedly. "And she could never never know what I saw and what I lived through." Esther is not sure Rose is right, but she is too courteous to say so. "My own parents sent me away," Rose says. "In the name of safety they abandoned me."

"Why don't you come here for dinner with Dorothy and Maury," Esther says. "You're wearing yourself out cooking."

"No, no."

"Because it's too much for you. Listen to the way you're talking. I'm worried about you, Rose. Look at this. I've got barbecued chicken. Ready to eat."

"He won't eat it."

"So I'll make him something else."

Rose must decline the invitation. Esther comes over to Rose's apartment to try to persuade her, but Rose has to say that he is really too sick. Rose, Esther, and Dorothy stand watching Maury sleep in his chair by the window with the sun coming in. "This is my dear neighbor," she says, introducing Esther to Dorothy.

"*Shalom. Ma shlomeich?*" How are you? Esther asks Dorothy in her new and childlike Hebrew. "*Shmi Esther. Eich ohevet* New York?" My name is Esther. How do you like New York?

Dorothy turns up the palm of her hand as if to say she can take it or leave it. "I did not come to see New York," she says.

"*At garah bimoshav? Osah tapuzim baboker? Ovedet maher?*" What she means to say is, It must be terribly difficult to raise tomatoes on a farm and live the life of a farmer, getting up before dawn. What comes out is: Do you live on a farm in the morning? Do you make oranges? Do you work fast? Dorothy grins. "*At mivinah kitsat ivrit sheli?*" Do you understand my little Hebrew?

"Yes," Dorothy says.

"You know," Esther tells Rose later, "a year ago I would never have tried to express myself in Hebrew like this."

Rose does not answer. She is sick at heart. It seems to her that she is completely alone. Her sons call her on the phone and ask her how she is doing. How can she explain it long-distance? "If you were here, it would be one thing," she tells Edward when he calls from Washington.

"We were there two weeks ago, remember? We came for winter break."

"But that was before all of this," she says.

"All of what?"

She hears Dorothy padding around and she dares not say anything. "He is weaker," she tells Ed. "He is far weaker than before. He can't get up from the chair; I can barely lift him."

"Ma, I wish I could get on a plane right now," Ed tells her. "But now I have to teach. Ma?"

"Yes."

"I just want to hear how you feel."

"What is there to say?"

"What do you mean, what is there to say?"

She says nothing. It seems to her that there is no point in describing how she feels, when he tells her he can do nothing about it. What is the point on the long-distance telephone? He has his classes to think about, his family. Even her grandchildren are wrapped up in school; they are wrapped up in multiplication and arts and crafts. How she had loved it when they were small and spoke in breathy voices about nothing at all.

Then her older son, Henry, calls her from Venice, California, and she is thrown from one extreme to another. From the ice into the *shvitz* bath, he is so wrought up and fraught with anxiety. "Mother! How are you? How are you managing there? Promise me you aren't taking a single step outside. I heard the ice is terrible." It has always been that way with her sons. Ed all business, and Henry just overcome, so that she must comfort him whenever he calls—or get off the phone first. He has been in therapy in California, so that he can understand himself. Fine. But now, when he calls, he tries out the therapy on her. He tells her how she feels, and when she tells him about Maury, he says with the utmost empathy, "Mother, you must be so afraid."

"Don't *say* that," she tells him. She feels it coming from him just as it emanates from Dorothy, this foreboding like a faint but undeniable smell, mildew in a sponge.

The one who truly comforts her is Ed's wife, Sarah, her darling daughter-in-law. Henry has not married, although he is now forty-five. He is living in a world of his own. But Rose does have one daughter-in-law, a beautiful girl. She says to Rose, "I don't understand why Dorothy is still sleeping on that sofa. It's ridiculous!"

"What can I do?" Rose tells her.

"She must have relatives, cousins." Over the wire Sarah

is thinking of something, coming up with a plan. Rose has always loved Sarah, because she truly thinks about others. Her own sons, for all the brilliance of their minds, do not have that quality. They take after Ben, their father.

In the dead of night Maury wakes up gasping. He is having trouble breathing. Rose props him up on pillows; she turns on all the lights. Then Dorothy bounds into the room dragging the telephone with her. She is calling an ambulance, shrieking into the phone.

"No, no," Maury gasps. "No ambulance. I'm fine."

Dorothy pays no attention to him.

"He doesn't want it," Rose says. "He doesn't need it." If Dorothy would just leave him alone, if she would just give him a few moments of peace, he would recover, Rose is sure of it. Instead, the medics in white tear through the apartment. They lift Maury out of his own bed and strap him onto the stretcher as if he were a piece of meat.

They are killing him jolting him through the streets, pounding at his chest. He does not even have a blanket in the bitter cold. The cold is terrible, and the noise! "Stop it! Stop it!" she screams. They are attacking him, beating his frail body. She fights them off and they just push her away roughly against the back window, icy black. The lights streaking through the night. She is not even wearing a coat. They screech to a halt and open up the doors. Climbing down, she falls to the ground; one of the orderlies saves her, and brings her in. They are racing him into the hospital.

Dorothy did not fit in the ambulance. They did not take her. She comes later to the hospital, like a shadow, to Maury's bedside. She stands over his bed shedding doleful tears. "Father," she says. He lies still and pale.

Rose cannot bear it. She opens up her purse and gives

Dorothy almost all the money she has in it. She puts the bills in Dorothy's hand. "Please," she says, "I beg you. Go back."

"Go back where?" Dorothy asks.

"Go back to where you came from. You must go; you must. Can't you see? You're causing him to die."

"What kind of nonsense?" Dorothy booms out.

"Yes, I tell you. Are you so thick that you can't see it? Before you came, he was eating and reading, he was walking downstairs. You've sapped his strength; you've bled him dry."

"And what have I done to sap him like this?" Dorothy demands. "What have I done but come to be with him, spend time and talk to my own father?"

"And look where he is now," Rose says. "You've done enough."

"It is not for you to decide when I come and when I go."

"You've outstayed your visa," Rose declares, giddy with exhaustion and anger. "And if you don't take this money and take your things and get yourself out of my apartment, I'll—I'll call the authorities on you."

"I'm a U.S. citizen," Dorothy answers stolidly.

Rose picks up her purse again and takes out her checkbook. She writes out a check with a trembling hand. It seems to her a matter of life and death. Maury's life hangs in the balance. It is a check for five hundred dollars. She puts it on the broad hospital windowsill. Neither she nor Dorothy looks at it.

For three days Maury breathes in and out, drifting in and out of consciousness. Dorothy speaks to him, but for the most part he does not reply. On the fourth day Dorothy takes the check. "Goodbye, father," she says to Maury.

"Goodbye, dear," he says in his light, dry voice. Dorothy looks at Rose, triumphant.

In the night, Rose sits by his bedside. She does not sleep for days; she cannot count how many days and nights she has gone without sleep. "Taking a little nap?" the nurses ask her. Rose opens her eyes and glares at them. She does not sleep at all. If only she could sleep. Instead, she watches Maury breathing in and out. "Oh, Mother," Henry says to her on the phone, "how horrible to feel yourself standing on the threshold of such—such—"

"Such what?" she asks him.

"I—I suppose, just—it's the unknown," he stammers.

She simply puts the phone down. This is no fear of the unknown, as she sits by his bedside. Henry cannot even remember that she has been through all this before, with his own father. She watches Maury, and she is stricken tenfold, because she remembers it all. Ben had lain for two weeks in his bed, and she had watched over him every minute. She had fallen sick; she had been hospitalized for days. Of course, this was many years ago, but it has never left her.

Ben and Maury could not have been more different. Ben was serious and had no patience. He was always gloomy, always shutting himself up with his books. Sometimes he wouldn't talk to her for days. Maury was another story altogether, always full of jokes. Even their first meeting had been something of a lark. Rose's dear friend Millie persuaded Rose to let her put an advertisement in the Jewish papers: "Charming English widow . . ." That was how she met Maury. That was the truth of it.

Were they happy together? They traveled here and they traveled there. Unlike Ben, Maury loved to see new places—even later, when his health did not permit it. He would laugh it off when he found himself in emergency rooms. They were always busy; they went to shows, went out to eat. He was careless about everything from A to Z. Drank, smoked cigars, walked outside after dark, and money just slipped through his fingers on bets, restaurants, and disreputable stocks. He would say to Rose, "Don't worry, kid, I've got a little cash squirreled away." But that wasn't in his nature. He was a grasshopper, never thinking about a cold winter day. His one economy was that he didn't pay taxes, and he did that because of his political convictions, as he was a staunch Socialist, very near the point of Communism. Rose could say this about her dear husband Ben: he had been an ant. She and Maury squabbled constantly.

"Maury," she says to him as he lies there on the white sheets, "the time you were locked out. I'll never forgive myself." Just a few years ago, they'd had a fight, a horrible fight about the drinking, and he stormed out without even a coat. Then, when he got outside, he saw it was too cold to take a walk, so of course he came back. But he'd walked out without his key, and he was locked out. He was standing downstairs in the outer vestibule of the lobby just pressing the buzzer when two great men came and mugged him. They dragged him out on the sidewalk. She saw it all from the window, but she could do nothing about it. She was up on the eighth floor. She screamed, she called the police, but by the time they came it was too late, the men were gone and her poor husband was left battered. It was lucky the muggers hadn't taken knives to him, or worse. "I'll never forgive myself," she tells him now.

"Forget about it," he says. It frightens her to hear his voice. The white bed has swallowed up the rest of him.

Those are his last words. He dies that night when the polished hospital is empty and not a single person has come to check on him for hours. No one knows he has passed away except for Rose. No one even notices. It is she who must ring the bells and rush through the corridors.

"Are you determined to assume complete and utter negligence?" she bursts out to the night nurse.

The children come. Ed with dear Sarah, and Henry from California with sunglasses folded in his pocket. Ed paces around the apartment and issues orders; they must contact a rabbi, they must have a plan. Rose feels faint. He is like a general, short and compact, with iron-gray eyes, small hands and feet. He does everything impatiently—even the way he opens doors, jerking the doorknobs with a flick of the wrist. And then there is Henry, tall, heavy, and rueful, simply lingering in corners and examining the pictures on the walls, leaning in doorways, stammering, as he always does at the most inconvenient moments, tearful all the time. She can hardly bear it.

"He did not want a rabbi," Rose tells Ed. "He did not believe in them."

"Look, Ma, he was Jewish, and I think—"

"He told me a hundred times, he wanted to be cremated and scattered," Rose says. "Please, I don't have the strength to argue. Please, do as he asked."

"Mother," Henry says, "we will."

"Thank you," she tells him.

"But where did he want to be sc-sc-scattered?"

That question is all she can take. "I don't know that, why are you asking me that? I tell you, I don't know. Why are you interrogating me like this? I haven't slept at all for ten days. I haven't eaten anything, not a bite. Why do you come here to drill me with questions?"

Sarah gets her a tissue. She says, "Mother, can I make you some fresh coffee?" Rose nods, mutely.

The coffee is wonderful. No one can make coffee like Sarah, they all agree. "But, Ma," Ed starts in, as soon as she feels the slightest warmth, "you have got to start thinking about the future." The future? The question is absurd. She has been to the future and back, to the hospital gates and beyond. She has seen the future. The white hospital bed, the silvery intravenous tubes. She's seen the end. Now, he says, she should begin to think about it?

"You must invest your money," Henry tells her.

"I can't think about that now," she wails.

"You're going to have to think about it," Ed informs her, quick as always with the ultimatums. "You've got enough money to live comfortably, very comfortably, even after you pay the back taxes and the penalties."

"I don't want it," she tells them all.

"But, Mother"—Henry leans down over her—"you can leave the city."

"Give up the apartment?" she gasps. All her treasures swim before her eyes—the framed needlepoint birds above the sofa, the secretary, and the black-and-white pictures of Ed and Henry in their adorable sailor suits.

"You can have a better apartment," Ed says.

"And where am I going to get seven rooms for two hundred eighty dollars a month?" she asks.

"Maybe not rent-controlled, but in a good neighborhood," he pleads with her. "Where you can walk outside. Where you aren't going to get robbed if you leave the building. If you do some, um, financial planning, you could live a safer, happier life."

She is disgusted that he would speak in such a way just two days after Maury's death. To talk about finances and about happiness, and to speak of them together. She stands up and clutches the back of her chair. "I don't *want* a happier life," she says with great conviction.

She won't go to the bank, and she won't go to Shearson. The only one she will see is Dick Gorham, because he was Maury's dear friend. Dick was the lawyer for the union when Maury was the accountant. It was in the days when the union could not afford a C.P.A., and so they hired Maury, because he was not certified. Dick is almost eighty, but he is a lawyer and has not retired. He still keeps up his office on Eighth Avenue, a one-room walkup full of files and stacks of papers. There are yellowing newspapers, some Yiddish, and paperback books; there are plaques from the union. The walls are covered with photographs of the testimonial dinners. Dick comes from behind his desk and embraces her. He asks her how she is, but already Ed, Sarah, and Henry are crowding in behind her. There are not enough chairs. They all begin talking at once. She should get C.D.s, she should get tax-free municipal bonds. Ed is for the C.D.s and Henry for the bonds. Sarah tells her these are good because she can spend the interest and keep the capital. Rose opens her mouth, but she cannot speak; they are all talking at once. She feels she might suffocate.

"C.D.s are good, conservative investments," Ed says.

"But the pen-pen-penalties," Henry interrupts.

"What penalties? They're negligible; she won't incur any—"

"What about some combination? Or a fund—" Sarah suggests.

"I don't like those funds, and I'll tell you why," Ed declares. "Anything they call a product is something that's packaged to be of the utmost convenience to *them*, and anything they call a—"

"Out! Out! All of you," Rose bursts out. "I can't bear it."

"Do you want to do this another day?" Sarah asks sympathetically.

"No!" Ed says. "I don't have another day."

"I want to speak to Dick. Alone," Rose tells them. "Out, please. I beg you."

They hesitate. Sarah motions for them to go.

"And where are we supposed to wait? On the street?" Ed grumbles.

She and Dick are alone. He comes around to her side of the desk. "Rose," he says. He takes her hand. He offers her a butterscotch candy from his big glass candy dish. She unwraps the yellow cellophane and puts the candy into her mouth. When she tastes the butterscotch on her tongue, she starts to cry because it tastes so good. She had forgotten.

"I don't want the money," she says.

"I know," Dick tells her. He has earnest blue eyes and a high dome of a forehead, pink and slightly freckled. "But he left it to you, you know."

"We left all our money to each other," Rose says. "Isn't that true?"

"That's right. That's how we wrote it up in the will."

"How was I to know he had any?" Rose folds and refolds the butterscotch wrapper.

"How could anybody know?"

"And *then* where does it go?" she asks suddenly, remembering something.

"The money? The way you've got it down, after you it goes to the children."

"The children?"

"That's right. Of course, you can do whatever you want."

"I don't want to do anything," she says miserably. The butterscotch is melting away on her tongue. The dent on the top is wearing down into a hole, sweeter and sweeter. "I would like to see Jerusalem; I would like to go there once. I would like to see Paris again."

"You could travel, sure."

"But I don't have the strength for it."

"But in time—"

"If I went on a boat." The idea or wish returns to her, the thought of sailing away over the ice and into the Atlantic. She would take one cabin, and Esther would take the mirror image next door. "I could sail on ships," she says.

"Well, of course, you'd be spending capital." Dick pushes around the papers on his desk. "But you only live once. The way I see it, you want to stay liquid, you want to dip in if you feel like it."

"But I can't," Rose says.

"Why not? It's your money; you can do anything you want."

"Even—write a new will?"

"Sure you can. You can write a will anytime you want."

~

"I said C.D.s, Henry said bonds," Ed explodes in the cab.

"We wanted you to spend the int-int-interest," Henry says.

"And preserve your capital so you will have something left," Ed says. "What do you do? You invest in Fannie Mae, so you can spend the interest and the capital and have *nothing* left."

"Ed," Sarah chides from the front seat.

Rose is sitting in back, wedged between her sons. They are frightening her to death, waving this and that prospectus in her face. "Don't you see, Ma," Ed tells her. "With bonds you get your interest and then when the bond comes due you get your original investment back. You put your money into the fund that buys mortgages, you understand? You'll get your money back as all these people pay off their mortgages, but then at the end you don't get any lump sum—you don't get anything. All the money is paid back as you go along. And if you spend that money that's being paid, you won't have any more for later. That's it—it's finished."

She is clutching her purse in her lap in the lurching cab; she is closing her eyes. Strange flashes of dreams fill her mind. There she is, strapped into the ambulance in the night, and her two husbands on either side of her, one lecturing her, terribly stern, the other whining and kvetching. She opens her eyes and sees spots; she sees her sons and her two husbands. "Stop it. Stop it, all of you!" she shouts.

In silence they help her out of the cab. Silently they take her up the stairs. Sarah carries the purse into the bedroom for Rose. "Why don't you take off your girdle?" she says to Rose. "Why don't you lie down?"

The sheets are smooth against her skin. There is no one else in the apartment. Dorothy and her jogging suits are gone; the children are gone until tomorrow.

⁓

In the night she gets up and puts on her robe and slippers. She walks through the empty apartment, turns on the lights. She begins to look at her things, to look at each one as if for the last time. She adjusts her pictures of the boys in their sailor suits. She examines her needlework, all the tiny stitches in her needlepoint birds. She holds up her photograph of Ben to the light, a picture in which he looks very stern and old. He would not approve of putting money in Fannie Mae. He would call it frivolous. She folds up Maury's plaid lap blanket and touches his large-print library books in their clear plastic library jackets. He used to say, "What's money for but to enjoy?" All the time he was saving a hundred here, a thousand there, in all those little bank accounts. Ben spent on the big things, the old Brooklyn house, the car, furniture, college for Ed and Henry. Maury never bought big-ticket items. As for Rose, she hates the thought of money. She has never had a head for mathematics or money. She loves beauty, and that is all.

Then she remembers something. There is something she must do. She goes to the secretary stocked with stationery. She still has her stationery and her old address labels: "Mr. and Mrs. B. Markowitz." She never changed her name, even after she married Maury. She had been Rose Markowitz for too long to change—and besides, Maury's last name was Rosenberg, and Rose Rosenberg was a name she could not bear. She couldn't bear it. She takes out her note paper, cream-colored, with a single coral rose at the top. She begins to write on it, covering the paper lightly in ballpoint. Her letters are round and large, with a great deal of space above and below. She leaves her *a*'s and *o*'s open at the top, as if they were bowls to be filled up later. *Will*, she writes at the top of the page.

> *Thank God I am still in sound mind, although my body is weak, still grieving for the loss of my dear husband still in shock from the way he was torn from me when they were claiming to be reviving him.*
>
> *The whole of my estate if there is any left from Fannie Mae, I leave not to my children or to Maury's daughter, Dorothy, not out of spite, but because I choose to give where there is most need. My son Edward is a renowned professor of the Middle East and although a good man is deeply absorbed in his own career and foreign affairs with little time for other matters. Within him lies a good heart, although self absorbed. With many successes and articles, he is*

standing on his own two feet. My son Henry is now in the art business in California. He has given up teaching for business however he has still not married. Although he breaks my heart being a bachelor, he does not do anything about it. He is living for himself only, and what way to live is that?

If however, my son Henry does marry within five years I will give his wife all my jewelry with the exception of my garnet ring which I leave to my dear neighbor Esther Rabinowitz. If he does not marry, then to my darling daughter in law Sarah will go all the jewelry.

As for Dorothy, I bear no malice toward her but I cannot forgive her for coming to push her own father into the grave.

All the money and goods will go to The Girls' Orphanage in Israel, to the fund for brides to prepare them for their weddings and their Jewish homes. I too was an orphan like them and I too know what it was like to be sent away to a foreign land.

The only exception is my diary, which I leave to my dear Sarah, because she is a writer. Although it is unfinished, she will know what to do with it.

Rose has covered six small pages of her cream stationery. She is exhausted. She gets up and walks back to the bedroom. But as she gets into bed she realizes she has forgotten something. What is it? She agonizes, imagining what it can be, but she can think of nothing. Then, in the early morning, before dawn, she wakes up and glimpses the stern picture of her husband Ben staring down at her from the wall. He seems to be following her with his eyes. She hurries back to the desk. *Codicil*, she writes.

I cannot forget also about Dad's dissertation which has never received recognition. I leave this also to Sarah to translate and to publish as she sees fit because she can appreciate its scholarship. When he passed away I planned to translate it in his memory but the difficulties I encountered in my life were too great before I met Maury and afterward Maury insisted I spend my time on other things for he believed that it was better to enjoy life while living than to spend time with the dead. However, I still hoped to translate it while I had the strength, but in recent years when he became ill I found I did not. It is not Maury who is to blame for this it was simply his disposition. Despite his many other qualities he was not a scholar.

She reads the will and codicil over to herself and sighs with relief. It is not that she feels better, but that it comforts her to write this down. Maury didn't write down much. He never wrote letters, or even postcards. But Rose feels she must leave some description of her feelings and ideas to her children. She cannot bear the thought that she will not be remembered. As for whether they'll approve of her will, she cannot worry about that now; it is hers to write, and they won't know about it for years and years. She won't say a word.

The Art Biz

In the cool, California night, Henry Markowitz is closing up Michael Spivitz Fine Art Gallery. He has to stay open until ten on Thursday nights to take in the evening crowd. The tourists tracking in sand from the beach and the open-air cappuccino bars. Henry hates the sand and the bathing suits, but, as Michael says, this is the reality of selling art in Venice. Henry has often had to resist the urge to turn these people away. At least the ones without shoes. The one thing he cannot abide is bare feet—as if this were the concession stand at the beach and not a gallery showing work by some very important twentieth-century artists. Admittedly, the artworks aren't originals. There are Chagall prints and signed Dalí lithographs. They sell a great many lithographs, but they are all signed. It seems to Henry that there should be a modicum of respect shown to these wisps of authenticity. Sandals at the very least.

He sweeps the parquet floor with a big push broom he

keeps in the back. There is a cleaning service, but he can't help himself. Five years ago he would not have envisioned himself sweeping a gallery in Venice Beach. His thought when he went into the art business was that he would be dealing in antiquities: cataloging, negotiating with collectors and museums in paneled rooms, and, of course, using his expertise—a Ph.D., two monographs, several articles—in early books and prints from England and France. This seemed the natural course for him while he was retooling at the Wharton School, putting a negative tenure decision and a failed grievance behind him, and, as his therapist put it, recognizing how many different life paths there really were once you opened yourself up to them. But one thing did not lead to another. Prints and manuscripts at Sotheby's was not forthcoming. The job at Christie's in London turned out to be only seasonal. He did have a firm offer from a friend of his brother's, but assistant manager at the Laura Ashley in Short Hills was not for him.

"Why not?" his brother, Edward, demanded.

"Why not? It's got nothing to do with art," Henry said.

"It's retail," Ed said, brutal and succinct.

"It's women's ap-ap-ap-"

"It's a job," Ed said.

"Apparel!" Henry burst out.

"So what," Ed said, always pragmatic. "I thought you wanted to be in New York."

"Short Hills is not, is not, New York," Henry cried. And he refused to discuss it further.

The path that did open up for him was manager at Michael Spivitz. It was not New York, but it was art. And Henry has been working on bringing in some original contemporary pieces. He is working on a show for a fabulous lesser-known sculptor who works in brass, creating seed forms with uncurling stems, or sometimes miniature human figures unfolding from a central root like earthy homunculi. Henry has given up New York, uprooted his elderly mother and moved her to Venice, laid down his life learning to drive on the L.A. freeway, but he is still in the art business.

He is just turning off the lights when he sees someone rattling the glass doors. It is a woman with a frenzied look and flyaway hair. He gestures that the gallery is closed and she gestures that she needs to talk to him, so he lets her in. As the heavy glass opens, her voice explodes into the gallery, frantic, with a heavy Israeli accent.

"My son! My son is in trouble."

"Has there been an accident?" Henry asks.

"Yes! Yes, an accident."

"Where is it?" Henry peers out into the dark street.

"Not in a car. He has disappeared."

"I don't understand," says Henry.

"You understand Hebrew?" she asks him.

He shakes his head.

"My name is Amalya Ben Ami," she says. "I'm staying at Venice Sands. I came just a few weeks ago with my son from Haifa, and now he has disappeared."

"You've lost your son? Did you call the police?"

"Yes, yes. They can do nothing. I need you to help me."

"I?" Henry stands there in his Indian cotton shirt and stares at the Israeli woman. She wears a good deal of jewelry and carries an enormous leather handbag. It sounds like some delusional fantasy, what she's saying, but the strangest thing is the way she tells it to him slowly and deliberately, as if he were some kind of moron who can't follow her.

"The police cannot help me," she says. "Michael Spivitz has got my son. He has my child."

"Michael Spivitz?" Henry asks, aghast.

"Let me explain this to you. Your employer has got my son," she says. "He is keeping him."

"That can't be," says Henry.

Then she breaks down in front of him, just sobs in frustration, like a teacher who has tried to explain the simplest problem and has not gotten through at all. "He has stolen him," she sobs, the glow of the track lighting shining on her flyaway hennaed hair.

"That's impossible," says Henry. "It doesn't make any sense at all. My employer does not steal children."

"It's true," she says. "Do you disbelieve me?"

"But I have no idea," Henry pleads with her. "You're distraught, you're—"

She simply puts her enormous handbag on the floor and begins pulling out papers, her passport, her airline tickets, a letter on consular stationery. "This is his picture," she says, and holds up a photo of a tanned teenager with dark eyes. "His name is Eitan Ben Ami."

"Look here," says Henry, "I must get home. May I call you a cab?"

She seems crushed at this and cries even more. "You don't believe me." Henry doesn't answer. "You don't listen to me."

Henry is beginning to feel nervous standing there alone with her in the gallery. "If you've lost him, this is a matter for the police," he says.

"I tell you, I've gone to the police," she cries out. "They do nothing."

"Well," Henry stammers, "then there's noth-nothing to be done. Now I must close up, I must get home. Please let me call you a cab for your hotel."

She stands there silent for a long time. Motionless. He begins thinking he should call the police. The police are very good in this neighborhood. Prompt and courteous. "I want to talk to a rabbi," she says suddenly in a small voice.

"I'll call you a rabbi then." Henry hurries anxiously to his desk and begins telephoning synagogues listed in the yellow pages under houses of worship. He leaves flustered messages on several answering machines. "This is Henry Markowitz. There is a woman here, Amalya Ben Ami, staying at Venice Sands, and she needs to speak to the rabbi as soon as possible. She is quite dis-dis-distressed."

Henry's condominium is ordinary and white, identical to all the others from the outside, but he has hung up his herbs and garlic braid in the galley kitchen, filled the second bedroom from floor to ceiling with his book collection. In the living room a Persian rug covers most of the gray wall-to-wall carpet, and the sliding glass doors are adorned with long flowing curtains and a custom-made scalloped valance in royal blue silk. His old prints cover the walls, and in a place of honor away from the light he has hung his small but real Dürer sketch of a rabbit. He takes off his clothes as soon as he gets in, puts on his silk bathrobe, and runs a hot bath. He needs to soak; he needs to close his eyes and forget the day. He pours himself a drink and takes out the leftover prime rib, beets, and potatoes au gratin to heat up. Although he lives alone, Henry cooks. He is one of those rare people capable of cooking a full meal just for himself. He spends time planning delicious and attractive meals, buys flowers for the table, even when he has no one else to entertain. Good food on good china, fine crystal, and old silver are necessities for him, essential to his existence. What is life without dinner? An afternoon without a good wine? A bed without fresh cotton? A house without flowers?

He sinks into the bath and the water flows over him.

He is a tall man, fleshy and pink, his curly hair receding, his deep-set eyes heavily shadowed from compulsive nocturnal scholarship. For Henry still keeps up with the literature in his field, and still works at writing articles—actually, one article—late at night propped up in bed. The water flows into his pores, relaxes his muscles; he feels his whole body uncoiling. Then the phone rings. He closes his eyes. He called her from the gallery hours ago, but she is calling anyway. The phone rings eleven times. He gets up with the water streaming off him, wraps a towel around his waist. "Hello, Mother," he says.

"I've bought seats," she tells him.

"Seats for what?"

"The seats for Yom Kippur," she says.

"Mother, I've already told you I can't do it."

"I don't understand that," she says.

"I can't take off the whole day."

"The whole day! Yizkor. Half an hour in Dad's memory. And Maury's."

"But, Mother, it's an hour drive each way. I simply cannot take off the entire afternoon."

"If I could take the bus—" she says.

"You can't take the bus."

"If I could, I would take the bus. I bought the seats today. I don't think they have refunds."

"Mother, you should have talked to me before you bought them."

"I did talk to you."

"And what did I tell you?" Henry asks wearily.

"You told me the same thing you're telling me now."

"And then why did you buy the seat when I said I wasn't going?"

"Because you should be going," Rose says. "One day a year you should stop and think."

"I do think about Dad," Henry says. In fact, he has

been thinking about his father a lot lately. He and his therapist have spent hours in the past year and a half working through Henry's feelings toward his father.

"I mean, you should think about me," says Rose.

"Mother, I haven't even had dinner yet," Henry says. "I'm exhausted; I've been on my feet the whole day, and I think my prime rib is drying out."

⁂

The next morning at the gallery Michael says, "Henry, you look tired."

"Michael, I've had such a night. A woman came here looking for you. A lunatic insisting her son was missing and you had him. Twice I nearly called the police. I thought she might pull out a gun."

"Oh, I know," Michael says. "She's been harassing me for weeks." He sits down at his desk. "I'm sorry she gave you such a fright." Michael is Canadian, and when he says sorry he pronounces the word soh-ry. He is a fair-haired man, tall and slender with a blond mustache and blue eyes.

"But where c-c-could she have developed these fantasies, these delusional fantasies?" Henry asks.

"I don't know. She seems completely obsessed," Michael says. "She calls me constantly. I'm having my number changed."

"Good God," says Henry, who is not English, but often speaks with an English inflection when moved. He thinks for a minute and then says, "She's clearly blaming you for her son's disappearance. But why? How did she meet you?"

"Well, through him," Michael says. "He's staying with me."

The blood rushes to Henry's face. "The boy?"

"Well, yes," Michael says, looking up from his paperwork with limpid blue eyes.

"With you? You? But why?"

"Because he wants to," Michael says.

"But he's fifteen," Henry exclaims.

"Actually, he's sixteen," says Michael.

Henry is gasping. "But he's a child."

"Henry." Michael comes around to the front of the desk and touches his arm. "I'm not *keep*ing this boy. He's had some problems with his mother, that's all. He asked if he could stay with me."

"But the police! But he's a child!"

"We've all spoken to the police. I asked him. They asked him: Do you want to go back to your mother? And I'm afraid he said no. Apparently he is a U.S. citizen, and so he can stay as long as he wants. His father is American."

"Michael, I'm—I don't know what to say," Henry tells his boss. He can feel himself blushing, his cheeks hot.

"Henry, Henry, Henry," Michael murmurs, his voice patronizing and sweet. Henry is probably fifteen years older than Michael. "But such an innocent," Michael would say during those years they lived together. "Henry, Henry," Michael would soothe and chide him, alternately smoothing and ruffling his feathers. It took Henry a year to work up the courage to leave. A year to give up Michael's house, his cars, his sleek kitchen, his beautiful things, his quick glances, sure touch, his sweet voice with just the faintest tang of sarcasm.

Henry lies face down, naked on the table for his massage. "So how's the art biz?" Jason asks him as he kneads Henry's back and shoulders.

"It's—it's—" Henry begins.

Henry lies there on the table, stiff as a corpse, his big fleshy body tight and unyielding to Jason's soothing touch. His mind is full of Michael and Michael's nonchalant news. That this boy, this very young boy is staying with him. He has no trouble believing the boy is staying there of his own free will. In that house? With the view, that spa and swimming pool? With Michael's wines? He wouldn't appreciate the wines, but the ambience, Michael himself . . . It is all intoxicating. And to one so young. How could he? The thought is utterly horrible, and, yet, Henry cannot chase it out of his head.

"Wow, you're just so tight today," says Jason. "I feel like I can't get under your skin." Henry looks up at Jason and feels his anxiety compounded with embarrassment. He can't relax. He just can't do it. And he had always found Jason's hands so beautiful, and Jason himself so amusing, with his surfer talk and his classical face, the long eyelashes of which Jason is vain, always curled, so that he looks like one of those rare Greek statues with the agate eyes still left in the sockets and lashes of beaten and curled copper. If it had been Jason it would be one thing. Jason is grown up, not an adult exactly, but a grown-up boy. This fifteen- or sixteen-year-old—what difference does the year make? —this little one can't possibly understand. He couldn't possibly know what Michael is about. Henry has been there, as they say, been there and back, been through it all. How many different euphemisms are there for that web? The spidery path of Henry's anxious youth and innocent middle age.

Already, before he gets home. Already, while driving, Henry feels a migraine blossoming, opening like an enormous Magritte rose into every empty cavity of his head. He feels its manifold petals pressing against his ears, against his eyes, even behind his jaw. As he enters the apartment, he holds this terrible flower high and still so as not to ruffle it. He takes his medication, lies on his bed with all the curtains drawn, and watches the colors behind his eyes. Hours pass. Far away he hears his neighbor's television, the condo's yard service with the leaf blowers. Slowly he gives way to nausea. Then he sleeps.

How is he to look at Michael without thinking of this terrible thing? This boy in the house. For several days, Henry can barely look him in the eye. And yet, Michael has done a great deal for him. He took him on when he had no experience, and gave it to him. He believed in Henry's managerial skill and trusted Henry's taste. He befriended Henry when he had almost no one and introduced him to a first and then a second therapist. He was an agent of change in Henry's life, a messenger from outside the gates of the academy. He gave him courage, declaring, Open your eyes to the world, come out and scale the walls! Exchange your scholarly obsessions for a new career. Leave the shadowy libraries for the bright, blinding California sun. Henry continues, steels himself each day at the gallery. He says nothing, but as he works, he argues with himself. He sits and does the books at his table in the back. Of course, there are certain feelings, desires, but must every passing interest turn into an acquisition? Henry sits there and he is ashamed. He doesn't deserve to make the analogy, desire and the collector's acquisitiveness. After all, he is in the business, pricing and selling lovely things. He looks at Michael and feels indignation mixed with guilt. If only he could tell him off. If he could speak to him with some authority and say, This is wrong, this is foolish. But he is too close to pass judgment. Confounded, compromised. He has been in the past a little like Michael and a little more like this boy. He has felt them both within himself, the tiger and the lamb.

⁓

The evening before Yom Kippur, Henry has to go to the dermatologist to have a sebaceous cyst looked at. His dermatologist is Stephen Goldwasser, cheerful, something of a yenta, with thinning red hair, a big fleshy face, and skin soft as a baby's. Goldwasser is a big advocate of the drug Retin-A.

"I think we'll have to freeze it off," Goldwasser says. "Are you going to Kol Nidre tonight?"

"I have an engagement," Henry says. "But tomorrow, perhaps, I'll—my mother has tickets."

"That's what she told me," says Goldwasser. "She was here Monday. Let's go get some liquid nitrogen and freeze this baby." He ushers Henry into the little room where he freezes off cysts and warts. "Have a seat, make yourself comfortable. Turn this way. Did you read about the Israeli woman in the *Jewish Opinion*?"

"I don't get—"

"This will sting just a little bit. I love this. I tell all the kids dermatology is just like *Star Trek* with the nitrogen—"

"Ow!"

"—and the laser guns. This is going to shrink right up. The woman apparently lost her child here in Venice. He's run away. They've found him, but he won't come back. She has no money, no connections. The federation actually made an appeal for her so she'll have somewhere to stay for the holidays, and she's staying with the Fleishmans. You know Leon?"

"N-not intimately," Henry says.

"I think he's giving her legal advice. Here, did I give

you this pamphlet on sebaceous cysts? Here's what it looks like under your skin. You see? And there's the wax formation. It's truly bizarre. Apparently the kid went by himself to one of these clubs and never came back."

Of course Henry doesn't breathe a word to Goldwasser. He simply makes his next appointment and leaves.

He is hardly in the mood to go to Michael's party that night, and yet he has to go. It is Michael's fortieth birthday. This is the engagement he mentioned to Goldwasser. Not at all a social engagement; all business for him. The art biz, as Jason calls it. Hours of talk with prospective clients, networking with buyers, lawyers, and possible sources. It is business that tires the legs and wearies the soul as one makes the rounds in a dark and rollicking room, drink in hand. And what of the art? Where is that elusive beauty to be found? The vision of life, the line that makes you look and look again. The form of suffering, the vessel of light. The art is nowhere to be seen. Like the little nightingale in Hans Christian Andersen, she has flown away.

He was determined when he left the academy to open his eyes to the world. And, yet, how vulgar that world is. Is it simply that he's hidden behind university walls for too long? Is he thin-skinned? In fact, his skin is delicate, Goldwasser has told him. He had felt better when he was hiding. He had felt more confident. When he came west, he still had the capacity to be shocked by it all. The people, the cars, the sun shining without seasons, the pursuit of material things. When he was shocked, he sees now, he could still enjoy it. He could take a kind of indignant pleasure in it. And now? Now he is weary, knowing, and regretful.

When he arrives at the party, Michael embraces him amid a throng of people, and Henry almost puts his hands up to protect himself. His charming fair-haired employer, mentor he might have called him, now embracing him with his slender arms, enfolding him in his Mephistophelean wings. The party is at a private men's club and is full of dealers. There is music; there is wine. Strips of teriyaki steak on little sticks. There are erotic ice sculptures, showy kisses, shouted conversations. The conversations are about cars. It is all horrible. Not merely commercial, not merely work, but a horror. The party is loud, and gets louder. People communicate in pantomime. The music and liquor flow through the crowd. There is singing at the piano. Henry feels his head buzzing. Soon his headache will unfold, like a pale night-blooming flower. The pianist bangs louder and louder. He strikes up a fanfare, and then waiters wheel in a birthday cake, a float on wheels, gargantuan in proportions, and out of that cake springs a boy, the boy, wearing a G-string.

The next morning on Yom Kippur, Henry oversleeps. His mother calls at eleven o'clock.

"I'll have to take a taxi," she says.

"All right," Henry tells her.

"Even if it's a hundred dollars."

"How could it be a hundred dollars?" he asks her, his voice muffled in the bed. "I don't think it will be more than forty."

"Forty dollars for a taxi! How can that be? I've never spent so much on a taxi in my life. I've never had to go to the temple in a taxi. I don't know the way."

"Mother, don't cry." He cannot bear the sound of her weeping on the phone.

"I don't understand why you won't go now, when before you said you would take me," she says.

"I will go, Mother. I will," he promises. He struggles

out of bed and showers, gets down half a cup of coffee and two pieces of toast for breakfast.

~

"I think it must be finished," she tells him as they park their car in the temple lot.

"But look at all these c-c-cars," Henry says.

He stops in the men's room on the way in to catch his breath. He cannot believe he managed to drive to the temple without an accident. He can't see straight. He washes his face and dabs his eyes with a scratchy paper towel. Then slowly, he walks back through the social hall with its mural depicting Solomon sitting in judgment of the two women, the great king dressed in what looks like Masonic robes, holding a saber over the head of the innocent babe. He walks past Chagall's twelve tribes of Israel reproduced as twelve hooked rugs hanging on the wall. His mother is sitting near the front, gesturing impatiently for him to take the seat next to her. All around her sit couples and families, squirming children, widows, all listening to the rabbi's sermon.

Henry looks at the rabbi standing there in his rainbow-colored talis. The rabbi is young and slight, with a thin face, and rather limp, thin hair. His voice is reedy, high enough to pierce Henry's muffled ears. "Why is it," the Rabbi asks, "that on Yom Kippur we Jews stand together and read off the list of sins together? Murder, adultery, burglary, slander—whether we did it or not as individuals, we beat our breasts as a community. This is our tradition. One of communal, rather than personal, guilt, and one of communal redemption. We make a confession as a group. We stand up and speak to God as a group. We hear the verdict as a group. I said at the beginning I was going to speak about connections. This is what I mean by connections. When we stand and recite our sins, when we ask for redemption, every one of us is connected to everybody else. Ultimately your sins are my sins, and my sins are yours. We are all in this together. We are all interconnected at the most intimate level there is."

Henry shudders in the chill air of the sanctuary. He feels almost feverish. He does not want to be sitting there in that congregation, does not want to be connected to that mass of people, or, in fact, to anyone. He wants to go home. Back to his bed. He wants to be absolutely alone except for his books.

"Let's pause for a moment," the rabbi says. "Let's pause and meditate on what it means to be connected to each other. What we mean to each other with all our faults. Let's think about what it is to say: You and I are all mixed up together, and it doesn't matter who has done what in this past year. We've all done it. As the great theologian John Donne wrote: It doesn't matter for whom the bell tolls. It tolls for me, for you, and for all of us. No human is an island who can survive by him- or herself. We are each clods of earth on the continent. We are attached. So let's take a moment for silent prayer. Take the hand of the person next to you, if you will. Connect yourself."

The organist plays softly, wisps and tendrils of music, and Henry finds himself in the strong grasp of his mother on one side and the sticky grip of a little girl on the other. For several long moments his mother sits with her eyes closed. "Mother," he whispers. "Mother, are you asleep?"

"Sh," she hisses, jerking awake.

The organist plays on, and Henry feels himself perspiring. He needs to extricate his hands, but he cannot. Instead, he sits miserably, pinned to his seat, the events of recent days clouding his head. The sight, again and again flashing through his mind, of the boy blasting through Michael's birthday cake, his perfect, hairless little body. Must he, Henry, be connected to that? Is he, Michael's manager and right hand, meant to be part of—to be co-author of that? And then Henry sees something else. Just in front of him he sees Amalya Ben Ami, the mother, with her hennaed hair and enormous handbag, this woman supposedly distraught and penniless, sitting next to Fleishman and his wife, her hosts and benefactors, according to Goldwasser. And she is sitting there with her hand in Fleishman's and ever so slightly, Henry is sure of it, massaging his knuckles with her thumb. Henry's eyes open; he gasps into the silence around him. Can this be? That this woman who has lost her son is now using the opportunity to carry on with this middle-aged married man? This attorney? And at this moment Henry feels, with a cathartic inner sob, pain and relief together, so that now his disgust floods and overwhelms even his inmost guilt. It seems to Henry in this moment that his whole world has cracked open to reveal a garden of grotesqueries, a garden worthy of Hieronymus Bosch with the variety and surprise of its cunning little monsters. It seems to him, as in a horror film, that the synagogue, the art world, the whole city of Los Angeles is infested. Insect-ridden just underneath the skin. He sits up in his chair, heart racing. He pulls his hands out of the communal hand-clasping and rubs them with his handkerchief.

"Henry, we'll have an accident," his mother tells him as they speed home. He grits his teeth and keeps driving. "Henry, you're going too fast." She is clutching the shoulder strap of her seat belt. But he barely hears her. His mind is full of voices. "How is the art biz?" Jason asked him. "It's retail," his brother exploded when Henry told him

Laura Ashley was not what he wanted. "Look, there are many paths in life," his therapist said, "and it's not like one road is necessarily better than the other. The question is, What's better for you, given that you are at this place right now." And what is this place? Henry asks himself now as he speeds home, eating up the gray freeway, devouring the blazing sky. What is this place I have gotten into with the lithographs and the Chagall hooked rugs? With Michael and his child lover, and the boy's own mother peddling herself in the temple. What is this place? What is it? He has uprooted his mother and brought her to live near him. He has learned to drive. And yet he can see it all now, can permit himself to see it with righteous certainty: this place, Venice, with its art and beach, and all its local color, is really Sodom. It is really Sodom and Gomorrah put together. Nothing but thievery and uncovered flesh. He sees the dichotomy with great clarity. Venice on the one hand, brazen and rotting in the sun, and, on the other, the East Coast, all cloistered and covered, all petticoated modesty. Dear Princeton with its old trees and towers, all his dear universities, even NYU, bastions of books, art, and learning, pockets of civility, where the rituals and niceties of life are still observed. Where iron gates hold business, all that whoredom, at bay.

"Henry," his mother is telling him, "I thought the rabbi was very well spoken." He will have to go back. He will have to find a way. "Henry," Rose says, "is that a police car? Is he chasing us?" Somehow he will support art. In the private sector, if he must. He will go back. He will rededicate himself to beauty. Not to the dealing, not the business, but to art itself. He will leave, will leave, and he won't look back over his shoulder. He will leave, and he won't look back. He is already trying to remember the name of his brother's friend in Short Hills.

Oral History

Rose volunteers once a week for the Venice Oral History project. They send her a girl, Alma, on Mondays, and Rose tells her the details of her life. It can be tedious, but it is important that it be done. "The irony is not lost on me," she tells her son Edward when he calls.

She is an attractive girl, though she walks around in rags. They all wear them, of course. Rose sees them advertised in the catalogs. She gets them all. Ninety-nine percent schlock for twice the money. The bargains, so-called, are the worst. You could take the prices, but for that merchandise! Rose sits and waits every week and she can never predict what Alma will wear. Never the same rags twice; she doesn't iron. A divorcée, of course, is what she is. She told Rose herself. Last time she wore earrings made out of scrap metal. She has two holes pierced in each ear. But really, apart from that and her hair, she would be a nice-looking girl. No raving beauty, but she has feminine hands, and Rose is very particular about hands.

It was the one thing Rose disliked about her own Ed's wife. Even in the wedding pictures, she had the most ungainly, thick-fingered hands. The photographs are all away in boxes except for the pair on the secretary. Those were the boys in their angelic days. Two and five. She took out the old pictures of the family for the research project. The other things left from the old house are the sofa and the Chinese carpet, green. The carpet was the first thing she bought when she worked in Macy's Ladies' Dresses, her job before she got the position at Tiffany. The second thing was the beveled-glass mirror, which broke. The mounting was loose, and it fell one night with such a smash Rose was trembling for a week. The dining-room table and the six chairs Ed forced her to leave behind, because in Venice she got a studio at the senior citizens' residence. But the nesting Chinese tables came as a set with the wing chair and the cloisonné lamps. Rose's other son, Henry, wanted them, but Rose wouldn't let him have them when he moved to England. He had uprooted her from Washington Heights so she could be near him in California, and then he moved to New Jersey and then to England within three years of her coming. She told him when he left her he wasn't taking the lamps back with him. Rose put them on the chifforobe beside the bed. For reading she bought a seventy-five-watt lamp.

Alma saunters in with her hair windblown. "Sit, sit," Rose urges, and she sinks down, folders denting cushions. It annoys and fascinates Rose, the way she flings herself about. If you asked her, she would tell you Alma doesn't know what manners are. But Rose enjoys disapproving of her. She always loved an impossible child. Even now that Henry's grown and only impossible, he is her favorite.

The girl shuffles the files about and rewinds something in the tape recorder before she even asks "How are you?"

Rose considers the question. "I feel fragile. And you?"

"Great." They look at each other for a moment. Wrinkled again, Rose observes mildly. She turns down the volume on the radio, miniaturizing an Ives symphony. Alma watches, squinting. The white afternoon sun still burns in her eyes, blinding her to the shadowy contours of the apartment.

"You look ill, dear," Rose says. "You look flushed."

"Sunburn. Not to worry."

"I was always so very fair," says Rose.

Alma breaks in. "At our last session, you spoke about your childhood. Maybe we can pick up from there. Back before World War I. How did you manage to survive, domestically, under the great oppression?"

Rose settles back in her chair, revealing the knee bands of her tan stockings. "I'll tell you about the Depression. That was when we lived in the Brooklyn house. Thank God we had the house." She waves her hand mystically over the maze of furniture. The secretary especially was an agony to move. They had to take out the louvers and hoist it through the window. Rose had a time of it. She was wringing her hands waiting for it to come through, and she was certain the men wouldn't see the finials on the top.

"*Before* the Depression," Alma urges. "I want to talk about prewar oppression. How did your mother bear up? Where did you live?"

"Well, the war was dirty and dangerous. I would never go back to Vienna. Never, *never*. I was sent to England and became very English. All I can remember of Vienna is filth."

Alma leans forward. "Can you be more specific? This is very important for the project."

"Alma," Rose murmurs, "I said I would help you, but some things should be forgotten."

"Try to remember. You're like a witness to those times—to that suffering."

"Oh, nonsense," Rose scoffs. Even so, she smiles, touched by Alma's interest in her life.

"I need your cooperation."

"Well," Rose says sweetly, "we'll make something up, dear. The university will never know."

"Mrs. Markowitz!" There is something in Rose that baffles Alma. Something blithe and cunningly oblivious. She tries again. "All right, I'd like to rephrase my first question in a less technical way. When I speak of the oppression, here's what I mean. As a member of the European, rising bourgeoisie and as a woman, did you feel that your ambition was stifled in Vienna?"

"I was a *little girl*!" Rose protests. "This is before the first war, remember. Don't make me out a *completely* desiccated old fool. Besides, we were Jewish. That's why we came here."

"So you were really part of the Jewish intellectual elite. Is that a good description of the family?"

"I had six brothers," Rose says thoughtfully. "Some were smart, some weren't. Joseph, yes. Joel, yes." She ticks them off on her fingers. "Saul, no. Mendel, yes. Nachum—died too young. Chaim, smart? *Definitely* not—may he rest in peace. He had a heart of gold. Maybe half the family was elite, the rest, not."

"Well, I meant economically. Anyway, let's move on."

"Economically, we had the house," Rose supplies. "That was what saved the family."

"In Vienna?"

"No, *here*. In America. The city. Brooklyn. I was the baby. They sent me to Hunter College, but fortunately I married Ben halfway through. A horrendous place. You see, I never knew any mathematics. Couldn't add two numbers together. It was because of the way I was brought up."

"Ah," murmurs Alma. "As a woman, you were socialized to be afraid of numbers."

"Well, they tried to teach me, but they gave up because I was so stupid."

"You thought you were stupid?"

"No. Artistic. I sewed dresses. My life goal was to go on a transatlantic cruise. Which I did. Several times."

"So you aspired to the upper classes," Alma concludes.

"Oh, we were upper-class. My brother was a teacher. We went to college. My sister-in-law painted, played the piano. We spoke German and French. We were very cultured people. Our home in Vienna was a beautiful work of art. In Brooklyn we lived even better."

"Whoa," cries Alma. "In my notes from last session you said you only knew poverty and hunger."

"That's nonsense."

"You've changed your mind since last week?"

Rose lifts her chin. "Are you saying I can't remember what I said a week ago?"

"No," Alma says. "I'm trying to compile a consistent record."

"I am consistent."

"Well, which is the truth?" Alma demands. "Were you poor and ignorant or were you cultured?"

Rose folds her hands. "We were cultured at heart."

Starting the car, Alma glares at the Venice Vista condominiums, their avocado-green walls and cement paths under date palms. Every week Rose changes her mind about when she left Vienna. They all have their tricks, of course, the women of Venice and Mar Vista, the retired piano teacher in the valley. But the others trail their gambits more predictably: Eileen with her great-grandchildren, Simone and her long recipes. Rose is more subtle than this, more eloquently inconsistent.

Alma drives past Venice Beach and thinks how the old ladies on park benches used to inspire her. She went to see *Venice People* while still in Romance languages at Berkeley, and it struck her then that this was what she wanted. She was tired of insinuating meaning from fiction. She needed to read lives, not texts. She needed to hear real voices. Her adviser tried to talk her out of switching programs. "You're doing brilliant work here!" Professor Garvey protested. "You'll write a publishable dissertation." But Alma had decided by this time that he was a fatuous, exploitative swine. So she left Garvey and his department, and now field work replaces MLA computer searches. People replace books. Her mother is distressed by all this. She is distressed by Alma's graduate work in general. She pleads softly on the telephone from Palos Verdes, "Alma, why do you drive yourself like this? You don't have to go to school all over again. You're thirty-one years old, and if you don't like your program you can just leave. There's no shame in that. Or take a year off and see how you feel."

"What would I do with a year off?" Alma demanded after one such speech.

"You don't need to do anything," her mother answered. "You could just come home and rest. Or we could travel together, just the two of us. You don't take care of yourself working like this." She didn't say anything about Alma's boyfriend, which was how Alma knew he was on her mind. Mom met him once and talked to him briefly, but she never speaks *of* him, never utters his alliterative, flat Jewish name, Ron Rosenblatt.

Ignoring her mother's offer, Alma moved to Venice and

bought the Toyota. She drives across Los Angeles interviewing. But work with live characters has its own frustrations. Alma's women never provide quite the testimony she is looking for. They record scant evidence about their time and instead fill cassettes with soap-opera reviews, reports of gastrointestinal symptoms, readings of their letters. Here, again, Rose is the most dramatic, unfolding yellowed papers from her secretary, holding them close to the light as if some great historical record were at hand—all to reveal a thank-you note from her oldest brother's bride or, in last week's interview, a copy of her surreal letter to the IRS. "My dear husband was a Maoist. Please excuse the lapse in taxes." Rose is the worst.

⁓

The apartment is almost as hot as the car. Alma's cocker spaniel, Flush, sprawls, ears drooping, on the couch. The dog is recovering from a virus. At the round table Ron works under the blast of a three-speed fan. He is writing a scholarly work on the folksinger John Jacob Niles, but lately he's been helping Alma with her data analysis. She wonders sometimes whether either project will ever get done. Though he loves gathering material, Ron has a laconic way of writing. He knows hundreds of ballads, but was already bored with writing about Niles when he and Alma met. The year before, he had wanted to take his sabbatical in Appalachia and check Niles's sources, but Alma told him it was a ridiculous waste of time and she wasn't going to sacrifice her project for it. He grumbled for a while and wrote a chapter.

Now, Ron sits with Alma's transcripts weighted down against the fan's narrow breeze with ashtrays and glass coasters. "Darling," he says, "I don't think this stuff is usable."

Alma slams the door. "Don't darling me."

"Ms. Renquist," Ron says, "this data is shitty."

"It's not my fault!" She sinks down next to Flush. "You should see what I have to work with. The way they change their stories. Rose Markowitz doesn't even seem to know whether she was rich or poor."

"But I can't see," says Ron. "That's the problem. I have no idea what these women are like. All I've got here are your interruptions. You've been asking all kinds of biased, leading questions."

"I'm just trying to guide the discussion," Alma retorts. "You want me to listen to them babble about constipation?"

"*Guiding?*" Ron asks. "Look at these transcripts. Every other question is about class struggle. Come on, this is supposed to be a federally funded grant. This should be very straightforward: the lives of women before and after the wars."

"Are you telling me how to run my study?" She bristles.

"Alma," he says, "use your head. These women don't know what you're talking about. First of all, stop trying to indoctrinate them. What does Eileen Meeker know about patriarchal power structures?"

"Plenty."

"But not by that name."

She stamps into the kitchen. "It's my thesis," she says. "It's my idea. You think you can do a better job, you interview them."

"Yeah, why not," Ron growls from the other room. "Why not the interviews, too?"

"Come in here if you want to talk to me." She pours herself a glass of Chablis and feels some remorse, partly because Ron is right; she has been interrupting too much. It's an old habit. She's always worked to get a jump on arguments, to press her own conclusions. Even in high school Alma wouldn't let a statement lie unchallenged. She interrogated her classmates in discussion. After class, teachers would lecture her apologetically. They gestured with exhausted hands in front of the cloudy blackboards. "I know you're very bright, Alma. But you shouldn't act so dogmatic." Ron doesn't flare up the way she does. She dances around him in their arguments, and he watches, infuriating her as if he were holding her by the wrists. It's better to back off than play his games. "Ron?" She leans in the kitchen doorway. "It's just so hard to sit there and listen to them. I get punchy."

"I know," he says. "Tell you what; I'm starving. Order a pizza."

She phones for a pizza with everything—anchovies on her half—and cannoli for dessert. They clear off the table and Alma folds her printouts back into her rolling file cabinet. Ron complains that the apartment looks like a suite of offices, but Alma loves office furniture, the wall systems and built-in cabinets. She's attached corner fittings to the bookcases and nested drawers under the bed. She's installed folding tables, armless chairs, a layered printer stand, every kind of space saver. She indulges in the minimal. Ron's sprawling reel-to-reel tape player (needed for research) and his shaggy ferns look like loose cargo next to Alma's modules.

The pizza comes with double cheese, olives, mushrooms, onions, green peppers, and eggplant. Ron surveys the crust for Alma's anchovies and slices her a piece, which she cuts neatly with a fork and knife. He lifts a long curling piece straight to his mouth trailing cheese. But the doorbell interrupts him. The delivery boy is back, standing in the doorway. "Can I use your phone?" he asks.

They can hear him talking in the kitchen. "Hi. It's

John. Dad there? Hi. Fine. Two more. I, uh, locked the keys in the car. I'm on Elk." A long pause and then he reappears, avoiding their eyes. Silently he walks down to wait in the parking lot.

"God," Ron says, "how embarrassing. Poor kid. You forget what it's like to get an earful like that."

"I don't," says Alma.

"Well," he teases, "if you hate interviewing so much, go back to Cervantes."

She sighs. "But I want to work with people!"

"As opposed to the rest of us?"

"Oh, you know what I mean. It's just Rose who gets to me. The woman is driving me crazy. One session tears and suffering. The next week she laughs and laughs."

"Maybe she's senile," Ron suggests.

"No," says Alma. "She's too damn manipulative."

"Poor kid." He stakes out another piece. "You've just never had an Aunt Rose, that's all. You don't have the background for old Jewish ladies. Caroling at rest homes in Palos Verdes just won't do it."

"Very funny," says Alma. "I did *not* go caroling."

"It was a metaphor. Let me tell you, though, you've got to fight Rose on her own ground. She gets emotional, play on her emotions. Don't analyze out loud, sit there and cry with her. She'll pour out her heart."

Alma looks at him.

"Trust me," Ron says.

At the next session Alma tries. "We've been skipping around a lot," she tells Rose. "So I'd like to go back to your childhood. This time I'm going to try to talk less and let you talk more. Where did you live as a child?"

Rose picks off a dead leaf from her African violet. "We

lived outside Vienna in a little house on the grounds of a castle. When the soldiers came, all us children and women were locked in the castle, and one soldier had my mother roast them a pig! A whole pig! And then they left. Can you imagine?"

"How did you feel about that?" Alma asks.

"I just told you."

"I mean, beyond the bare facts. Emotionally. How did that make you feel? Didn't you feel violated when the soldiers came in? Do you still dream about it?"

Rose shakes her head. "This was *many* years ago."

"Yet you remember it so clearly!"

"No, actually," says Rose, "it's gotten very fuzzy in my mind."

"You're trying to forget it?"

"No, I just can't remember it that well. Alma, I haven't thought about this for years and years."

Alma glares at the needlepoint bird framed on the wall. "You're sublimating this."

"Pardon me?"

"You're purposely forgetting. Pushing it out of sight."

"Alma," Rose says gently, "when you forget something you don't *try*, you just—forget what happened."

"But can't you remember the feelings? Weren't you frightened?"

"I suppose we were."

"Couldn't you have gotten *killed*?" Alma bursts out. "I mean, really murdered. Raped, then murdered."

"Oh, definitely." Rose's voice quavers. "Sometimes when I think of the wars I could just cry."

Alma leans over taut with expectation, urgency, and sympathy.

"But I don't think about them very much."

What *does* she think about, Alma wonders, staring at

Rose's shadowed eyes. In fact, Rose is thinking about her slipcovers. She regrets that she gave them up. For forty years they covered the sofa where Alma sits. Rose brought them with her from New York when she moved into the residence, but the same day, Gladys came to introduce herself and examine Rose's things (she was sharp as a whip to the last day, and mean), and she picked up the cover on the sofa and said: "Rose, what are you waiting for?" She embarrassed Rose into it. She wanted them for the flea market, Rose found out later. Gladys used to visit all the residents, spying for the flea markets. They gave her awards. Now Rose has to keep the jalousies closed so the cushions won't fade.

Alma bends over her tape recorder. "Let's move on to the family you lived with in England during the war."

"She was a monster and became senile," Rose declares. "When they lost their money, she went mad because they couldn't afford plates."

"Plates?" Alma asks.

"China, porcelain. She broke something every day. She threw plates across the dining room. But *he* was an angel. The only one who understood me. There was also the most cherubic little boy, Eli. With golden hair. I went back to see him in 1954. He was a great big hairy man. Horrible! I couldn't believe my eyes."

Upper-middle-class industrialists, Alma writes in her notebook.

"They were very observant, that I know. We went to services every week. Alma"—Rose picks up the tape recorder—"I insist you turn off the machine and take some cheese cake. Listen. In my day we were taught to eat. I was a size eighteen at your age." She sees Alma writing and amends, "Well, maybe sixteen. Come. *Sit,* dear. Just let me get the cake out of the Frigidaire. You know, I've always thought Alma was a lovely name."

"Really?" Alma looks up startled. "I hate it."

"Why?"

"Rose," says Alma, "are you trying to sidetrack me?"

"No, I'm really interested."

"Oh, I don't know." She rattles her notes. "It sounds so—spinsterish," she finishes carefully. "And on top of that, Almas are never famous in their own right. They're always married to famous males."

"Now that's not true." Rose emerges from the kitchenette. "I've heard of many famous Almas. Let me think. What about Alma Mahler?" She presents the piece of cake. "Let me tell you about this cheese cake. I got the recipe from Esther Feurbaum. F-e-u-r-b-a-u-m, my dear neighbor in New York. This woman was a legend in her time in the New York Hadassah. I'm telling you so her name won't be forgotten. If there were any justice in this world, *she* from all of us would be alive today recording her life for your book. Such a tragedy."

"What happened to her?" Alma asks. "What kind of tragedy?"

"Very great," says Rose. "If you won't taste, take a look at her recipe. You'll see what I mean."

Ron watches Alma from the bed. Brushing out her wet hair, she stands with a towel draped over her cotton shirt. Plain and expensive, her clothes seem young for her. Not incongruous, but unforgiving. She buys jeans and dresses cut for her younger self, the waist she must have had in college, hips and breasts not yet thickened with extra weight. It makes him a little sad. Not because he didn't know her when she was younger; he believes her when she says she was a little bitch. It's just that it saddens him to think she dresses as she remembers herself. Still, she does it more out of habit than vanity. Her money is like that, too. A habit outgrown, but not outworn. It was something of a joke at his department when they first started going out. "She only wears jeans and old T-shirts!" everyone said. "But have you noticed, they're never the same jeans and T-shirts?"

Alma's cousin Liz is showing her pen-and-ink animals at the Royce Gallery, so they are going to the opening. They both hate gallery openings. Ron hates the people and Alma hates the art. It's one of her inherited pretensions; her mother is a collector.

"Tell me again why we're going to this thing," says Ron.

"Because it's her first show in three years!" Alma says. "This is a very stressful point in her life. She really is marrying Tom this time, and she needs reinforcement or she'll run back to Yosemite, and you know she doesn't take care of herself out there—we've been through this before."

"Yes," he says, "but it's so funny."

She misses this last in the roar of her blow-dryer.

From the Royce Gallery Ron can see two other artists. One sells handpainted silk scarves and holds classes Mondays. The other offers handcrafted wood furniture—that is, if working out back with a Sears router counts as handwork. Besides the galleries, there are boutiques with their starched Indian rags and ice-cream stores, bright and blank—room for standing customers only. Galleries are like that, too; nowhere to sit. Ron thinks of Venice's old attractions. He used to take his day campers to Muscle Beach for snow cones—strawberry, orange, grape, no gourmet flavors—and then for a tour of the Hyperion Treatment Plant. "How old are you?" his seven-year-olds asked him, and he told them he was ninety-nine. They believed him, too. Later on he went to the endangered-programs beach parties. Ethnic Studies would challenge Women's Studies for volleyball, and afterward everyone sat on the sand and stuffed themselves with homemade food. Then a few people would stay and get stoned quietly under the stars.

In the chatter by the drinks table a long-legged woman leans toward him companionably. "I miss Venice," he tells her.

"This is Venice," she says.

He cups his hands and whispers in her ear, "I mean old Venice."

She clutches her drink. "What, Venice, Italy?"

Across the room, Alma squeezes her cousin's hand. "Hey," she says. "How do you feel?"

Liz stands with her arms at her sides watching the crowd. "I'm okay," she says. "What are you doing nowadays?"

"Oral histories of women in Venice."

"Oh, wow," says Liz. "That must be a lot of work—"

"It is," Alma cuts in, "but it's worth it. There's so much great material out there." She smiles quickly at Liz's fiancé and moves on to avoid his frozen black eyes.

The drawings crowd the walls in distressed wood frames. "Such fine draftsmanship," muses a salesman. Alma nods, but the fine detail disturbs her. The lines seem unnaturally concentrated, like leaf veins under a magnifying glass. Every quill on Liz's hedgehog is equally important, every hair on a mouse is equally focused. She draws with a hawk's vision, Alma thinks, but there must be a way to draw with human sight. There has to be a rule for finding significant details, a method of selective focus. Moving to the open door for air, she finds herself staring at a small bronze of the Indian maiden Sacajawea. The stern figure stands slit-eyed against the elements. So powerful. So angry. Her hair thrown back in the wind. Her baby lodged like a stone against her heart. Her lips mute.

The living room is stifling when they get home, because whenever they leave the house they have to close and lock the windows for security. "I'm getting central air-conditioning," Alma announces.

Ron looks at her aghast. "That's ridiculous! Alma, this is just a brief heat wave!"

"This happens every summer," she says. "It's just beginning." She flips on the answering machine.

"Alma, it's Mom," enunciates Nan Renquist from the tape. "No message except I look forward to seeing you Saturday."

Ron scowls at the machine. "I'm not supervising any air-conditioning while you're gone," he tells Alma.

"No one asked you to." She watches the machine cycle through two hang-ups. Suddenly it crackles.

"This is Rose Markowitz. I am feeling very ill, my dear, and I would like to cancel the interview for Monday. Simone passed away yesterday . . ."

"Shit!" Alma throws herself down on the rug.

"I haven't slept all night," Rose continues, "which is not unusual for me except that I had a terrifying dream which I hardly ever do. She was standing above me dressed in her terrible blue gown. An evening gown which she wore to the senior citizens' dinners."

"Jesus!" Alma moans. "Simone was fine last week. I've got five weeks of tapes on her! What happened?" She flicks off the machine.

"Hey, I was listening to that." Ron flips the button.

The voice stretches on. "I told her at the time I thought the dress was inappropriate; it was foolish to wear a thing like that and threadbare, too. It looked shoddy, to tell the truth, and it was inappropriate to wear on this so-called bingo night. They all wear them of course . . ." Her voice fades for a second. "When I saw her there, she looked at me and looked and she wouldn't say anything, and I kept calling her but she wouldn't answer me, and I felt sure I was growing mad. There is a gentleman here they just took away with Alzheimer's mad as a hatter; he couldn't remember his own wife they said—she died two years ago . . ."

"Would you turn that thing *off*?" Alma goes into the other room, but Ron bends over the tape.

"So she wouldn't answer me. She just stood above my bed like a ghost until morning, and now I feel terribly ill. She used to dream like this, you know, and now I'm dreaming the way she did. She used to smile and smile; she loved to sleep more and more, she said, and just before she passed away she dreamt she met her sweetheart, looking just as he used to look—she saw him at Marina del Rey in her dream—and he told her, '*Je me souviens. Je me souviens, Simone. Je me souviens.*' And I asked her, Who is it who remembered you? She would just smile and smile. 'It was one of them,' she said. 'I'm not sure which.' " The tape cuts off.

Ron finds Alma curled up on the bed. "They'll all be dead by the time I finish," she says. "And I'll never get this done anyway, because they don't understand what I'm doing at all! I talked to Rose's doctor, you know. She takes tranquilizers. Half the time she's blowing her mind on some form of Percodan. You heard her just now."

"She was great," says Ron. "I think she's fascinating. You should copy the tape from the machine."

"You don't understand," she cries. "You think it's funny, but don't you see, all I have is tapes like that. Hours and hours of trivial reminiscences, insignificant data."

"Alma—" He puts his hand on her shoulder but she shakes him off.

"Can't you see," she says. "They're incoherent. They can't tell past and present apart. Half the time they don't know when they're awake or sleeping. I can't get facts or dates from them. Only these muddled stories. What kind of vehicle do I have here? What can I do with this shit?"

"Calm down," says Ron. "It's not worth getting upset about."

"Yes, it is worth it! I'd like to see you just once get upset about an idea!"

"Well"—Ron smiles—"I don't have a religion like you. The thing is, though, you have to work with what you've got. I'll help you, but I'm not Robert Coles—what can I say?"

She laughs a little at this and turns over. "Oh God, Ron, I'm such a fool. Could you tell me in a nonpatronizing way that you'll take care of me?"

"Give me a minute," he says, but she's up and washing her face.

"At least I won't have Rose on Monday," she says. "I'll have a respite this weekend."

"Now *that's* dangerous. She'll convince you to give up. Your mother will talk you out of the whole thing."

"Thanks a lot! She's not talking me out of anything."

"We'll see," says Ron.

Ron doesn't know Alma's mother at all. When she calls, she asks for Alma without identifying herself. And she never leaves messages with him. Only on the answering machine. He pictures Nan as Alma describes her—someone who smoothes away and subdues all opposition. He has his own private image of her, too, more place than person: windless rooms and vapid water. He imagines her house surrounded by still blue swimming pools.

He senses Nan's presence while Alma is away. He feels the way she pulls invisibly from her house outside the city so that Alma changes her plans and comes when she calls. Alma, otherwise strong-willed, indignant, earnest. Those were the qualities he first liked in her, and, above all, her energy. Not her arguments, he realizes now, but the way she argues, the way she jumps out of her chair, the way she laughs when cornered, as if she could sweep away objections with her hands.

She's wonderful at protestations, manifestos. An orator at picnics, flushed with sun and wine. He's heard the stories about her riding lessons, Mount Holyoke, her wedding afterward. They're in Egypt on their honeymoon and she's riding this stinking camel when these Bedouin women start following them. They're watching her, talking among themselves, and finally the old one comes up to her guide and starts pointing. The guide says, "They want to know how much your husband paid for you." So here she is, with this camel shitting underneath her, giving them the big speech about how in America you marry out of love; the man doesn't pay for you. The guide translates, and the Bedouins start up again, talking among themselves. Finally, one points to her engagement ring. The guide says, "They want to know how much he paid for that." And seriously, she knew right there she was going to leave her husband. She's not going to get bought again.

He's laughed at this, and he's waited straight-faced not to give it away and then watched the rest laugh. And now the story and the laughter afterward cycle together in his mind like dust and a record needle. It scratches him, it hurts him to remember how she tells this standing next to him, arms folded, eyes for her audience. Each time she loses something in the telling. Her tapes are like that, too. It shocks him how cheap she sounds. Everything fresh about her stripped to an insistent, alien voice. It's strange how delicate the old women sound in contrast. They speak without an end, and it's a kind of music, the long, slow ramble of their voices.

"Now did Rose tell you about the ferns?" Eileen asks from tape E.M. 3. "Well, I came in to water; the two of them looked just pitiful to see. So I boiled some water because I'd read years ago tea was the fertilizer for ferns. I watered them with tea, cooled off, of course, and when I came in next morning they'd just perked right up—looked so much better, and all in one night! I kept house for my daddy in West Virginia: I dug up two ferns from somewhere and planted them one on each side of the porch. I used tea, pots of it; kept it in the fridge and heated it a little to take the chill off, of course, and pretty soon those ferns were big like *this*. They used to stop on the road to take pictures of them. It was a cream farm. We sold cream once a week. The milk was for the pigs and the calves in spring. May to July, or was it August? I forget when the calves got milk. We raised most everything. Sold what was left over—we made certain there was plenty left to sell. That was the advantage for us children. If we raised tomatoes we got the cash. Yes, we took them to the produce market; the prices came from Pittsburgh—you could read them in the paper, and when radios came along you could hear them. When Dad died I didn't want to go back . . ."

"But why? Why didn't you?" That was Alma.

"Oh, you know how it is."

"No, I don't know. Tell me why!"

Alma has trouble sleeping at her mother's house. She unbinds herself from the tight sheets and slips downstairs. She wants to take a walk but can't remember how to turn off the new alarm system. It's as cluttered as Rose's place, she thinks as she paces around. Mom's clutter is older, though. Hopi pottery and shards of ancient blue glass, Roman coins, hand puppets and bas-reliefs bought together in Indonesia. Mayan wood carvings. Most of the things are broken, and usually in a set there is one thing missing. Dad would point this out when Mom returned from her excursions. He would line up a set of graduated gold-wire circlets and ask, "Now where are number two and five? Your mother buys seconds," he told Alma.

Even before Dad died, Mom traveled alone. In the summers she took Alma with her—mostly to excavations. They went to Ashkelon once, and after high-school graduation, Pompeii and Herculaneum. Albums of pictures crowd the bookcases. It's frightening the way she keeps them among the artifacts. The photos themselves are such a mixture of dead and living things. Nan and Alma Renquist grinning in Pompeii among the corpses preserved where they went about their business. As Alma flips the album pages, it seems to her the ashen bodies on the streets look more alive—clutching themselves, doubled over—than the tourists frozen upright in the photos. What, after all, has Alma to do with the girl in white shorts? And what relation has her mother to this younger woman holding out something invisible and now forgotten in her hand? Rose and the others with old photo albums talk about themselves as girls, but they are speaking really of other people. She forces the albums back on the shelves. They'd planned an early start to go riding the next day, but Alma sleeps through her alarm and Nan doesn't wake her.

"You're exhausted," she murmurs when Alma appears for lunch.

"No, I'm not," Alma says.

They take a trail up above the canyon, and riding slowly they can feel the sky burning against the red hills. The clouds evaporate above them. "I can almost understand Liz out here," Alma tells her mother.

"She's really marrying him!" Nan says wonderingly. "I can't imagine what sort of children they'll have."

"They won't have any."

"You never know." Nan smiles.

Alma bends over her horse. "I know."

"Are you still seeing—"

"Yes," says Alma. "We're sifting data."

"And then what?" Nan asks.

"Oh, God, I don't know." They stand at the edge of the canyon where the red walls break away to the bottom. "Maybe we'll break up." She looks at Nan slyly. "Maybe we'll get married. Mommy, I was teasing! I didn't mean anything. Besides, we're never *going* to finish the project, so you don't have to worry about what'll happen afterward."

"I do worry," says Nan. "I worry about the way you throw yourself into these projects without an end in sight. You don't consider what they cost you in time or—"

"Oh, say what you mean," Alma says. "It's not the project you're upset about."

"Don't finish my sentences. You work yourself into the ground with these interviews just the way you did with your thesis. And I don't care what kind of feminist Marxism they taught you at Berkeley; you're acting compulsive.

Just tell me honestly if you think this history project is going anywhere."

Alma blinks, but counters, "First, you tell me if you're talking about the project or about Ron. You can't seem to separate the two."

"No, it's you who can't separate them," says Nan.

"Rose called while you were gone," Ron tells her.

"I don't want to hear it," she says.

"Giving up on her?"

Alma flings her backpack down. "Look, I don't have to transcribe every goddamn phone message. I don't have to be on call every waking hour. And that does not mean I'm giving up!"

"Welcome home," he says. "Glad to see you had such a good weekend."

She turns away. Sliding out one of her filing cabinets, she begins sorting the new batch of transcripts the typist delivered.

He picks up the paper. "Did she ask about me?" he asks.

"Sort of."

"What did she say?"

"I don't know. Nothing much. How am I supposed to remember blow by blow?"

"You're supposed to be an oral historian," he points out.

"Well, she's my *mother*, for God's sake. People don't listen to their mother." She brushes the hair out of her eyes. "I'm getting central air-conditioning. We can't work like this."

"Don't do me any favors with her money," mutters Ron.

"Who said it was for you?" she challenges, hurt. "I'm worried about Flush. Look at him. He's suffering in this house. Look at those eyes!" She tosses one of Eileen Meeker's files on the floor. "What do you make of this stuff?"

"I listened to some of it," he says.

"Here's what I've been thinking about Eileen," Alma says. "The key is, she doesn't go back to the farm. It's just after the war began. The Depression is over; she joins the Women's Army Corps. Now what do you make of that? The resources of the farm are depleted."

"If you want my opinion," Ron says, "what she's describing is how to revive dying ferns. And then she remembers the farm. Stop pushing it. Stop pushing all the time."

She slams the file drawer. "If you don't want to think about the analysis, then leave me alone and don't interfere with my work."

"Terrific. You wrap up the inquisition and I'll finish my book."

"Oh, your book," she snaps. "As if I'm the one dragging you away from that! It was your idea, remember. You wanted to help me."

"That's right," says Ron, "and now I want to stop. I have perfect confidence in you. You know exactly what these women should say, and I'm sure single-handedly you can lead them to the truth about their lives."

She forces open a window. "You never wanted to help me. Only criticize my work. You just want to control what I say. You don't want me to be independent."

"Oh, I don't!" says Ron. "Why don't you try that little speech on Mom. I know it works better on men, but I think if we're talking about control—"

"She does not control me."

"Prove it," he says. "If she didn't—if you ever had the courage of your convictions—you would have married me."

"Don't flatter yourself," she says.

He looks at her. "You're right," he says. "She doesn't control you. You're already just like her."

"You don't understand."

"But I do," he says. "Your mother wants us to break up."

"Of course she does," Alma says. "I'm her daughter!"

"So," Ron says, "does she object to me on principle or does she also object to Jews?"

"You don't even know her," says Alma. "And I hate you and the way you twist what I say. Do you have to call my mother a racist to understand that she doesn't want me to marry you? Can't you comprehend this on any other level? It would destroy my relationship with her—"

"You mean she'd disinherit you. That's what you're saying."

"No! I don't care about the money."

"Oh, Alma," he says, "you're such a hypocrite."

"A girdle," Rose tells her. "I'd never wear anything else. Some women over here wear whalebone. These old ladies promenading at the Dorothy Chandler Pavilion in their whalebone and gold lamé. Oof! They are so antiquated. I did see one whale, however. During the war, they took all the children to the Isle of Sandwich before they transported us to England. The Isle of Sandwich—and there was a whale on the beach; I still remember it. I was so small and frail they had to carry me everywhere. But after a few months at the convent I blossomed out. How I blossomed out!"

Alma doesn't have the energy to find a chronology in this. The Isle of Sandwich must be the Isle of Man. But she doesn't ask about it. Rose spins out her own chronology, and she knows the places she has been.

"I still remember the day Caruso died," she continues seamlessly. "I was playing by the sea. Extra! Extra! Read all about it! The place is ordinary now, but in the twenties the resort was chic. Our governess had an operatic voice. She spent evenings at the piano and it was not unusual for a crowd to gather at the window. She was a lovely girl, but married quite beneath her." She frowns searchingly. "He was in the chicken business, I believe. When I came here from England, other girls my age were dating, and I was just a child, size seventeen, incidentally. How my cousins stared at me! Shainey called me the Grina Cusina—she got the name from the song, you know. But I had something they didn't. My complexion was like perfect makeup. It was peaches, it was pink, people turned around in the street. For my first date—do you know how old I was?" Alma looks up startled. "I was twenty-three," Rose says.

On their first date, Ron and Alma had gone to the opening of *The Birds* at UCLA. Swinging on trapezes above the audience, the actors merged Aristophanes with lampoons of Reaganomics. Alma got a crick in her neck watching, but somehow they made it to intermission. "Dive Bomb!" headlined the review in the *Daily Bruin*. Then they went to a recital series by a cellist friend who looked so exalted when he played, Ron used to moan, "If only they could turn off the sound!"

"There was a young man I was sweet on," Rose says. "And Shainey said to his real young lady: You have black eyebrows and yellow hair! That was unheard of. In those days it was unheard of to—to dissect people like that. But he wasn't the one, you know. When I first got engaged, my brother and my parents said they would never speak to me again. Alma! You're not listening."

Alma shakes herself. "Yes, I am."

"But you look terrible! What is it, dear? You haven't said a word. What was that?"

"Nothing," Alma whispers. "My boyfriend left."

"Oh yes," Rose says, with perfect cognizance. "That's just what I was saying. My brother swore never to speak to me again or even utter my name in his house. He did it, too!"

"He was Jewish," says Alma.

"Of course he was. All my fiancés were Jewish."

"No, Ron." She wants overwhelmingly to run away, to break away from Rose and the long, cryptic history of Rose's life.

Rose considers Alma's case a moment. "Well," she concludes, "if he was Jewish, it was a good thing you parted. If you had married, it would have broken his mother's heart! Anyway, they all thought he was no good. It turned out they were right, too. So I broke it off. Can you imagine? Don't cry, dear. It was only my first engagement. It was very sad; but you know, somehow I lived through it! Don't feel bad."

The Wedding of Henry Markowitz

Henry sits at the oval claw-foot table, expandable to seat twelve—his find at a Wantage estate sale, a jewel of Victoriana, refinished down to its griffin feet. It's big, but it's the table he always wanted, and that's why he bought it. He simply hired piano movers. The flat is full of his discoveries, his rare books, and his antique decanters. There is a special case for his maps, his charts of the heavens. He designed it and had it built by a cabinetmaker. Everything fits; the colors are warm library hues, deep green and cinnabar.

"Describe the expression on her face," Henry says to his younger brother, Ed.

"Flabbergasted," Ed says. "Ma was completely taken aback. Well, we were all so surprised. I mean, to hear you were *engaged*! Ma was in shock! But we were so pleased." He looks at Henry. "Well, I mean, what do you want to know?"

"I just wondered how she looked," Henry says, fidgeting with the place cards on the table.

"Oh," Ed says. "Well."

"Tell me about your work. How is the book coming?"

"What, the anthology?"

"No, no—your history of the Arabic-speaking peoples."

"That was fifteen years ago, Henry!" Ed says with some annoyance. "I haven't worked on that for fifteen years."

"That long?" Henry says. "What a shame. I was thinking about it just the other day. There was an exhibit of Persian miniatures at the Ashmolean, and I was thinking about your book, your idea about the art and politics—the art especially. It's so rich—the compression, the landscape, and the men with their swords, and a waterfall like a thread into an oasis, all in one little frame. They were like jewels. You've got to go back to it; you could just do the art, you know. Even if you just did the art—"

"Well, I'm not an art historian," Ed says. "And I'm not Albert Hourani, either. I just do the best I can."

Henry looks at him and feels flustered. "What do you think of these?" he asks, holding up the place cards. "We had the calligrapher who did the addresses for the invitations. The printing was a nightmare, of course. There are scarcely any engravers left. Would you believe invitations these days are nearly all done thermally? Run your finger over the verso and you can feel the difference."

"Huh." Ed stares at him, head propped up on his fist. He has been flying most of the night and isn't acclimated to Oxford in June—the birds singing at four-thirty in the morning and the searing blue sky.

"Won't you have some coffee?" Henry asks him.

"Some tea? Earl Grey? Black currant? How was Yehudit's graduation?"

"It was fine," Ed says. "It was beautiful. It rained. Here, I brought you pictures." He takes out the snapshots of his daughter, of the family under umbrellas.

"Oh, it looks like it was *pouring*," Henry says. "Oh, the poor thing—she looks drenched. Those umbrellas! My God, what if it rains at the reception? We checked the almanacs, of course, for the chances. Oh, look at Sarah with that plastic bag over her hair!"

Ed is gazing out at Henry's living room, at his brocaded armchairs and his stacks of books. Leather-bound quartos, damp and a little ragged. The huge dark table stretches through the living room, grotesquely out of scale.

"And these are the sibs!" Henry bursts out, holding a photo of Ed's two oldest before him. "They're huge!"

"They're—they're nineteen and twenty-one years old," Ed splutters.

"Really! I had forgotten they were so old. The time just, just— Are you angry at me?"

"What's to be angry at? I'm jet-lagged, can't you see that? I get on the plane at Dulles, and here you are in the same apartment with these little books and these chairs—these *things* of yours."

Henry flushes to the tip of his nose.

"Well, I'm sorry," Ed says. "I thought by now you'd know the ages of my children."

"I *did* know," Henry protests. "I used to know. I lost track!"

"Well, we're all supposed to keep track of you," Ed snaps. "We just picked up and schlepped across the Atlantic on two months' notice."

"Don't be upset," Henry says.

"I'm not upset. I'm trying to tell you it wasn't easy for

us to get here, let alone bring Mother. Sarah and I have *very* complex schedules. I'm overextended, I've got papers promised, I've got a conference in July with half the funding gone, since the Institute went belly up. I've got graduate students covering my classes right now. Sarah is missing her conference completely."

"I'm sorry," Henry says.

"It's okay," says Ed. "I just want you to see. We don't just pop over to Oxford—"

"I know," Henry says. "And I'm grateful, Edward."

"So don't talk to me about paper!" Ed bursts out.

"What paper?"

"Just stop with the paper; that's all I ask."

"I was talking about engraving," Henry says. "I thought it would interest you."

"All right. Okay, look—" Ed stares at Henry's grandfather clock. In the clock case a gold moon shines against a background of midnight blue.

Henry watches from the window as the rented Ford Fiesta lurches off, scattering gravel. He and his brother have not become close friends. Periodically they write letters, but there is always this barrier: Edward can never imagine him as a human being, not as he really is. He's always insulting Henry's collections, his passions for art and manuscripts and rare editions. Edward looks down on him for leaving America. But, of course, Edward is part of it all—what America has become. Those sprawling universities Henry left behind long ago. America, with its mass-produced undergraduates processed through seedy lecture halls where, under flickering lights, they slump with their knees up and take in lectures as they might see movies. Where the familiar passes into the wide pupils of their eyes and the rest dribbles down the aisles to collect with the dirt and candy wrappers at the professor's feet. Has he not been a professor at Queens College and then NYU? And the graduate students. Hasn't he seen them at Princeton clustering at the office doors? Young Calibans eager for praise. They can tear open the Italian Renaissance before lunch, strangle a Donne sonnet and crush its wings, battering away with blunt instruments. As for the older scholars—like students at a cooking school, they cook up Shakespeare, serve him up like roast goose, stuffed with their political-sexual agendas, carve and quarter him with long knives. For Henry, reading had always been a gentle thing, a thing as delicate as blowing eggs. Two pinpricks and the meaning came, whole, unbroken, into the bowl. Now reading is a boiling and a breaking, something to concoct. It's a deviling of art, history, social theory, politics—all mixed and piped back in and served up on a platter. These are the scholars in the journals now. They are at war with the beautiful; they are against God and metaphor. They deny, as Edward does, all of what Henry believes; in fact, all that he lives for: texture and artistry. And Edward is more than a part of it. He has become a shaper himself of the tawdry yellow thing they sell now as the humanities. The cheapening of craft and light, intuition and sensibility, into the social sciences. Edward had begun as a Near Eastern historian and now is nothing more than a political expert. Another cog in the grant-getting, TV-interview machine.

Henry has left all of that—the academic mills, the illusion that scholarship can persist in those ugly industrial institutions. And this is the best America has to offer. The rest of it is so ugly, so corrupt, Henry can't bear thinking about it. He took his business degree and left the country to live like a human being: manager of Laura Ashley by day, artistic impresario by night, amid the bells and turrets of a true university, with gentle old walls, lichen-covered and printed with season after season of lilacs and the thick, corded stems of roses. He walks in the deep silence of these courtyards, especially in the weeks in September, when the tourists have faded but the late flowers still bloom in their second and third ranks under the mullioned windows, and especially in March, before the students have returned from vacation and the willows begin to show pale green—those last weeks in September and March when Oxford is completely his own.

But Edward can never see any of this. He's caught in the American rituals. Food, kids, cars, commercials. How could one expect Edward to look up and enter into the wedding? Henry paces into the kitchen and mists his African violet. He counts to ten, simply because he can't allow himself to get upset.

The suite in the Old Parsonage Hotel has dark-green curtains, and Ed draws them closed and sinks down on the bed beside his wife. "Where's Mother?" he asks.

"End of the hall. Taking a hot bath." Sarah closes her eyes again. "How is he?" she asks him.

"Same as ever."

"And what about her?"

"Who?"

"The bride. Ed?"

"I don't know, she's fine. She wasn't there; she was working."

Sarah rolls over and looks at him. "What did you talk about?"

"We talked about him, of course. And his *things*."

"Did you ask him when we're supposed to come tonight?"

"No. Wasn't it eight o'clock?"

"Why didn't you ask him?"

Ed sighs. "Because he amazes me. Because I walk into his apartment and he's still doing *Brideshead Revisited*, with those brocades and those clocks! Those rotting leather bindings. His eighteenth-century *peklach*!"

"Oh, stop."

"And that ridiculous table. I'm not going to make it, Sarah." Ed swings his laptop onto the bed and unzips the case.

Sarah says, "I think it's sad that you can't just—"

"Have a normal conversation with him?"

"No, I meant just lighten up. This is your only brother getting married."

"So to speak." Ed fiddles with the keyboard, as if he were typing up the book review that was due a month ago.

"What do you mean?" Sarah asks.

"You know what I mean."

"Oh, come out and say it," she says. "You've got such an attitude, Ed. It's unbelievable."

"Well, it's so obvious," he exclaims. "You thought so, too. For years."

"Not necessarily," says Sarah, who is a writer of fiction and believes in change, secrets, and revelations.

The last time they were in Oxford was ten years ago, when Ed lectured at the Wantage Center—the Oxford Center for Peace in the Middle East. Henry had them over for dinner and cooked everything with heavy cream. The kids were sick, Ed turned green trying to make conversation, Ed and Henry's mother, Rose, took a glass of Drambuie and fell asleep. And there they all were. They've seen Henry since then, in Washington; and he's had his turn feeling ill, looking up with mournful eyes from their clamorous dinner table all sprawled over with teenagers. He wrote them letters, as well. "There is a pale gold in the walls," he would write, "and toward evening a kind of glow in the stone—the kind of color one glimpses in the last flicker of sun on the river—the last lingering warmth of the day, such a poignance, and the tracery so frail, the stained glass in Corpus Christi like the last glowing embers of a fire, the last opalescent, bluest flame." And Sarah would write back, speaking for the family, "Ben is at band camp and Ed may now have the grant application in on time." They kept up the correspondence, as the two letter writers of the family. It was a strange match. The lyrical, if sometimes muddled, estuaries of Henry's fountain pen and the updates from Sarah's Uni-Ball. Ed rolled his eyes at Henry's letters, and the kids groaned when they heard them, but Sarah kept some of them. The truth was she liked them. She'd had all that kind of writing beaten out of her in workshops, but she secretly liked it. Once when she went to pick up Ed at Georgetown she stopped and watched for the last light on the tracery. It was too early in the evening, however.

"I'm not up for a four-hour dinner," Ed tells her.

"It starts at eight?"

"I said I don't know."

"I said you have to call him and ask," Sarah says.

"I'm taking a nap."

There is a knock at the door as Ed takes off his pants.

"It's your mother," Sarah says.

"I am aware of that," Ed says, and he puts his pants back on again.

Rose appears at the door in jet-black wraparound sunglasses because of her recent cataract operation. "Where is Henry?" she asks, her voice surprisingly strong for her eighty-six years.

"We're meeting him for dinner," Ed says.

"But you were picking him up and bringing him to the hotel."

"He has errands today. Last-minute—"

"Why are we here at the last minute?" Rose sighs.

"I'm already missing a week of school," Ed says. "We discussed this, Ma; remember? And you wouldn't travel by yourself."

"I would have," Rose says.

"Well, that's not what you said before."

"I would have if it meant I could see Henry. If I could have spent time with him."

Ed looks at her. "Well, we discussed this before, and that was not what you said."

"But that's what I was thinking," Rose says. "How can we meet the family three days before? Where is the bride?"

"We're meeting her for dinner," Sarah says.

Rose takes off her sunglasses and snaps them shut with disgust. "What kind of dinner could *that* be? Without any introductions. What kind of thing is that? You go to a wedding to be with the family. You go to meet the community. *You* had a beautiful wedding," she says to Sarah and looks at her so yearningly that Sarah feels she weighs one hundred and twenty-five pounds again. "Everyone was there except for the Feldmans and the Richters and Natalie, may she rest in peace, and the Yarchevers." There had been a band that was not to be believed and they all danced so long that Sarah's father, Sol, paid the men for two extra hours. Sarah just floated on Ed's arm, layers and layers of tulle in her gown. She was so slender—and Ed, too; they were twenty-two years old, Ed just three months older. "Apart from that, everyone was there," Rose tells them now, "and they still talk about it. Who is going to remember this wedding?"

"Well, he invited two hundred fifty people," Sarah says.

"But who that we know?" murmurs Rose. "Who? How many? No one."

"I'm going to take a nap now," Ed says.

After Rose goes back to her room and they lie down, the phone rings. Ed realizes he has a splitting headache.

"Hello?" Sarah answers.

"Hello, it's Rose. Tell me her name again."

"Susan McPhearson."

"I know that; I mean the spelling."

Sarah spells it for her.

"That's not a Jewish name," Rose says.

"It's not a Jewish person, Ma," Ed calls out. He can hear Rose's voice over the receiver.

"You tell Ed," Rose says to Sarah on the phone, "that there are a lot of women and gentlemen in this world pretending they are what they are not."

"I don't think anyone's pretending," Sarah ventures.

"Fine," Rose says. "Remember, I told you about the Winston couple on the Alaska cruise. At the Chopin concert I met the couple, last name Winston. I looked at this old gentleman. Winston? Never. A Weinstein. 'Where are you from?' 'Tenafly, New Jersey.' 'But where were you from before that?' He admits originally he was from Vienna; he'll only go so far, you know. So during the intermission I speak to him with my good *Hochdeutsch*. We all spoke *very* good German, growing up. He and I and Mrs. Winston become friendly. We sit down again, and this young pianist, this young boy, begins banging the Chopin—it went right through my head, because he had no feeling for the music, not the slightest understanding. So I lean over to this old gentleman—Winston, as he calls himself—and I whisper in Yiddish, referring to the pianist:

'Vos veist a chazer fun lukshen?' What does a pig know about egg noodles? He nods his head. Weinstein! That's how I caught him and his *Hochdeutsch.* He understood Yiddish perfectly."

Ed grabs the receiver from Sarah. "Susan McPhearson doesn't know Yiddish, Ma."

"Neither do you," Rose points out. "Let me tell you—"

"She's not pretending," Ed says.

"I wasn't just thinking of her," Rose says. "There's also Henry."

"What do you think she meant by that?" Ed asks Sarah after he hangs up the phone. "That Henry is pretending?"

Sarah looks up at the ceiling. They are lying together on the bed. "That he's pretending he's English, I guess."

"Oh, he's been doing that for years," Ed says. "I really think she's wondering what he's doing taking up with a woman after all this time."

"All this time? You don't have the slightest idea how he's been living. You barely looked at his letters."

"He never said anything in his letters."

"Yes, he did," Sarah says. "Just because they were all about bridges over the river—"

"The wind in the willows and the antiquarian book sales at Fyfield Manor. I think basically this is going to be a companionate marriage."

"Oh, no, it won't be," says Sarah. "They'll go to Stratford, and they'll go punting—"

"Yeah, I can really picture Henry standing up in a punt."

Henry is at his Laura Ashley office, on the phone with Unwin's about the champagne. He has shopped for the wedding in the European way, at little specialty shops all through town, and he would have done without a caterer altogether if he could; catering seems to him so much like the supermarket approach. As it is, he has the crusty rolls ordered from his own bakery, Mrs. Thomson's Victorian Bakery. He drives there every afternoon for the day's bread, because it is simply the best there is. Mrs. T. uses a brick oven in the wall, with its cast-iron door embossed "Bendick & Peterson, 1932" above a sheaf of wheat. How many times has he asked to watch as Mrs. T. opens that door and slips the loaves out with her paddle? The cake is being decorated by a specialist. Henry designed it himself. Six tiers in ivory with sprays of lilacs pouring down, all done in royal icing and tinted buttercream. There is a filigree skirt to it, like antique lace traced in sugar. He wouldn't tell Susan how much it cost. "We'll only have a wedding cake once in our lives," he said.

"I never liked sweets," she said, "but I suppose we must eat some *gâteau.*" That shocked him; not that Susan didn't like sweets but the idea that their cake would be eaten. He hadn't thought of that at all.

"All right, then," Unwin's assistant says on the phone. "Never fear. We've got all the champagne here in the store, and we'll wheel the bottles in on our hand trucks."

"Around the back?" Henry asks.

"Round the back, sir."

When he gets off the phone he locks the office and finds his assistant, Mary. "Where is Susan's gown?" he asks her.

"She picked it up yesterday," Mary says.

"So she did. I'm a little distracted," he confides. "Just between us." He runs out to the car.

Susan is filing papers at her desk. She is assistant registrar at Merton College and knows where everything is. In forest green and an antique shawl, her graying hair pinned up loosely, she flicks off the lights in her office, closes the door, and goes out to meet Henry. They are a tall couple, and complement each other. Where Henry's ears and nose are knobby, Susan's face is fine and rather flat. Henry rubs at the last curls on his head and Susan walks on sensibly without fidgeting at all.

"I asked him about his book," Henry says, "and he's given up on it altogether. The good book, the one he was going to write on Arabic thought and art. He's just given up on it, does the political thing now. It's so sad, Susan, so terribly sad, what he's become."

"*He* may like it," Susan points out.

"Oh, I don't think so," Henry says. "How could he? Giving it all up to be some sort of apologist to the media for the P.L.O. or the Arab League. When there was such beauty to uncover, such a history there. And he's just a pardoner—selling indulgences on TV."

"It can't be as bad as all that," Susan says.

"I shouldn't have brought it up with him," Henry sighs, "but that's the problem, you know, there's nothing we can't fight about. We're going to sit there tonight at dinner, and I'll spend three hundred pounds, and what will we say?"

"At Elizabeth? We can talk about the wines. The wines alone . . . Besides, the others will be there—Sarah." She looks at him encouragingly.

"And Mother," Henry says.

He has booked the private room upstairs at Elizabeth, and it's terribly expensive, but Henry couldn't face cooking on such an occasion. He is a perfectionist about his cooking; he exhausts himself worrying. The room is dark with rich paneling, and there are candles set in antique sconces. When he opens the door, Susan steps in and sees his family for the first time, pale and a little startled in the dim light, blinking to see her, like cave dwellers. Then Ed jumps up and clasps her hand. Sarah is kissing Henry on the cheek. "Hello, dear," Rose says to Susan. "Henry, we thought you would never get here. I was sure it was the wrong restaurant and I was afraid we wouldn't be able to see you."

"Mother," he says, "this is Susan McPhearson."

"It's a pleasure to meet you," Rose says to Susan. "Tell me, how do you spell your name?"

When the terrine arrives, Sarah takes the conversation into her own hands. "Where will you be living?" she asks Susan and Henry.

"In Henry's flat," Susan says, "until we find something bigger. I've still got my books up in mine, and—"

"And we've got a cottage in Wantage," Henry tells them. "I'll drive you out there tomorrow afternoon."

"Out in the country?" Rose asks. "I've always wanted a sweet cottage in the country," she tells Susan, "ever since I was a little girl; a thatched cottage with roses. I grew up in London, you know. I was evacuated . . ."

"Really?" Susan exclaims, but they are interrupted.

"Ma," Ed says, leaning over, "they don't have any plain chicken."

"You know I can't have sauces," Rose says. "Not with my digestion."

"It doesn't come without sauce," Henry says.

"In the beginning it all comes without sauce," Rose says.

"Have a little fish," Sarah suggests.

"Where is your family, dear?" Rose asks Susan.

"My sisters are coming up Saturday for the wedding. Dad is here now, but he doesn't go out at night."

"Hmm," Rose says. "And who is performing the ceremony?"

"The Junior Chaplain at the College. We got him because I'm staff."

Ed leans back in his chair. "So you get him free?" he asks lightly.

"You're having a priest?" Rose asks.

"A very liberal one," Susan says. "Very young. Vegan."

"You told me a justice of the peace," Rose tells Henry. "I thought you said a justice of the peace."

"We were considering it," Henry says.

"That was when we were going to have a simpler wedding," explains Susan.

"But no one told me about this—"

"Ma, we discussed this in Washington!" Ed exclaims. "We discussed this at the airport. I told you ten times about this wedding."

The door opens, and the waiter backs in with a tray of covered platters. In silence he serves the family. Sarah smiles wanly at him. When he comes to Rose she holds up her hand and says, "None for me, thank you."

"None at all, madam?" the waiter asks.

"Mother," Henry whispers. The waiter looks at him for direction. Henry gestures him to put the plate down on the table. Rose waves him away.

"Look, put it there on the sideboard," Sarah says. They all watch as the waiter covers it up and rushes about getting a stand for the dish, lighting the flame under it.

"Ed, I want to go home," Rose says after the waiter has gone.

"We're going to stay here and finish dinner," Ed tells her doggedly, and he begins to eat.

"Ed," Rose says, "call me a cab. I want to go back to Heathrow."

Sarah gulps down her wine the wrong way and starts to choke. Susan thumps her on the back.

"No, we're not doing that now," Ed is telling Rose. "We can't change the tickets. You're not going, and that's just it. I've had enough, Ma. We've come this far and we're going through with this thing."

"Ed!" Sarah coughs.

"This wedding," Ed amends.

Rose begins to cry. "What would your dear father say to this?" she asks. "Did I bring you up to give you away to a priest? Just tell me, Henry, what change has occurred in you to bring you to this?"

Henry looks across the table to the antique sideboard with Rose's covered dinner on it. What change indeed? It was an escape he'd planned his whole life, ever since he'd learned to read, when he uncovered Arabian caverns and climbed Scottish citadels and read Keats's odes in the bathroom. He was scribing the Romantic poets into memory as he walked to school, big for his age—he was always tall, while Ed was little and mean and played basketball, all speed and elbows. Henry has told Susan about this. How he wore lace-up shoes and carried a leather briefcase stained burnt orange from the snow, the buckles working themselves loose. It was stuffed with Norse myths, crammed with Arthurian romances—and, of course, his science books, his Hebrew books. He has told Susan how he and Ed schlepped to Hebrew school after regular school and every week he sat in Mr. Hurov's class and watched Mr. Hurov with his pointy teeth announce: "*Hayom nilmad binyan kal.*" "Today we will learn conjugation *kal.*" The first conjugation. The easy one. Every week and every year. The class moved up and up, into Intermediate and even Advanced Hebrew, and they never learned the other conjugations. There were girls sitting in back who made sure of that. Slender, cracking gum with little pointed tongues, like pubescent ladies of Avignon. They never listened, never let the class move on. And how Mr. Hurov sighed, how he fumed. He was a very cultured European man, and he wanted them to learn enough to read a certain poem by Bialik about a pool in the forest. The girls didn't even know about the pool. They weren't even listening when Mr. Hurov told the class about it. Henry knew about the poem, the pool in the forest, but of course he couldn't read it. He didn't know the other six conjugations. He didn't have the vocabulary. He told Susan how they made him practice for his bar mitzvah and he had to memorize the Hebrew and pretend he understood it. How he took comfort in writing his bar-mitzvah speech. His portion was the attempted sacrifice of Isaac, and he spent weeks reading about human sacrifice. He read W. Robertson Smith's book *Lectures on the Religion of the Semites* and typed up his speech on the ancient sacrificial cults, laboriously typed it —thirty-one pages—on his father's manual typewriter. And then the rabbi met with him to review his speech, read two pages, and put it down on his desk and said—this was what crushed him—"Where do you thank your family and friends for coming? Your aunts from Philadelphia? Why didn't you thank Mr. Hurov for preparing you and teaching you Hebrew?"

"Because he *didn't* teach me any Hebrew," Henry had muttered. But of course they made him do it their way. He told Susan how he sat smothered in the long, stifling service at the temple, where the cantor sang out of the right side of his mouth and the congregation droned in answer. How he rose and recited the name of each relative who had come to witness this milestone. How, naturally, all his research on human sacrifice was excised from the speech. In summer he had hay fever and sneezed in the dusty, airless rooms of the house, with its polished tables and tall, fringed, shantung lampshades, its twin beds with pale-blue candlewick bedspreads, its overstuffed chairs, heavy curtains, heavy meals. Rose took him and Ed shopping and tried to force Henry to buy jackets and shoes that never quite fit. In the shoe store he would stand on the fluoroscope and stare at the X-ray image of his feet. The green outline of his bones. Books and the museums beckoned to the other world.

He hadn't thought of it in years, when he met Susan. It was years since he'd left home, years since he'd bothered to remember it all—his childhood or even his first plans to escape the city and the department stores, the temple, the gum-cracking girls. Talking to Susan he remembered his first sightings of the Old World, completely new to him. He told her how he found it in Mr. Birnbaum's German and French classes at Tilden High School and how he started to read Flaubert and trail his fingers in streams of adjectives. How he discovered the Pre-Raphaelites and saw a reproduction of Millais's *Ophelia*, the figure floating downstream, her hair floating with the flowers, and how he wanted that painting, or rather wanted to drift downstream himself into that painting, to submerge himself in those colors, surrender to that shining water. Meanwhile, Ed was taking Spanish in Mr. Levinson's class so that he could become an ambassador to South America and then an official in the State Department. Henry hadn't thought of this in years, and perhaps that was why, when Henry began talking to Susan, he fell in love so quickly. They sat down together at Les Quatre Saisons, and he found himself telling her about Mr. Hurov and the shoe stores, the corridors of Tilden High School, his aborted bar-mitzvah speech. All of it tumbled out; she nodded sagely, without the slightest comprehension. That moved him deeply, to see her fascination with his childhood, the endless rituals he remembered, the embarrassments, the aesthetic violations—the maroon-flocked wallpaper in the temple's basement social hall, the mirrors, and the modern brass chandelier spreading across the ceiling like an arthritic hand, palm up. His cloying aunts. She had never heard of such things. He unburdened his heart there in the restaurant until the last crumbs of their strawberry tarts had vanished and she sat looking into his eyes, mesmerized. Dare he make the comparison? He felt like Othello, come from foreign parts. He could never say it—it would sound ridiculous—but it was true: "She lov'd me for the dangers I had pass'd, and I lov'd her that she did pity them." There were aspects of his past they didn't discuss, but, then, those things belonged to a part of his life which he had rarely if ever spoken about, even within himself—a part of his life that had narrowed over time, hemmed in by a lack of direct speech. With Susan it was all talk. He poured words into her ear, filled her open hands with his stories. The other kind of passion was not something he and Susan associated strongly with each other. This is not to say they never touched each other; only that it was talk the two of them loved best, and that Henry had wanted a listener, thirsted for one. From the time of this first dinner he was overwhelmed with gratitude, tenderness, relief. He had told her his whole childhood, down to the last bourgeois pretension, told her everything.

"I'm going to no wedding with priests in it," Rose is telling Ed, and her voice startles Henry, returning him to the dinner at hand.

"Mother," Henry says, "please don't upset yourself."

"She's tired," Ed advises Henry softly. "None of us got any sleep on the plane. She said she was taking a nap this afternoon, but—"

"Why are they whispering about me in the third person?" Rose asks. "I can tell you what I was doing this afternoon. I was writing seven postcards. I'm not tired," she informs Ed. "I'm upset, because I was told one thing and then another, and I don't like to be manipulated. If it was going to be a priest you should have told me the truth."

"Here," Sarah says to Rose, "try to eat some of your chicken; it costs a fortune." She puts Rose's dish on the table and pulls off the cover with a flourish.

"I don't want it," Rose says. "I want to go home."

"Absolutely not," Ed says, mortified for Henry, who has provided such an exquisite dinner, such delicate wines.

"I'll run you back," Susan offers, to Ed's surprise. "Why don't I drive her back to the hotel? It's just ten minutes." She takes out her car keys.

It's almost dark as Susan drives Rose back to the Old Parsonage. "You must understand," Rose declares, "I love everything English. My family sent me to London when the Great War started. When the English Jewish societies provided the opportunity, my parents sent me. I was just seven years old, but there was no food in Vienna. It was hardly better than Bukovina. When my English family took me in I was so weak and frail they had to carry me. But after the first month I blossomed out! We took tea, we had the theater, and at the seaside we played with our governess, who had an operatic voice and used to sing on the balcony—" She pauses, searching her memory. "In any case, he gets it from me," she says.

"Gets what?" asks Susan.

"England. He loves England, and it's because of me. I brought him up that way. I bought him books when he was a little child. King Arthur and the English poetry. Ed was never interested in England, but I would tell Henry about the countryside. The green meadows and fields of poppies. I learned all my English here in England, you know, when I was a child. My English family provided me with an education and even a tutor in Hebrew twice a week. They didn't forget that. They were a very wealthy family and they took us every year to a cottage by the sea, and our governess used to go out on the balcony and sing like a golden flute. That was how she would sing—" She loses the thought when the man at the hotel opens the door and helps her out of the car.

After Susan leaves, and Rose is alone in her hotel room, she takes two Percodans and lies down. Then she remembers what she was about to say.

The day before the wedding, Susan takes off from work, and Henry finally has a chance to drive his family out to Wantage to see the cottage. They have to coax Rose out of the hotel, and she tells them all again that she won't be coming to the wedding. She would rather sit in the hotel dining room alone. But when she sees Henry's cottage she sighs. It has a gray thatched roof and white walls. "The garden is still rough, but we're planting," Henry says. "Doesn't it look just like David Copperfield's Rookery? It doesn't have rooks, of course." The thatch is covered with chicken wire to keep the birds away.

Susan unlocks the door, and they all stand in the little front room and look at the gleaming pewter pitchers on the mantel and Henry's china cabinet, his Persian carpets. "Oh, it's a doll's house," Rose murmurs, and she sinks down on the love seat, ready to stay.

"I almost sold it," Susan says. "It was such trouble. I had it listed before I met Henry."

"How *did* you meet?" Ed asks.

"Oh, didn't Henry say? Dick Frankel introduced us at the Wantage Center. He thought Henry might buy the house."

Ed looks over at Henry and imagines the meeting at one of the center teas. Dick Frankel bustling around as center founder, fund-raiser—proprietor of the manor house he has acquired for his center for Middle East peace. A fixer-up manor house on the outer fringes of academic Oxford. Henry's cottage, Ed thinks, is a similar project on a smaller scale. Yes, Frankel would have introduced Henry and Susan at one of his garden parties. Long tables in the sunken garden at the back of the manor house. Israeli historians in short-sleeved white shirts, Henry in a lemon-yellow linen jacket and silk tie, a babble of Hebrew and the slight stammer of Oxford English under the trees, and Susan standing in the middle in a great straw hat and a billowy skirt—not at all impressionistic, quite substantial.

Henry is ushering Sarah upstairs to show her the bedroom. "Watch your head," he says as they sit down in a pair of chairs tucked under the eaves. "I wanted to talk to you about Mother," he whispers. "Do you really think she'll refuse to come to the chapel tomorrow?"

"I'm not sure," Sarah begins.

"Do you think she'd do that to me?" Henry asks.

"You know her better than I do," Sarah says. "She's capable of just about anything."

"But you've got to talk to her."

Sarah smiles wryly at her brother-in-law. "Look, we're going to try, but you can't let her ruin the wedding. You knew she'd make a scene. She's been practicing for months."

"Years," says Henry.

"No, not years. The truth is, she's in shock. She wasn't expecting it. Well, none of us— So tell, me, anyway." Sarah leans closer. "How did it all happen? When did you decide—uh, propose?"

Henry brightens a little. "Well, I was in the market, looking for a little cottage just like this, and after Dick gave me Susan's number we drove out here one Sunday and I saw this place—a wreck—and I said, 'Absolutely not,' and she said, 'How would you like to come round for a slummy lunch?' And we went up to her flat and talked books, and we talked about decorating. She was reupholstering and so was I, and we talked about the cottage, and I said she should redo it and then sell it. She could get estimates. And I took her to the store and showed her our new fabrics. She started buying, and we went in on it together."

"Quite a project," says Sarah.

"Oh, yes, an investment. We were going to sell it to a couple from London as a retreat. But we were both such perfectionists; we were spending weeks looking for period doorknobs; we were restoring a 1923 stove—"

"Henry," Rose calls from downstairs.

"*Aaagh!*" he screams, as, standing up, he slams his head into the sloped ceiling.

"My God, what *is* the matter?" Susan cries out as she races up the stairs.

"No, no, don't, don't touch me," Henry cries, clutching his head, and he stands smarting, face flushed red, in the center of the room. "Don't crowd me," he says.

"Let me have a look at it," Susan says.

"Just get me some ice," he moans, and sinks down on one of the white twin beds.

"I *thought* those chairs were too big for that spot," Susan says when she returns with the ice. "Oh, Henry, that's a nasty bump. What will they think tomorrow? Just take this pillow here and hold the ice."

"Henry," Rose calls from the stairwell, "what did you do to yourself?"

On the drive back to the hotel, Rose dozes off and Ed listens intently to BBC 3. Sarah imagines Henry and Susan spreading out fabric swatches over the furniture in the cottage. She thinks of them putting so much of themselves into the house that they belonged to it and to each other. Marriage was the only way to finish up such a project, such a detailed, intricate design—reproduction William Morris vines twining the kitchen walls. Sleepily, Sarah thinks of those poets and Oxonians who became Higher and Higher Church, seeking spire after spire until they were Catholic and their churches were cathedrals. Was Henry like that, marrying? Moving—she imagines—from young men to gardening, then to orchards, and finally to a cottage and a wife? A courtship more and more ornate. Sarah had thought Henry lived beautifully before; she had been a little disappointed to hear of his marrying. It seemed like a capitulation to the everyday world. But Henry hasn't given in at all. He has retreated into the more decorated nineteenth century.

When the gong sounds for breakfast at the Old Parsonage, Ed and Sarah dress quickly and march over to Rose's door. "Rose," Sarah calls through the door, "we'll be in the dining room." Then they go down to their porridge and their thin, triangle-cut toast. They don't wait for Rose to answer the door; they have a battle plan.

But Rose doesn't join them at breakfast, and she isn't waiting for them when they return. Ed runs out for the

Guardian. Sarah lays out her pressed linen suit on the bed and listens for Rose in the hall. Henry expects them at eleven for pictures. They read the *Guardian* in great detail. Henry phones twice.

"I can't take this," Ed bursts out at ten-thirty. He abandons the plan and pounds on Rose's door. "Come out, Ma—you're coming to the wedding!" he shouts.

"I am certainly not," Rose calls back.

"You're going to sit in bed all day? Is that what you came to England for?"

"I did not come to be bulldozed at my age," Rose says.

Ed stamps back into his room. "I thought she wasn't getting any attention for that kind of behavior," Sarah says. She is loading her camera, slotting extra rolls of film into the loops in the strap.

Ed picks up the phone and calls Rose down the hall. "We're leaving now, Ma," he says softly. "You don't want to make Henry miserable, do you?"

"Don't you browbeat me," Rose snaps. "Can't you see—I'm the one who's miserable?"

They wait a little longer, and then they leave for the wedding. After they have left, the man from room service wheels up a cart piled with covered dishes, a morning paper, coffeepot, and a vase with a rosebud. He stops at Rose's door.

Looking down the aisle of the chapel, standing in a storm of organ music, Henry watches Susan as she comes forward to join him. She walks serenely and slowly in her heavy gown, matching her steps to those of her eighty-three-year-old father.

Ed sits nervously in his high-backed pew and scans the faces of Henry's guests. He guesses that they are nearly all Jewish. As Susan helps her father to a seat, Sarah examines the wedding gown, a patterned cotton damask, white on white, with a bell skirt and full sleeves. Susan's hair shines silver in the jeweled chapel light. Ed fidgets and looks out at the Jewish community of Oxford, some twenty Israeli scholars among them, with dark-eyed children piping up in Hebrew and told to sit still, all of them sitting among banks of white lilies. But Sarah feels a particular joy watching Henry in his gray morning coat and Susan all in white. Surely Henry is living out a kind of fairy tale, or at least the sequel to one, marrying the fairy godmother. "Look, there's Dick and Irene Frankel," Ed whispers.

Henry stands transfixed, with Susan at his side. Above them, far above, stand the seven points of the chapel window, and above that, the rose window, floating like a pendant in the dusty light. The chaplain's voice and the green dusk of the place fill his mind. The dark carvings of leaves, the glint of gold, and rich sound. He has seen and heard but never lived the place as he does now. He forgets everything else and does not realize that his mother has actually arrived and is standing at the back of the chapel, putting the cab change into her wallet, snapping her pocketbook shut.

"The aspic is melting," Henry tells Susan anxiously under the tent on the Wantage Center grounds. They couldn't get the Merton College Fellows' Garden for the reception.

"They'll eat it all, I'm sure," Susan tells him.

"But tell them to get more ice for the buffet," Henry says.

"All right." Susan walks off purposefully. She has on a good pair of low-heeled shoes under her gown.

It's a stifling summer day. The guests drink cases of the chilled champagne. Henry bustles about; he kisses his mother. The string quartet plays on manfully, flushed with heat, and Henry sighs to find the cool shadows, the wood-glen shade of the carved chapel so soon replaced, and even the wedding cake sweating a little in the sun. Susan fans herself cheerfully and sets out a pair of lawn chairs for her father and Rose in the deep shade of an oak tree.

"Oh dear, yes, it is hot," Dick Frankel says, and Ed thinks that Dick hasn't changed at all since the days when Ed was lecturing here at his summer institute, and the kids were roughhousing on this very lawn. "Welcome just the same," Dick tells him. "We must have you again for the West Bank conference next summer." Sarah takes a picture of Ed and Dick standing there, Dick gesturing toward the manor which houses his institute. She gets a nice shot of Susan as well, as Susan whirls around in her bell skirt, pointing with her index finger toward the long white dessert table.

"I love everything English," Rose tells Susan's father under the tree. "I grew up in London, you know, in an English family, and I did everything an English child can do. We had teas and holidays at the sea—our governess had an operatic voice, in fact, and she used to sing on the balcony by the sea. Passersby used to stop and listen. They were very kind to me—my English father particularly. But," she concludes, "my real family was in New York—I was sent to England before they had the opportunity to emigrate, and my visa was delayed. All that time in England I was waiting to leave, you see. I only wanted to go home to my real family. Only, only wanted to go home."

"It's time," Susan says under the tent. "It's got to be done." She takes the knife and plunges it deep into the center tier of the cake.

"Oh, God," Henry says, "I don't think that's the right place. Look, you hit the support. Get the caterer—"

Henry turns away when the caterers dismantle the wedding cake. "It would be rather silly to spend all that money and not eat it, wouldn't it, darling?" Susan asks. "We've got the pictures, in any case."

Henry carries Rose's piece out for her himself, along with some strawberries. "Thank you, dear," she says.

"Thank you for coming," he tells her, and his voice shakes.

"It was very nice," Rose replies. "This gentleman here is asleep, however."

"I'll get Susan." Henry strides off in his sweltering morning coat.

"I never wanted to *stay* in England," Rose muses as she sets to her cake and strawberries.

Mosquitoes

There is no one behind the desk at the Airport Green Shuttle Service, and no customers are waiting at the counter. Ed thinks he must be in the wrong place. He's been traveling for ten days. Customers mob the other shuttle counters. Ed waits fifteen minutes and then tows his bags over to a pay phone. "Markowitz?" someone calls out. An enormously heavy woman rushes up to him with a clipboard. "Peterstown?" she asks, out of breath. "Christians and Jews—Ecumenical Institute?"

Ed nods grimly.

"All right." She heaves herself behind the desk. "Let me do this—receipt. Mark you paid for."

"Where is the bus?" Ed asks.

"I have to bring it out front," she says. She picks up his suitcase, and he follows her out to the curb, where a young man is waiting, reading Origen.

"Are you going to the Peterstown conference?" Ed asks him.

"No, sir, I'm going to St. Peter's College to join the faculty. My name is Pat Flanagan." The young man says all this with such alacrity that Ed stares at him. Flanagan shakes his hand vigorously.

"Theology?" Ed asks.

"Primarily philosophy." The van pulls up with the heavy woman at the wheel. "I'm interested in *demonstratio Dei*—natural theology, proofs of God's existence," Flanagan explains, as they drive off.

"Descartes?" Ed asks.

"Oh, yes."

"Yeah, I remember that from college." Ed had never liked philosophy. "But what was the story with him? His whole proof turned out to be circular, right?"

"Circular?" Flanagan ponders this. "I've never thought so."

Ed leans against the rattling van window. He'd accepted the Peterstown invitation because the honorarium covered his trip out to the Hoover Institution and the Berkeley conference on the intifada. But after ten days and three speaking engagements in the Bay Area, he just isn't up to another conference. He can't wait to get back home, to D.C.

They drive out on the highway into the cornfields, past gleaming silos and Howard Johnson restaurants—each set back from the road on landscaped acreage. There are cows, as well, and some city instinct in Ed makes him want to say aloud, "Cows." He looks at Flanagan and holds it in. "When do we get there?" he asks the driver.

"We stop about one o'clock," she says.

Not for another hour, he realizes, and he tries to sleep.

At last they pull up into a Holiday Inn parking lot, and he staggers off the van after the driver. She looks at him. "Can I have my bags?" he asks, fumbling in his wallet.

"This isn't Peterstown," she says. "This is the bathroom break."

"Where the hell are we?" Ed asks Pat Flanagan in the men's room.

"This is St. Cloud. Peterstown is two and a half hours west of here."

Ed dabs his face with a wet paper towel.

"It's a little remote," Pat admits. "But it's very pristine."

St. Peter's College stands on a sweeping hill above a lake. Beyond the lake there are trees. There is no sign of a town. Flanagan shakes hands again with Ed and strides off into a huge cruciform building on the crest of the hill. Then the van rattles down a side road to the lake. There is no institute in sight, no sign of human habitation. The driver unloads Ed's suitcases, and Ed stands with his bags on a grassy meadow in front of the broad lake, the water rippling slightly in the breeze. "Wait!" he calls after the driver, but she slides the van door shut and leaves him there.

Staring at the hillside, Ed sees chimneys and vents poking through the lush green turf. He drags himself down to the lake and finds that the institute is composed entirely of terraced sod houses dug into the ground. Each opens onto the lake with sliding glass doors, and there are at least a dozen of these buildings, although they are nearly invisible from the road. A beaming man strides out from one of the houses—a large man, looking like a cross between a bear and a Buick, with a big chest, broad shoulders, and a polished dome of a forehead. "You must be Ed; you're the second to last. The others all came this morning. My name is Matthew."

"Matthew—" Ed hesitates for a last name.

"Brother Matthew. I'm just filling in as a liaison between the college and the institute—making sure you're all comfortable. Follow me. We've got you down at the end, in Lama House."

"What does that stand for?" Ed asks.

"The Dalai Lama. We've got each of the houses named after a spiritual leader."

"Quite a setup."

"We had a competition for the design ten years back," Matthew says, "and this concept really stole our hearts. The idea of living in the ground in complete humility in front of that view. The semicircular formation of the houses stands for tolerance and equality—there are a lot of symbols here—and of course all that sod is wonderful in the winter. We have our winter fellows living here with their families, and they love the insulation. Here we are. Let's just rap on the door and see if your housemate is around. Hello, Bob? He must be asleep. Let's just get your bags inside. Bob Hemmings is our Presbyterian."

"In what sense?" Ed asks.

"For the conference," Matthew says.

"Oh, you've got one of each flavor?"

"Yes, that's exactly right. Well, I'll let you settle in."

"Oh, wait." Ed calls him back. "Can I have my key?"

"We don't have keys," Matthew says. "It's easier that way. In any case, there aren't any locks. It was one of the special features in the design."

The front room in the little house is a combination living room and kitchen. Behind, in the shadows, is the bathroom, flanked by bedroom doors. Ed opens the door on the right and finds Bob Hemmings stretched out on his back in his underwear listening to a Walkman. Hemmings jumps up and pushes off his earphones. "Hi, there!" he cries out. He's a deep-voiced man, well over six feet. Ed feels suddenly exhausted from the earnest welcomes he has been receiving all day. He misses the peckishness of the academics in California, the sullen diffidence of his students in Georgetown.

"Listen," Ed says to Bob, after he has showered and changed, "is there any food in here? I missed lunch."

"No, we're having all our meals up at the college," Bob says. "See, here's your meal card. They left it on the table. The dining hall opens for dinner at six."

"Can we walk to town?"

"Well, I'm game." Bob stretches out his lanky frame. "It's a bit of a hike, though."

"How far?"

"Well, we could do it in an hour."

Ed flops on the couch. "Isn't there a convenience store around here someplace?"

"Not that I know of. Oh, but just a sec. I saved an apple from lunch. It's in my room."

"What is this, a prison?" Ed mutters, staring at his meal card.

"I love it here," Bob says. "I took my study leave here last winter."

"Where do you teach?" Ed asks.

"Well, I preach. I've got a ministry in Syracuse."

"Oh," Ed says. "Where's the conference schedule?"

"I haven't seen one. We're supposed to convene at dinner. I guess we'll find out what's up when we get there."

"Fine," Ed says. "Great." He strides into his bedroom and shuts the door.

"I'll leave the apple on the table for you," Bob calls after him.

"Oh, uh, thank you," Ed says.

"Sure thing!" Bob sings out.

Ed's room contains a bed and a chair, but no desk. He puts his suitcase on the bed and rummages through his toiletries case. He takes out his green roll-on mosquito repellent and rubs it all over his arms and neck. He hasn't seen any mosquitoes yet, but he's been warned. He's heard stories back in Washington. Then, of course, the airport concession stands in Minneapolis were full of T-shirts and coffee mugs picturing "The State Bird." He stretches out and falls asleep.

Pastor Bob is gone by the time Ed ventures out into the front room. It's after six, and he rushes out with his meal card to search for the dining hall. A thin, gray-haired man lopes up the path just ahead. He is wearing a yarmulke.

"You're going to the institute dinner?" Ed calls out.

"Oh, yes," the man sighs. "Who are you, Markowitz? My name is Mauricio Brodsky." He has a Spanish accent, Ed notices. "Tell me, how is it that they ensnared you and brought you here to the country? I arrived this morning. Already the silence is deafening. Already my migraines are flaring."

"What's that sound?" Ed asks. He can hear a tiny whine in the air—the soft, steady sound of a mosquito.

"This is my secret weapon." Mauricio unclips what looks like a cigarette lighter from his pocket. "It makes the sound of the male mosquito—to repel the female, who bites. She is already pregnant and wants nothing to do with him, and thus she flies away to bite someone else. Just two triple-A batteries. I got it by mail order from the Germans. Where else?" He gestures upward with long fingers, and Ed marvels at the way this man's accent combines with an unmistakably Yiddish kvetching lilt. He looks gray about the gills, like a New Yorker, and he wears charcoal slacks. His face is changeable, with sardonic eyes, hair and chin receding, a look of studious penetration, devil-may-care pessimism, a little mustache, a satiric gleam. "So how did they lure you here?" Mauricio asks.

"I was on my way back East anyway—"

"I heard they were short of Jews," Mauricio says. "Did they give you a thousand? Two thousand? Listen, you don't have to say anything. I'm in the business. I know. Catholic-Jewish is my specialty. It's like the theater business. Worse!"

Sweat soaks Ed's shirt, and the summer air hangs heavy and wet against him. They get to the top of the hill, and he is almost overcome by the heat. When Mauricio opens the glass door to the college dining hall, the chilled air from inside covers them in a sickening rush. An eager, blue-eyed man emerges from a crowd of young students, nuns, monks in brown cassocks. "This is Rich Mather," Mauricio tells Ed, "the institute director."

"Ed! Wonderful to see you!" Mather looks Ed in the eye. "Come up to the front of the line."

"Wait a second," Ed says, grabbing a tray, but Mather hurries him past the plates of brownies and red Jell-O cubes and the vats of mashed potatoes. Ed reaches for a plate of meat loaf, but the woman at the counter gives him a tray wrapped in layers of aluminum foil. "Your kosher meal," she says. He takes it, almost ill with hunger. "Listen, Rich," he says to Mather, "I've got a quick question on the time limits for the presentations. I've got two papers I could present—one that's more theoretical, running about forty minutes, or I have one that's more popular, on terrorism, tolerance, double standards."

"Ed, Ed," Mather says, "you don't have to worry about

any of that here. I think you'll see pretty soon that we don't care about formalities here."

"No time limits?" Ed asks.

"Oh, no. No papers, either. We just want you to say what you want to say."

"Well, I *did* say what I wanted to say. It's in my paper!" Ed turns in alarm to Mauricio, who looks at him with his thin-lipped, sardonic smile.

They sit down in a private dining room with Bob Hemmings and the other conference participants. There are eight in all: five Christians and three Jews. The fourth Jew got stuck in Paris, Mather tells them. He'll be arriving in the morning. Ed looks at the cafeteria trays piled high with potatoes and Irish stew, bowls of minestrone. He would like to go back to the line and explain that although he's Jewish, he doesn't keep strictly kosher outside the home —that he would gladly take some stew and potatoes. But Mather keeps talking. Ed peels away the foil layers on his tray. He pulls out a bagel-dog.

"Well," says Rich Mather, "I think it's time for me to open up this dialogue. Some of you have asked me about presentations and conference sessions. I'd like to re-emphasize that our goal here is to depart from the academic-conference style as much as possible. Our institute is a very unique place, not only bridging the gap between Christians and Jews but also between academics and clergy. Time, rules, and public speaking are not a concern here. Our tradition is not structured or formal but, rather, informal to the highest degree. And what we require—the only thing we require—is that all of you speak from the heart, talk with total honesty and sincerity, express the beliefs you hold deepest within you—"

Oh, is that all, Ed thinks, holding his bagel-dog, and he feels a sudden panic. He feels he is falling—had he ever really read the conference brochure?—falling as in a dream, his prepared paper snatched away, ripped from his flailing hands, while this rhetoric sways below him in roiling mud bubbles.

"What we do here is speak in the first person," Mather says. "We talk about our common subject by talking about ourselves. After all, there is no better way to talk about interfaith relations than to talk about inner faith. That's what we've found at each of these gatherings over the years. What is the study of religion but the study of life itself? The study of ourselves?"

Ed thinks he is going to puke. He swallows and looks across the table. Brother Matthew is still beaming as he puts away his mashed potatoes. Next to him a pale woman, blue-eyed and fair-haired, pores over a pocket Langenscheidt dictionary.

"So I guess what I'm saying is that we all come to this conference as—as—"

"Pilgrims," a woman on Ed's left fills in with assurance.

"Yes! Except that we don't really know where we're going or how to get there. But I think it's that process of searching that's really the key. We're going to follow an old tradition at the Ecumenical Institute—one of personal narrative. I'll just go ahead and begin, and any one of you can jump in when you're ready."

"Hold it," says Ed. "I want to understand what we're doing here. So basically we're going to spend these sessions telling about ourselves? You want us to sit here and tell the story of our lives?"

"Only as a starting point," Mather answers. "It's not the whole story we're after. Just the turning points, the epiphanies. And, naturally, we'd like to focus on the religious dimension. Your relationships on a spiritual level—with God, with Scripture. To begin—"

"Rich," Brother Matthew interrupts, "just let me distribute these." He hands out a red St. Peter's College notebook to each of them. "Gifts from the college," he says.

"Oh, and I also brought a little something," announces a white-bearded man with a big yarmulke. He passes around some little plastic tubes in folded papers. "Lip salve," he says. "One of my congregants has devised this new formula here, and he's starting out in business with it. Those little papers have his address in North Carolina for you to order. I think you'll like it. I often use it myself." He smacks his lips. "Especially in the summer," he adds.

"Thank you, Rabbi," Mather says. "Rabbi Lehrer comes to us from Chapel Hill, where he holds a chair in medieval history." Ed stares at the wiry little rabbi. A chair! What kind of chair could it be? Or is the man some kind of brilliant eccentric? Ed has never heard of him.

"I grew up in Cambridge, Mass.," Mather tells the group, "in the shadows of all those Mathers. They sort of dominated the landscape for me, like the red brick . . ."

Ed glances around the room. He is amazed to see all the others taking notes. He looks over at Bob Hemmings's notebook. "St. Peter's College," Bob has written. "We are all pilgrims. In religion, ourselves." Ed opens his own notebook. He stares at the blank page, then rips it out and writes a note to Mauricio. "What the hell *is* this?"

Mather hums on pleasantly like a lawn mower in the distance. "And I'd got to the point, by the time I lived in Eliot House, where I'd always won these academic awards, continually won these prizes—and I didn't know enough to let it scare me; I assumed I deserved everything that came to me. Until the day I found out I hadn't won that Rhodes Scholarship—that I hadn't been chosen. I see that as a turning point for me, because it opened my eyes to a new experience. I mean, I was experiencing failure—which, of course, was so much more important than all the successes I'd had before. I remember I woke up in the middle of the night and began walking along the Charles. I felt absolutely at peace and in love with this new, bittersweet taste—failure. I felt a humility before the world and before God. I felt that I was in fact *not* a chosen one, not set apart, created to excel. I was created only to live! Of course, at that stage of my life this heightened understanding couldn't last—"

Mauricio hands back Ed's note. His answer is in pale ballpoint, his letters elongated and aristocratic under Ed's black scrawl. "What is this, you ask? A conference in the old sense, no? A *parlement*? A convocation? A Decameron? No—it's a Canterbury Tales, or, rather, Parliament of Fowls. A medieval amphigory. Believe me, this is what ecumenicism comes to. New York burns and the Klan is marching. We are sequestering ourselves. We are retiring to the country. Mather begins the Book of the Unitarian Courtier. What do you want me to say? It gives me migraines—still, I love my work."

"My marriage was breaking up, and I had to confront that," Mather is telling them, "along with the other issues I had been harboring—my guilt, my alcoholism—and in that process I found that the Church held less for me. Spiritually, where I found myself was in my network of friends and my support groups. Then, slowly, I found that as one vessel emptied out, another filled—that my supports in terms of people and my therapy process came, for me, to be a church. I think it's happened this way for a whole generation coming to terms with dependency—"

"Excuse me," says the woman with the precise voice.

"Yes, Sister Elaine."

"I think you have to be careful about speaking for a whole generation. I, for one, am not dependent. I am a *sinner*"—she divides the air swiftly with her hands—"but I am not dependent. I'm sorry, I interrupted you."

"No, go on, go on," Mather urges, leaning forward in his chair. "Please, jump in. I was just getting the ball rolling, but I want to hear from all of you."

"No, you aren't done," Sister Elaine demurs.

"No, please."

Ed watches Sister Elaine as she gives in unwillingly. She is a thin woman with delicate features and short, wavy hair. Her skirt and short-sleeved top are brown and strangely autumnal. She drapes a cardigan over her shoulders. "I grew up in a functional family," she begins, "and remained close to my parents and my brother after I left home. I was still a very young girl when I lived in the mother house. I had my training there—the discipline. It was there I had the most important experience of my life. Two years after that—"

"Tell us about the experience," Mather says.

"Oh, no," Sister Elaine demurs.

"No, really, please, this is exactly—"

"Oh, no, I couldn't possibly tell you about it," Sister Elaine says. "It wouldn't be of general interest, though it was the most important experience of *my* life. And, of course, it's private. Paradoxically, in the mother house, where we lived in such close proximity, sharing rooms, schedules, and meals, we all managed to observe a strict degree of privacy. There would be a room for silence, for example, and when you entered it—left the corridor where everyone was bubbling over—you would find perfect quiet, almost as if you were alone. I taught in the primary schools until one day I was called by the diocese to get my Ph.D. in Scriptures of the First Testament. Now, of course,

I'm an assistant professor, subject to all the strains and pressures—the ruthlessness. I specialize in prophets from a form-critical approach, and I serve in the Washington, D.C., Jewish–Christian dialogue, on the Catholic Committee."

"Go on," Mather says.

"That's it," Sister Elaine tells him. "What else do you want to know?"

"Uh, well, I know you are a feminist, for one thing, and I was wondering about your feelings, as a feminist, living within the hierarchy of the Church."

"Well, I am a feminist," Sister Elaine says, "but I am not a revisionist. I won't change the liturgy."

"That's what I was wondering—I mean, why you won't," Mather says.

"Because I won't tear my heart out!" This startles everyone around the table, and one very old man wakes up suddenly and shakes himself.

"Well," he says, when he finds the others looking at him, "I believe I am the senior member of the group—"

"Just a second, Brother Marcus," Mather interrupts apologetically. "I don't think Sister Elaine was finished."

"Oh, I beg your pardon," the old man says, and he settles down again into his white beard.

"Yes, I was finished—absolutely," Sister Elaine tells Mather sternly.

"Well, you just tell me when you want me to start," Brother Marcus says in a deep Southern voice. "Give me a holler, so I can hear, because you are dealing with a very old monk here."

"You go right ahead," Sister Elaine tells him.

Ed feels a nudge at his side. It's Mauricio. "You see," he whispers in his breathy Spanish accent, "first the nun's tale, and now the nun's priest's." He quirks his eyebrow at Ed.

"Yeah, right," Ed says, not really sure what Mauricio is getting at, feeling exhausted, duped, self-deceived. It was his own greed, after all, that drew him here. The check from the Ecumenical Institute. It's agonizing sitting here like this, forced into this kind of voyeurism.

Brother Marcus just looks out at all of them, his beard startlingly white, his eyes the intense blue of the very young and the very old. "I believe I am the senior member of the group," he says again. "I am eighty-four years old. My name is Brother Marcus Goldwater, and I think I've been invited because of my life experience, ecumenically speaking. I was raised in Chattanooga, Tennessee, in a family of Reformed Jewish background. We went every year to the temple on the High Holy Days, and there was a dinner every year on Passover. Also, we children belonged to a Jewish social club, where we went to dances and singing parties. At the age of eighteen I got a job at the Sears and Roebuck Company and I stayed with the company nine years, where I fell under the influence of my immediate supervisor, who set out to court me into Catholicism."

"What do you mean, 'court you'?" Ed asks, shocked. He has never heard anything like this. He's stunned to come up against such a figure—the voice, those eyes, that bright white beard.

"By courting I mean that he never pretended he was doing anything different," Goldwater explains, more deliberately than ever, "and yet he never forced me farther than I wanted to go. He courted me the way a man courts a young girl. He never made any pretenses, though. He told me that he had converted five and he hoped I would be his sixth. It happened gradually. He used my natural curiosity, like this—'I'm going to a beautiful concert,' he said to me. 'I want to take you along, but you wouldn't understand it.' Well, that piqued me, of course. I insisted he take me. The concert was a holy Mass. I sank down on my knees, and I could understand."

"You are saying," Mauricio says dryly, "that this man seduced you into Catholicism."

"Oh, yes," says Goldwater, "he seduced me very deliberately. Yes, indeed. But I think that's what a conversion is. I surrendered myself up, body and soul. I fell in love with the Church. Yielded away. My supervisor at the Sears and Roebuck Company was not interested in an easy infatuation or a quick conversion. He insisted I take instruction, which I did for several years, and later, when I decided I wanted to take orders, he questioned me severely." Brother Marcus looks down at his hands, and Ed notices his ring for the first time; it's large and silver, a Gothic cross that reaches almost to the first knuckle—it's a little tarnished, so it looks at first like wrought iron. "So I was his sixth," Marcus says. "But this I remember him telling me, and I have always been grateful for it. He said, 'Never forget your roots. Never forget you were born a Jew.' And I have not. Some of you here will surely think I am an apostate, but I am not. I'm just the opposite, because I have preserved my identity. And I have *never* given up my Jewish name, Marcus Goldwater."

"Oh dear, oh my!" gasps old Rabbi Lehrer. He is convulsed with laughter, and no one can believe it. He sounds absolutely pixilated. "I had this one from a congregant of mine in North Carolina," he wheezes, eyes streaming. "There was a man—a Jewish man—and somehow his name got onto the solicitation list for the Republican Party. The girl calls him up and says, 'Mr. Goldwasser, may I put you down for a contribution?' Says the man, 'My name is Goldwater. Goldwater, not Goldwasser. My father's name is Goldwater, my grandfather, *olev hasholem*, his name was Goldwater, too!'

"But on one subject I must seriously disagree with you, Brother Mark," the rabbi says, wiping the tears from his eyes. "You are not the senior member of the party, because I am eighty-*five*. And, God willing, in November I'll be eighty-six! I was born in a little town that would now be in Romania if it had survived the First War and if what was left had been spared by the Nazis later on. This is history! One 'if' after another. But I had a beautiful, religious childhood, thanks to my parents, of blessed memory. My father had a sawmill and kept us prosperous and well. Always he instilled in us a love of education, and he kept a library in the house, where he himself would read and meditate. He was prominent in the synagogue and in the town. His greatest joy was to give to the poor and provide for them. But it was my dear mother who instilled in me my spiritual sense from the time I was a child, and I remember that once—it is one of my earliest memories—she was standing in the golden light of the window in late afternoon with a book before her. 'Mama, Mama,' I asked her, as small children do, 'why are you standing there with that book?'

" 'Because I am praying,' she answered me. 'Praying to the creator who made the world.' Small as I was, this impressed me deeply, and from that moment I also wanted to dedicate myself to God, the creator of this beautiful world."

Ed squirms. He closes his eyes and sees pictures. Embarrassing pictures. The kind that hang in the social hall of his temple in D.C. Fake Chagalls of the old country. A woman standing at the window, a babushka on her head. A pair of klutzy candlesticks. Does Lehrer expect them to believe he grew up in one of those pictures? It makes Ed sick, because he does believe it. He sees Lehrer in all those garish colors, that village with roofs tilted upward and rabbis with upturned eyes and frail Hasidic faces and Lehrer's mother floating at the window. He sees it all, and it is maddening, the way Lehrer triggers these clichés. Affirming that he, Ed, has roots in bad lithographs and the pictures on mortuary calendars; that he, Ed, originally comes from a Judaica shop, and that his cultural memory is bound in coffee-table books.

"My parents," Lehrer continues, as Brother Marcus nods off again, "had dearly hoped I would become a rabbi when they saw my love of learning in the little school my brothers and I attended. In any case, it seemed ordained that I should be a rabbi. Our last name was Lehrer, which means teacher, and my parents had given me the name Menachem, which means comforter. In fact, I was named after my sainted grandfather on the maternal side, who was directly descended from the famous Vilna Gaon, one of the greatest teachers and scholars who ever lived. Well, I grew into something of a *talmid chachem* myself. What can I say? It was not my intelligence but my love of the subject that spurred me on. I loved God's word—this was my gift."

Ed shifts in his chair. His right foot has fallen asleep. He writes a note to Mauricio: "I don't think I can take this much longer."

"How fortunate that we emigrated to Toronto when we did, in 1915!" Rabbi Lehrer exclaims. "I was only a small boy, but truly my life has been full of blessings. We settled in Canada, and, as before, my father prospered, this time in the retail business. My older brothers soon joined him in the company. Then it was my turn to choose a career. I remember the day clearly. My parents sat down with me, and they said, 'Menachem, you are old enough to decide on your profession.'

" 'Father, Mother,' I said, 'my dearest wish is to become a rabbi and devote my life to learning.' Well, they smiled, because this was exactly what they had hoped for all through my childhood."

Mauricio is signaling to Rich Mather, tapping his watch. He passes a note to Ed in his pale, spiky handwriting. "Stand it, you say? What else do we do in this world but talk about ourselves?"

"And so it happened that when my dear wife and I moved to Vancouver, where I took on the fledgling congregation—well, there another blessing befell me. By some chance my phone number was only one digit different from that in the immigration office, and, purely by mistake, some officials called me—officials deciding the cases of some of the Jews fleeing Hitler. Well, whenever they asked for my services I was more than happy to oblige them as an interpreter or whatever else was needed, and in this small way I helped several Jewish families seeking asylum. For this—only for this in my life—I can say I am truly *proud*."

"Rabbi," Mather says, hesitantly, "I sense some of the people in the room are feeling tired after their flights."

"Maybe we should end this session," Ed cuts in.

"But I'm only up to 1932!" Rabbi Lehrer says, dismayed. "I haven't even gotten to the war years and my congregations in Winnipeg and North Carolina, or my monograph—"

"It *is* getting late," says Sister Elaine. The others start to gather their things or even stand up. Brother Marcus wakes and looks around him.

"I suppose I have more to tell, having lived so long," Lehrer says.

"You should write your memoirs, Rabbi," Bob Hemmings tells him.

"I have two hundred pages," Lehrer says.

It is ten o'clock when they walk down the hill to the institute's sod houses. The sun is setting, and heavy clouds move rapidly across the sky. An instant later the sky blackens, and it begins to pour. Steam hisses up from the black asphalt road. "Christ," Ed groans. His glasses are steaming up, and water pours down his face.

"This is one of our storms," Brother Matthew tells the group, in exactly the tone he used identifying Bob Hemmings as "our Presbyterian." Sister Elaine is the only one with an umbrella. She insists on giving it to Rabbi Lehrer and Brother Marcus.

"Coming from where I do—Chattanooga," Marcus says, "I couldn't possibly accept a lady's only umbrella."

"Nor could I, nor could I," the rabbi tells her.

"But you are the senior members," Elaine reminds them, and she holds it over their heads.

Ed stamps into his sod house, shoes squelching, stomach churning. After he has dried off, he waits in the living room until Bob says, "Well, time to turn in. Pleasant dreams!" Then Ed seizes the phone. It's late in D.C. He doesn't want to wake his wife, but this is an emergency.

The phone rings three times on the other end. Sarah picks up. "Hello, what is it now, Rose?" she asks.

"Sarah, this is Ed."

"Oh," Sarah says, "I thought it was your mother. She's been calling from L.A. about her lawsuit."

"What?"

"She's suing Primo Cleaners—remember?"

"Oh. Listen, Sarah, I don't want to hear about that."

"Why not? She's your mother," Sarah says, "and I'm the one stuck here manning the phones. I'm at the end of my rope. She's met a retired judge at the center and they're working on the case full time. She's been calling me every night! Two, three times a night. I would have disconnected the phone if the kids hadn't been on that canoe trip. I was afraid in an emergency they wouldn't be able to reach me. Of course, she's having a wonderful time."

"Who?"

"Rose. She's getting more mileage out of that bedspread. It was polished cotton, and they laundered it and ruined the finish. Of course, she doesn't want a new one."

"Sarah, I don't care about that bedspread," Ed tells her.

"Neither do I!" she thunders.

"Don't you scream at me. I didn't call to be screamed at."

"Fine."

"Sarah?"

"What?"

"Are you there?"

"Yes."

"How are you?"

"I just told you how I was," she says.

"Look, Sarah, I've had a miserable day. I've been through hell."

"What's wrong?"

"What's wrong? I'm in some godforsaken hole in the ground. Literally! It's a hundred degrees when it isn't pouring rain, with a bunch of clergymen"—he lowers his voice, eyeing Hemmings's closed bedroom door—"with no academic qualifications whatsoever, at a conference which is being run like some cross between Stanislavsky and A.A."

"What have you been doing?"

"I have been listening to the participants talk about themselves. We're supposed to talk about ourselves."

"What do you do the rest of the time?"

"Anything. No structure. No schedule."

"It sounds nice," Sarah says. "It sounds relaxing. Why don't you relax and enjoy it?"

"No, no, you don't understand, Sarah. You don't understand what these sessions are like. There's some kind of senile rabbi here who just—"

"Is there a lake?" she asks.

"What? Yeah."

"Go for a swim. I rolled up your swim trunks with your underwear."

"I don't want to go swimming," Ed hisses. "I want to go *home* and get some—"

"You think I'm going to fall for that after sending four kids to Camp Ramah?"

"When I think of the referee reports on my desk. And the unanswered mail—the paper I promised Frankel! My time and energy—"

"Oh, Ed," Sarah says, "it's two more days. One and a half."

"I don't think you're catching on to what I'm saying. These people are making me physically ill! The bullshit here goes right up to the sky!"

"What's that from—*Oklahoma!*?" She giggles.

"And my roommate," he whispers, "is a small-town preacher out of Norman Rockwell. Just now he wished me pleasant dreams!"

"So what, Ed! What's wrong with that?"

"He doesn't even know me!"

"It's a good thing. Ed, I happen to have a meeting at the university tomorrow morning."

"Sarah?"

"What."

"I'm just exhausted."

"So am I," she says.

"You have no idea."

"Pleasant dreams," she tells him.

Ed finds a glass in the living-room cupboard and fumbles in his toiletries case for his Alka-Seltzer. Glumly, he drinks the fizzing mixture in the bathroom; he eyes himself in the mirror. His thinning hair is windblown, his eyes stare out, wild and confused—the remnant of a younger body. "I'm too old for this," he mutters, as he eases into bed. His ears ring with other voices. The Spanish Yiddish of Mauricio Brodsky, and Bob Hemmings's "Sure thing!" clanging in the air, Rich Mather's even tones, Rabbi Lehrer's tale of good fortune. Ed pushes his pillows to his ears.

At six in the morning, Ed wakes to the noise of cars or trucks on the college road. He jumps out of bed, ravenous, and finds Bob in the living room, writing in his notebook. "Good morning!" Bob greets him. "How did you sleep?"

"Okay," Ed growls, incapable of cheer at this hour. "What's that noise? Garbage trucks?"

"Tour buses," Bob tells him. "The British Special Olympics team is dorming at the college. I was just up there, looking around. They've got maybe six, eight buses from Minneapolis. It's something to see."

"What about breakfast?" Ed asks.

"I'll just wash up and we can walk over together," Bob says.

While he is waiting, Ed glances at Bob's open notebook. He sees that Bob has written his entire personal statement out in longhand. "I preach at First Presbyterian in Syracuse. Of course, we Presbyterians have a thing about being first. Just about all our churches are called First Presbyterian."

"Ready to go?" Bob asks, as he emerges from the bathroom.

Red banners festoon the dining hall—"Welcome, Special Olympians, England, Scotland, and Wales"—and the workers dish out scrambled eggs and hash browns, sausages and French toast. "I guess you'll want the kosher meal," says Bob.

"What did you do here in the winter?" Ed asks Bob at the table.

"Well, I studied, I meditated, I decompressed," Bob says. "You get burnt out in a job like mine. There's creative burnout, where you feel like you can't write another homily. Then there's the emotional toll—"

"Hmm." Ed stares into his cereal bowl.

"Troubled, troubled people," Bob says. "Just before I came here I was counseling a man whose life has really fallen apart, split wide open. He'd married late, and he and his wife had built their dream house. It took them five years. Beautiful place in the mountains. Custom furniture, folk art, antique-toy collection—unbelievable stuff. Then they prepared to have a child and lost the baby in the womb at nine months. They came in for counseling, but by that time the marriage was falling apart. The wife pulled away. I think they'll have a divorce. We had a ceremony for the child, a kind of funeral—and now the house is up for sale. The husband has been coming to me alone now, studying his Bible, trying to understand."

"What's to understand?" Ed asks. "It's the American way. First the dream house, then the toys, then death, then religion. It's so goddamn American."

Bob laughs and shakes his head. "It's true," he says. "Ed, that's very well put. Still, the pain is real. The questions are real." Bob's voice drifts off. Then he douses his French toast with more syrup. "You want to try out the lake?"

The lake is full of Special Olympians, swimming and splashing, diving off the dock into the cold green water. Bob jumps in and starts swimming efficiently, stretching out his long body. Ed looks around warily. There must be thousands of mosquitoes in the long, wet grass. Just thinking about it makes him itch. Millions of them breeding in the still water under the dock. He eases himself into the water and paddles around, cold currents seizing his legs. Then he turns back and clings to the mossy dock for support, despite the kids dive-bombing overhead. A small child wriggles by, swimming like a minnow underwater. Suddenly a little girl looks up into his face. Treading water, she stares at him. "Hello," Ed says, "what sport do you play?"

"Gymnastics," she says, and continues treading water, staring into his eyes.

"And what's your name?" Ed asks.

"Alison."

"Where are you from, Alison?"

"The green house at Burnham where the road takes the cliffs down by the sea," she recites for him. Then she pushes off again.

"Good luck," Ed calls after her. He feels cold in the lake, and helpless, with all this splashing life around him. All these people, and these scholars with such histories attached to them—these cosmological systems instead of homes, ancestral totems instead of parents, vocations instead of professions, paradigm shifts instead of childhoods. He'd never developed that kind of mythology about himself—or, rather, he would never discuss it in public! He feels all out of kilter. Since he arrived, he hasn't been able to hear himself think. Clambering onto the dock, he resolves to take his briefcase and get some work done in the college library.

The library looks like a cathedral. Desks line up against

a railing high up on a balcony. It's like sitting in a choir loft. Ed peers down at the stacks below. How can he get out of this mess? He could try to call the shuttle service and change his ticket with the airline. He could hide out in his sod house for the afternoon session.

"Dr. Markowitz?" someone whispers behind him. It is a young monk in a brown cassock and rope belt. "Pat Flanagan. Remember me? The shuttle bus."

"Oh!" Ed stares at the young man. He had forgotten about him—the new professor. "I thought you were coming out here to teach," he says.

"Oh, yes," Flanagan says. "But also to join the monastery. How do you like it here?"

"It's very nice," Ed says. "It's fine. I thought you said it was quiet."

"I guess it's not as quiet at this time of year," Flanagan says. "They rent out the facilities in the summer, and right now, in particular, we've got the Special Olympics, and a basketball camp, and the Elderhostel groups—I guess you've seen them."

"No."

"Well, you can't miss them—they all wear matching T-shirts. But in winter it's really peaceful. If you like to walk in the snow, it's the best place in the world."

"Yeah, I heard," Ed says.

He slips into the dining hall as soon as it opens for lunch. Then, stealthily, after checking to make sure that none of the conference people are around, he takes a tray and loads up with fried chicken, mashed potatoes, peas, and apple pie. He slips into a seat near the wall, where a long table of Elderhostel students camouflage him. Then he devours the chicken and potatoes. He goes back for seconds. He eats like a man rescued from captivity.

"Now, Margaret," says the woman next to him. "I told you before—this weekend we're having a wienie roast."

"Oh, yes, oh, yes, I remember now—and I want to bring something," Margaret replies.

"But you don't have to bring anything."

"But I really want to."

"Well, now, we always have more than enough food at our wienie roasts. I can't think of anything."

"How about potato salad?" Margaret asks.

"Well, I don't know."

"You don't like potato salad?"

"No, I love it."

"Oh, you don't have to fib to me, Eileen."

"No, no, I love it," Eileen says. "It's just that I don't think we ever have potato salad."

"Oh," Margaret sounds surprised. "We always have potato salad with our wienies. See, I don't eat my wienie on a bun. I like to cut mine up on the plate, with the potato salad sort of surrounding it."

"Eduardo!" Mauricio Brodsky cries out before the afternoon session begins.

"Well, you're happy today," Ed says.

"I was at the bookstore, and I loaded up! Catholic theology. An outstanding collection. I spent three hundred dollars—for my research, my detective work. Where were you this morning? You missed Mass."

"I'm Jewish," Ed says, looking at Mauricio with his thin Latin mustache and black yarmulke.

"It's true, and that's why it is imperative, vital, that you go and you understand! I always go, whenever I am near a cathedral, to immerse myself in the sounds and the sights. Of course, it means nothing to me, nothing!" he confides, flicking his long fingers. "But one should go. As a Jew, one *must* go. To—to—"

"Experience it," Ed finishes.

"No, no, so they can experience you. But let me tell you, the true joy, the joy of my life, is to bring my Catholic clergy to my own Young Israel—to sit with them in the congregation. It is a beautiful thing to sit down with them, to antagonize the rabbi."

"Hello, Professor Markowitz, Dr. Brodsky," says Brother Matthew. Beads of perspiration stand on his massive forehead. "Are you enjoying yourselves? Do you like your rooms?"

"Brother Matthew, it is all beautiful, excellent," Mauricio says.

"Good, good," says Matthew. "You know, we have a tradition here at St. Peter's. When you come here as a guest you become part of the family—and that means you can come anytime and stay with us."

"Beautiful," Mauricio says. "Excellent. So, Brother Matthew, when are you going to tell your tale?"

"What—me?" Matthew laughs. "I'm not in the conference, you know. I'm just a liaison. I just come down to listen to all of you."

"Oh, I think you must tell us your tale," Mauricio says.

"There is nothing to tell," Matthew says. "I entered the monastery when I was sixteen, and what with one thing and another, I never left. Of course, I was over at the Vatican for a couple of years. And I lived eleven years in Alaska with the Inuit."

"Well, that's something!" Mauricio says.

"Oh, I don't know. Life wasn't much different in Alaska," says Brother Matthew. "The rule is the same, wherever you go."

"So . . ." Ed hesitates. "You joined up when you were sixteen."

"I started on the path. I guess otherwise I would have become an auto mechanic like my brothers. I do the monastery auto repairs in any case."

Ed stares at the monk and thinks that he really does look like an auto mechanic. This makes him want to ask Matthew what he thinks of all this nonsense at the conference—Marcus, the Southern Jew converted to Catholicism, Sister Elaine and her mother house. He wants to ask, confidentially, whether it gives Matthew the willies. But Rich Mather is talking already.

"Let me introduce a newcomer, Avner Rabinovitch, our Israeli from the University of Haifa," he says. "His flight was delayed twelve hours in Paris, so he just got in this morning. He's a newcomer to the conference, but an old-timer here at the institute—a key member of our Third World Scriptural Caucus."

Ed perks up. He himself has a certain interest in the Third World, specifically fringe terrorist groups. He looks with hope at Rabinovitch, an actual scholar whose area of expertise connects to Ed's own field.

"I don't know about you," Mather is telling them. "But I've already got a pile of notes." He looks around the private dining room, where they sit exactly as they had the night before—Ed between Mauricio and Bob Hemmings, opposite them Sister Elaine and Rabbi Lehrer. "Marthe, would you like to—" Mather turns toward the woman sitting on the other side of Mauricio, the Langenscheidt dictionary on the table. She is extremely fair, with the beginning of a bad sunburn.

"You must pardon me for my English," Marthe says, looking up at them with pale-blue eyes. "Also, I must tell you that it was my husband originally to come here to this meeting, but he could not at the end and sent me, his wife, to represent him in his place. So, I must speak not only for myself but for him also, my husband, who is a true theologian—I, only his assistant and a graduate student."

Mauricio leans over and says to Ed, "Now, this is the wife's tale, no?"

"I must also say," Marthe continues, "I do not take it for granted—I who am a Christian, and a German one—what it is to sit down with you who are Jews. This is a privilege for me, and my husband says, as well, it is a lesson to us who have residing on us the guilt of our history. So I must deeply thank you.

"I grew up in Düsseldorf in a Protestant family, not religious but secular-cultural—devoted to books, arts, and music. On weekdays my father played on the piano Mozart, Handel, Schumann, and Brahms. On Sundays he played the works of Johann Sebastian Bach. I grew and married. Then, with Peter, my education began. Peter was searching in his religion. Now we married; we searched together. We were looking for answers to our history. How the Church had stood close by in the terrible events of Hitler. Peter wrote a book about the Protestant Church and the Nazis. Together we discovered the guilt of our religious people, and now, Peter believed, the guilt in our religion itself. Even the good scholars who refused to ally with the cooperating Church—these brought into their own theology a cooperation with anti-Semitism. It was the tenets of the religion which contained the sin, Peter decided, and I, who researched, must agree with him in this. The root of the Church we found corrupt, based on violence—namely, the violent seizure of the Hebrew Scripture by a latter culture. Peter asked me, What have the Christian interpreters to do with Jesus' own view of the Scripture? For Jesus read the text as a Jew. Yet it was seized and made over for new uses. Peter's book led him to despair the Church, passive in the evil time of this century. We thought together, How to reply to this history? How must we raise our two children? To the question of evil in the world, we know there is no answer. To the question of the Church, we did not know. Then Peter found an idea in himself. He said to me, This church failed us, but with us it may be changed. We must use theology to understand, and we must employ our historical scholarship to reform. In our own Lutheran tradition of Reformation, we may strip away the rotten and make new. This is my husband's idea in life, and for me, too, although I have returned only recently to university now that my children are growing. The Hebrew is for me difficult, but I study and grow to it so I and Peter may continue. We must continue. However, we have no escape from our terrible guilt—" Marthe's voice breaks; her eyes fill with tears. Mauricio reaches out and clasps her hands, and Ed sees that Mauricio is also crying. The two of them sit there together, clasping hands. "We must always ask pardon," Marthe weeps.

"We must give it," Mauricio says.

No one else speaks. Finally, Rich Mather says, "Well, I can feel the energy in the room. Marthe, it was a beautiful statement. Really. Maybe—Mauricio?"

Mauricio begins to talk, seriously, quickly. Of course, Ed thinks, Mauricio will offer no satirical comment on himself, no title for his own story. Ed looks down at his own open notebook, covered with spiraling doodles. He picks up his pen and writes: "The pardoner's tale."

"My parents raised me and my brother in Buenos Aires," says Mauricio. "The rest of my family died in the camps. They sent me to Catholic schools because they wanted me to be a lawyer, and there I learned not only the Christian but the Jewish Bible. On holy days I walked in streets scattered with leaflets, scattered like flowers, quotations from the gospels—' "Crucify him," said the Jews, "crucify him!" ' Here was my second taste of anti-Semitism—here my resolve to fight the bigotry, both in Jews and in Christians. I became a rabbi, and I settled in New York City to work in the Jewish–Catholic Dialogue Foundation. There, I met my great love—Catholic theology and canon law. My academic delight! My apartment is filled with Catholic missals, tracts, Passion plays, but, above all, canon law. I write for all the religious presses. Last year, when my daughter was engaged, we were having a little party for our new in-laws. Very observant Jews, dressed in black, wearing black hats—who knew whether they would eat our food? My wife looked at me. 'Mauricio,' she said, 'your books! They're all over the apartment. They are in the dining room! What will these people say to us? Shouldn't we do something? Hang a curtain? Put up a screen?'

" 'Anna,' I said, 'This is what I am—how can I hide it? My life is here. Is this so terrible? Is this like a skeleton in the closet?'

"Naturally, with my own religion, I have nothing but aggravations. It is too close to me to enjoy. Every Shabbat I go to my little synagogue and I am disgusted with the way the service runs. What can I say? I love to complain. Mistakenly, I turn on a light on Shabbat. Do I worry that God is angry with me? Certainly not. So he is angry with me. So what? I am angry with God! He let my family die. For this I will never forgive him. Always I have this argument with God. I ask him, why did you fail us? Men may fail. How can you, ever? What is this study of evil? I agree with Marthe—there is no answer. What is this thing, theodicy? My family went to the ovens, and that's it—" He breaks off, breathless.

"This is so *true*," affirms Avner Rabinovitch. Ed's hope in the Israeli scholar dies. Rabinovitch is obviously not going to speak like a scholar but like one of *them*. He speaks hoarsely, with a heavy Israeli accent, a haunted look in his eyes—either from anguish, Ed thinks, or from his sleepless night at de Gaulle. "What could it be? What answer is there from a God like that? I myself argue with God, talk against him in the night. I work at the university, teach my classes. At home, I pace, with the holy book in my hand. What can commentaries mean? How can the commentators explain evil? They talk about words and letters in words. They ask—empty questions."

"Now, wait a minute," Rabbi Lehrer puts up a hand. "There are many discussions of evil in the commentaries, and among our great philosophers. I myself have found many answers. There is the work of—"

"Rabbi," Mauricio interrupts, "what kind of evil could you see in Canada? We should all be so lucky to live in Canada during the major catastrophes, the world wars."

"I think that's an ad-hominem argument," Lehrer fumes. "I was making a point about theodicy."

"Well, my point is this," Avner breaks in. "I had a son once. Now he is no more. How can I justify his death in Lebanon? Who can justify a thing like that? Can I find solace in the Scriptures? I read the sacrifice of Isaac and find there the death of my son. His death, over and over, in the letters of my book."

"Hold on," Bob Hemmings says, puzzled. "Isaac didn't die. He was saved."

"Yes!" says Avner, and his fleshy face reddens with emotion, surprisingly young. "That is exactly the point. Isaac was saved. But my son was not rescued by any angel. He is gone, but I must live and teach, and argue why with God. And this is my work, to ask these questions, while my colleagues in religion debate—fine points. And this is what I am saying. The true scholar must consider the texts with his own experience. What can my colleagues gain, counting words? I take up the Scriptures in the dark night of my soul. I demand it—speak!"

"Get me out of here," Ed whispers under his breath.

"What did you say, Ed?" Rich Mather asks. "Did you want to respond? Share your own statement?"

"No," Ed says.

"But it's your turn," says Sister Elaine.

"I believe you're the last one," Brother Marcus points out.

"Pass," Ed says. "I pass."

"Oh, Ed," Mather chides him. "I think we've built up enough trust—I think there's enough warmth in this room—"

"Okay," Ed stems the flow of Mather's assurances. "You want a statement from me? You want to know what I think? I think this is the most disorganized, disjointed conference I have ever seen, and as a professional, a historian, and an academic, I feel sick—*sick!*—listening to this. I have never seen anything like this. I have never seen navel-picking on this scale! Self-congratulation, self-flagellation! What are we doing here? This is surreal! What am I doing here listening—you should excuse the expression—to these *bubbe-mayses*? And what are these little scenes played out here, which are supposed to be so terribly moving, where Marthe begs forgiveness for crimes she did not commit and Mauricio pardons her for suffering he did not feel? That's not moving. That's sick. Since when were you appointed to speak for the Germans and the Jews? When did you assume the mantle? I'd love to know. And Avner, I'm sorry your son was killed. What kind of license does that give you to write off historical techniques and scholarly analysis? How can you possibly sit here and—"

"You have completely misunderstood what I was saying," Avner breaks in. "I was making a critique of my profession, the scriptural discipline—the academics, like you—which looks only at minutiae."

"I am a scholar!" Ed bellows. "That means every once in a while I stop picking my nose and focus on something outside myself and my own pain. I work on achieving some distance. I work on some objectivity. I take a decongestant for my ego! That's what a discipline is!" he shouts. "It's about discipline! You're sitting here massaging each other with Cheez Whiz, and I'm sick of watching!"

The silence is different this time. Bigger, not solemn or full of energy. The only sound comes from Marthe, flipping frantically through the pages of her dictionary.

It is a terrible quiet, and no one is willing to break it. Rich Mather stares down at the table, something closed and tight about his face. "Well," Mauricio says at last. "Suppose we take a break."

"No," Sister Elaine says. "If there is a problem here, we certainly shouldn't run away from it. I'm not going to take a break."

"So you agree there's a problem here!" Ed says. "You agree we have a bullshit problem here!"

"Ed, Ed." Mauricio tsks. "That kind of language—"

"That is the appropriate language!" says Ed. "That is the correct term!" He's starting to feel good in his mutiny. Starting to feel like himself again. He is sitting at the conference table and he has a bit of a paunch, but figuratively he stands on the deck of a ship, Captain Blood, saber drawn, challenging all comers.

"I'd like to ask our leader how to proceed," says Sister Elaine.

"Look, I speak as a member of the group," Mather says at last, "and I can only say, as a group member, that I sense a lot of anger here. But I've found in situations like this that sometimes, when we're at the lowest point of confusion, we're really on the verge of something."

"I am not confused," Ed says. "I am rejecting this project!"

"You are rejecting ecumenical dialogue?" Mauricio asks.

"No, I'm rejecting therapeutic back-rubbing! Interfaith tick-pulling."

"Ed," Mather says. "Don't underestimate the opportunity we have here. I've sat in this room and seen the Nobel Prize winner in physics connect with process theology. I've watched a new generation of astronomers talk about God and find him in themselves. I've seen Protestants, Jews, and Catholics come to terms with anti-Semitism, poverty, and the environmental crisis, and I've watched great scholars break through—break free from academic jargon. Don't underestimate the process."

Ed leans forward in his chair. "Look, am I asking too much when I say I want to process as a professional—as an adult? I'd be happy to hear about Rabbi Lehrer's work. Why do I have to hear about his mother? Avner, I'd be delighted to discuss Scripture in the Third World. I don't want to hear about the dark night of the soul, okay?"

Avner glares at Ed. "I do not want to hear this abuse at the conference. This is an insult! Unprofessional!"

"You're lecturing *me* about unprofessional?" Ed bursts out.

"Stop! Stop!" Marthe wails. "I feel here too many tenses—"

"Tensions," Elaine amends.

"And they make me too painful!" Marthe says. "We

cannot go on like a garden, everything growing into each other. We must have a leader to make prunes—and—and—cuttings, so," she illustrates with her hands. "If Rich will not, we must choose another and a new idea. This one is finished, and can do no more."

"I think," Elaine says, "the personal statements had a certain limited value. But they can carry us only so far. Maybe it's a good thing Ed provided that critical perspective for us. We may actually owe Ed a vote of thanks."

"Well—" Ed begins.

"No, don't answer me, Ed." Elaine holds up her hand to scattered laughter.

"I do think it's time for something new," says old Brother Marcus. "Everyone has spoken, anyway."

"Actually, I haven't yet," Bob Hemmings mentions shyly, "but I guess that's not important." He puts aside his notes with a slight gesture of regret. "I'd like to offer a suggestion, though, because we've had some hard feelings. I know most of us, being Biblical people, turn to the Bible for guidance. I know I do. I even listen to it on tape—in the car, on my Walkman—and I always hear new things. And I thought maybe we could turn to some passage now, and read or listen together. I was thinking about something like Isaiah 40."

"Oh, yes, excellent, Isaiah 40," Elaine says. "It's so—"

"Comforting," Mauricio finishes.

"No," Elaine says witheringly, "that's not what I was thinking of at all."

"I don't have my Bible, I'm afraid," Brother Marcus says.

"Neither do I," admits Bob.

"I have not brought it with me," Marthe says, blushing into her sunburn.

"All right, wait a minute here," Bob says, laughing. "Can it be that not a single person at the table has a Bible?"

"I do," Rabbi Lehrer tells them. "Of course, it's all in Hebrew."

"I could run to the college library and get some Bibles," Brother Matthew offers.

"But which edition?" Bob asks.

"Each translation mangles worse and worse," rumbles Avner.

"I'll recite," Elaine breaks in, with a clarity that comes, Ed imagines, from her years of teaching primary school. "Isaiah 40," she announces, "King James version: 'Comfort ye, comfort ye my people, saith your God. Speak ye comfortably to Jerusalem, and cry unto her, that her warfare is accomplished, that her iniquity is pardoned: for she hath received of the Lord's hand double for all her sins.' " Elaine is an unfulfilled actress. This much is clear. She recites with passion. She looks her listeners in the eye and declaims ferociously, as if she were the rebuking prophet: " 'Who hath measured the waters in the hollow of his hand, and meted out heaven with the span, and comprehended the dust of the earth in a measure?' " Her memory finally fails her at " 'Behold, the nations *are* as a drop of a bucket, and are counted as the small dust of the balance.' " They all applaud her, and Rabbi Lehrer, who has been following in his own book, picks up where she leaves off, chanting in Hebrew in a surprisingly deep bass-baritone.

"Let us hold hands!" Marthe whispers.

"Let's not and say we did," mutters Ed. Nevertheless, he is amazed by the old rabbi's performance, his beautiful phrasing.

Brother Matthew shakes the rabbi's hand afterward. "The traditional chanting!" he says.

"You read it so faithfully," Elaine tells him.

"Well," says Mauricio, "may I propose we break for dinner? The main dining hall will close, you see, and for the kosher meals—"

"But we should make plans for the morning," Elaine says. "Rich, what should we do? It's our last day."

"Small groups, I think." Rich looks exhausted. "I think we'll have to move into small groups."

They get up for dinner, but Brother Matthew calls them back. He has a little camera. "Let me get a picture of everyone," he says. "Over there by the wall. Rich, Ed, could you kneel down in front? Mauricio, you stand between Elaine and Marthe."

"Ah! Like the Latin lover!" says Mauricio, with his arms around the two women in the group.

"Bob, can you lean in a little? Now, everyone, say *celibacy*!"

At dinner, Ed takes a table with Mauricio and Bob. Then he gets up and steps outside. He needs to cool down. Standing on the dining-hall steps with his bagel-dog, he looks out at the magnificent late-afternoon sky. The birds are gathering in the trees, and he listens to their rippling voices. He breathes deeply. It is only his imagination, he tells himself—his own paranoia: that tiny sound gathering force in the grass by the lake. That maddening, delicate whine, the rising voices of mosquitoes.

Fantasy Rose

*R*ose is making herself at home. She pads around in bedroom slippers and enjoys the soft, dusty-rose carpet in her granddaughter Miriam's old room. It's her favorite color, and her favorite room in the house.

"We cleared out the top two drawers," Sarah tells her mother-in-law.

"I don't need much space," Rose says, neatly stacking her nightgowns in a corner of the top drawer. "It's such a big bureau."

"It's been through a lot." Sarah looks at the dresser. It had been hers as a child and it's still in good shape, except for the top, where the kids used to keep their fish tank and their fish supplies: purple gravel, glass wool and carbon for the filter, toothbrushes stained algae-green. The fish had been quite a production—especially since they never lasted. The little blue neons would die off in weeks and the angelfish would bite each other and swim around with notches in their fins. When Yehudit went off to college, there was just one fish left—a great, morose plecostomus that slunk around the bottom of the tank or hung for hours onto the glass with its suction mouth. Miriam's brothers had named it Hoover. Sarah ended up feeding it. "We have to get the top refinished," she says now, looking at the water-damaged wood.

"We should get the whole room redone," Ed puts in from the doorway. "Look at these curtains."

"Faded," Sarah says. The pink curtains are almost white now.

"Faded! They've shrunk." Ed tugs at one of them and laughs. "They're getting smaller and smaller. They're absurd. Where did we get these—Woolworth's?"

"No—it was that place, Wigwam."

"Right!" Ed snaps his fingers. "Wigwam. That was before they became Cost-Less." He turns to his mother. "We're going to redo this whole room."

"Why?" Rose asks. "It doesn't need anything but new curtains. I could sew you a pair of curtains."

"No, no. No, thanks, Ma." Rose hasn't sewn since she was seventy-five, and when she did sew, her shortcuts were legendary. She made dresses with asymmetrical necklines and blouses with one sleeve longer than the other. She whipped up a pair of pants without a fly for one grandson, and for the girls she made doll clothes that didn't come off. She just sewed the clothes onto the dolls.

"It's my favorite room in the house," Rose says. She sinks down on the bed.

"We call it the shrine." Sarah gestures at the paraphernalia that her daughter Miriam has left behind. There are the stuffed animals lined up neatly on top of the bookcase. There is the mineral collection and the rusting music stand—a purple rabbit's-foot key chain hangs from it.

There are the dolls representing different countries. They are all actually from China. The souvenir collection from the family's summer at Oxford—a series of English and Scottish guard dolls, some headless, some with heads toppling. They all have weak necks. "We were going to redo it when she went to college."

"Then she went to medical school," Ed says.

"And then she got engaged," adds Sarah.

"It's time."

"It's time," Sarah agrees.

Rose shakes her head. "You were never a sentimentalist, Ed." She smooths down the tulle skirt of the Madame Alexander bride doll.

Rose is staying with them for ten days. She flew in from Venice, California, after her dear friend Eileen Meeker passed on. The shock was terrible. Eileen was supposed to come over for brunch on Sunday at eleven o'clock. Eleven came and Eileen did not. Rose walked over to 7-B. She stood on the landing and pounded on the door. "Meeker!" she screamed, because Eileen was hard of hearing, although too stubborn to admit it. "Meeker!" Not a sound. It was up to Rose to alert the staff. Then Rose watched Eileen's nephew sell off all her possessions. Just one week later they moved in poor Juliet Frazier with her companion, and now Rose is left to watch them wheel her up and down, poor thing. Frazier doesn't know whether she is coming or going. Rose is very, very happy to be in Foggy Bottom with Ed and Sarah. She cried when they met her at the airport. "I've been so miserable!" she told them. "I've been so ill."

"We'll take you to Dr. Maltzman," Sarah said.

"No, no, it's my stomach."

Ed looked at Sarah. "It's those pills. You know they're bad for your digestion. You have to cut back on the pills."

"I have been cutting back," Rose told them, "except when the pain is too much for me. The pain is what I can't take, and only the pills will do for the pain."

"Yeah, well, we've been through that before," Ed said.

"Of course I can't live there any longer," Rose tells them at dinner that night. "Not after what happened."

"You'll feel better in a few days," Ed says.

Rose stares at him. She puts down her fork. Sometimes she thinks her son has no heart.

Sarah changes the subject. "There is a movie I wanted to see. The writing workshop at school is showing *Waiting for the Moon*. I thought we could all go on Sunday."

"Sure. Fine," Ed says. "You want to go, Ma?"

"If I can, I'll go," Rose says.

Ed gives Sarah a look. Sarah frowns back in warning.

"It was a terrible thing the way they treated her," Rose says. "They came in and they liquidated her apartment. I watched them. In and out, in and out they carried her things. Her most precious possessions. For years she dusted. In the end, what was the difference? She had no roots there. They just wheeled in Juliet Frazier. I said to them before I left that they could look for another tenant for number 3-C."

"What?" Ed says.

"I gave them notice. I said, Look around for someone new, because what happened to Meeker isn't going to happen to me. But be sure to tell your prospective tenant about the thermostat in the oven and the TV reception. Warn her she'd better be prepared to fork up for an exterior antenna. I said, My son Henry brought me here when he was working for the gallery, but he's gone now, in England, and has been living there for years. Now he's settled and married in Oxford. My younger son lives in Washington. My grandchildren are in the East. I don't need to stay in Venice—in *dr'erd auffn deck* on the West Coast. This is not where I'm going to finish my eighties, where my dearest friend is left alone to drop dead in front of the television."

"Oh, Ma," Ed says. "Don't cry. It's late, and you're exhausted. You've been through a long, long flight and you need to rest."

Rose puts her hand in his. "In the winter I'll stay with you, and in the summer I'll visit Henry. I love Oxford in the summer. It isn't humid there like Washington. It isn't unbearably hot like it is here."

"What are you saying?" gasps Ed. "You're completely settled in Venice. You have all your furniture there just the way you like it! You have your friends at the center!"

"How would you like it if you had to spend all your time with old, sick people?" Rose asks. Her voice is stern, her gray eyes plaintive.

"No, we're not doing this now," Ed says. "We're not going to discuss this."

"I want to call Henry," Rose tells Sarah.

"He's asleep. It's the middle of the night there."

"I'll call him later tonight, when it's morning in England. I'll be up in the night. I'll call from downstairs."

"Why don't we call him on the weekend?" Sarah suggests. "We'll have more time—and you'll feel better. Don't you want to finish your dinner?" Rose is standing up from the table.

"No. Thank you, dear. It was very good."

"Do you want some coffee? Decaffeinated?"

"No, thank you. I might come down for some later. I haven't been sleeping at night."

Ed can't sleep, either. He never sleeps well when his mother is staying with them, and now he lies in bed thinking about her plans to leave Venice and come East. "Sarah," he whispers.

She sighs and turns over.

"Sarah, she's going to move in with us."

Sarah doesn't answer.

"She's not going to move in with us, is she? Sarah?"

"No," Sarah answers suddenly. "Go back to sleep."

He lies there and looks out into the dark room. He stares at the dim crack of light between the bottom of the shade and the windowsill. Tomorrow he has to teach, but he's thinking about his mother, feeling that she is now going to stay with them in their house—that she is going to live with them. He knows she is lonely and bored. He wants to give her some companionship. To take care of her. It's the thought of doing all this that fills him with panic. It has nothing to do with her age. It's that she makes him nervous. At long stretches she drives him crazy. She has too much power over him. He hears her now as she pads down the hall to the bathroom. It's three-twelve in the morning. She is taking a hot shower. He listens as the water pours on and on. He hears her shaking her medicine bottles. She is taking her pills. She took some after dinner, of course, because he upset her. That isn't completely true. She would have taken them anyway. He feels guilty all the same. He imagines she'll go down to the kitchen and try to call Henry. Does she have his office number? Ed nudges Sarah's shoulder. "I can't sleep."

"Go to sleep," she replies distantly, like an echo.

"Sarah."

After a moment she speaks to him in a rapid, clear voice. "Don't be ridiculous. She is not going to move in; she just needs to feel wanted. She'll have a big fight with you tomorrow and refuse to live here. So calm down and go back to sleep." She turns toward the wall with most of the quilt wrapped around her, and Ed lies alone under the white sheets, listening to the slight creak of the stairs.

His lectures go badly that week. It's only the second week of the semester, and he sees that students are dropping out. He blames his poor performance for the dwindling enrollment. It was always a popular class in the past—Terrorism and Conflict Resolution—and he's known at Georgetown as something of a showman. "Energetic and full of insight," the student guide summed up in its evaluation. "Markowitz spices his lectures with lurid details of covert operations all over the Middle East. The slide lecture on the World's Most Wanted is a must-see, and the open discussion 'Friend or Foe?' also rates high marks." But Ed is flat this week. He comes in to school worn out from lack of sleep, from listening to Rose as she walks around the house at night, from watching her as she nods off during the day in the living room. When Ed comes home she doesn't bring up her idea about moving in. She looks up at him and talks in a lazy, druggy voice. She is taking her pills. She's got the orange bottles stashed away in Miriam's room and she is taking them every few hours. An opium eater among the stuffed animals.

Sarah was wrong that he and Rose would fight. They haven't fought at all. It's Ed and Sarah who have been fighting all week. "How am I supposed to get any work done?" Sarah demands. "I work at home. This is my office.

How can I write when she comes in and talks my ear off about herself and her symptoms—"

"It was your idea to have her visit," Ed says.

"Because it was the right thing to do! Because she was bereft of her friend!"

"Bereft?"

"*Bereft!*"

They face each other over the kitchen table.

"I said this was a bad time," Ed tells Sarah. "You insisted—"

"It's not a question of timing. You are leaving me to bear the entire responsibility. You stay in your office until six while I am here making dinner with her *watching* me! Then you keep me up at night."

"Sarah, I can't sleep because I'm tense! My head is pounding. You don't understand what I'm going through. You have no idea how nervous I am—"

"You sound just like her." Sarah storms out, nearly running down Rose in the hall.

Rose seems to take more pills each day. Either she is taking more or Ed is watching more closely. He hears her rattling in the bathroom at night. He watches her steal off to her room to take them. They send her spinning into reveries and long family stories in which she scrambles generations. In her accounts she is always the child or the niece, younger than everyone else. Always, strangely, an only child. She can't seem to remember herself as a sister or a cousin. In memory she stands alone as the only member of her generation, just as she stands alone now. It alarms Ed. He corrects her sharply, and Sarah hisses at him later over the dinner dishes. "Let it go! What's the difference?"

"The difference? She's taking drugs!"

"What are you going to do? She's eighty-seven."

"This is not eighty-seven speaking. This is enforced feeblemindedness. Synthetic senility!" He lowers his voice. "And she's doing it to get back at me. Because I didn't invite her to move in with us."

"Oh, she is not, Ed. She is not getting back at you. You've always got a conspiracy theory. Why don't you just work on being a better sport?"

On Sunday they go to see a movie in Georgetown. It's a rambling film about Gertrude Stein and Alice B. Toklas. The kind of film that glides from one old country house to the next and hovers over fields in the South of France, lingering on the remains of picnics. It's the kind of film Ed hates because it doesn't go anywhere. Just stews in its own juices. The vintage cars are more interesting than the characters.

Sarah is enjoying herself, though, and Ed is glad, because she deserves something for putting up with him—and with Rose—all week. Late-afternoon sun, and then moonlight, suffuses the movie screen. Gertrude and Alice sit in silence looking at each other. "What is the answer?" Alice asks at last. There is a long pause. Ed glances at his watch and looks up just in time to see Rose slumping in her seat. "Ma?" he whispers. "Ma? Sarah? What happened?"

"We need an ambulance," Sarah says, as the three other audience members turn around. "Pull her up. We have to get to a phone."

"No, don't move her!" Ed cries.

"Okay, wait with her while I call."

He looks down at his mother collapsed in her seat, breathing ever so slightly in the flickering moonlight of the movie.

They follow the ambulance in their car, and at the emergency room Ed tells his story at least four times.

"She just fell forward in the theater," he tells the triage nurse. They are wheeling Rose in on a gurney.

Sarah is carrying Rose's purse, a massive black wedge of a bag with short, round handles. "I think this has something to do with it." She hands the nurse two of Rose's orange prescription bottles.

⁓

That night Ed lies in bed imagining tiny sounds, tricking himself into hearing the stairs creak and the cabinets close—as if the house could twitch by itself, and the floorboards could have pins and needles. Rose is in the hospital for tests, and the doctor is concerned.

"She overdosed on the Percodan," Dr. Ing explained. "She must have lost count."

"She's been taking it for years," Ed said.

"Oh, yes, she's addicted to it."

Ed hated Ing for saying that. He felt his face burning there in the office.

"I have to call Henry," Ed says now to Sarah, who lies awake beside him.

"I thought you were going to call him in the morning."

"No, no," Ed groans. "I'm going to worry about it all night." It has to be done. He has to call his brother, who is hard enough to talk to under normal circumstances. His Anglophile brother, the collector and obsessive chef, the Laura Ashley manager in Oxford. The publisher of bleak poetry books in tiny editions.

"So call him." Sarah takes the phone from the nightstand and lays it on his chest.

"I don't have his number up here. I've got to go down to the kitchen and get the Rolodex." Ed heaves himself out of bed and thumps down the stairs. After a moment Sarah struggles up, puts on Ed's bathrobe, and goes after him.

They sit at the kitchen table, which is strewn with the remains of the *Times*, and one of Ed's yellow legal pads with a list of things to do, and a cluster of blackening bananas. Sarah has been meaning to make banana bread. "Hello, Henry?" Ed calls into the receiver. "Hello? We've got a terrible connection. It's Ed."

"Good God, what's the matter?" Henry cries on the other end. Ed's jaw tightens. It's true that he almost never calls his brother, but it offends him that Henry should assume some disaster has occurred the minute he hears Ed's voice. And, of course, assume it with that surreal British accent. All Henry's Briticisms seem to come out of books, and now, as Ed speaks, Henry's gasps of horror have a Dickensian quality—with subtle Brooklyn harmonics. "Gracious heavens," Henry exclaims. "Oh, poor Mother! Poor Mother. What are we going to do?"

"I don't know," Ed says grimly. "There isn't much we *can* do."

"Oh, God," Henry says.

"Look, can you get Susan?" Ed glares at the bananas on the table as he waits for Henry's wife to come on the line. Then he picks them up and throws them into the kitchen garbage. They land with a satisfying thump.

"Hello, Ed? Susan here." Her clipped voice soothes him.

"You heard what I said? I think you'd better send Henry out here."

"Yes, of course," Susan says. "We'll book him a flight today, and I'll ring you with his arrival information."

Ed feels much better when he hangs up. "She's one in a million," he tells Sarah.

By the time Henry arrives, Rose is home from the hospital. She was there for three days—unconscious part of the time. But then she came to, and she left the hospital, frail but radiant, a bunch of helium balloons from the grandchildren tied to the back of her wheelchair. "She has an amazing constitution for a woman her age," the doctor told Ed. "There is absolutely nothing wrong with her—except that she's taking massive doses of Percodan."

"So let's get her off it," Ed said.

"You'd have to get her into a clinical detox program," the doctor told him. "This is not something you should try at home."

Rose is recovering in Miriam's room. No one has mentioned a detox program. No one has mentioned when she will be going home. She lies on the pink twin bed and reads Danielle Steel, Belva Plain, and Andrew Greeley. Henry, after his first transports, has collapsed, exhausted with jet lag and stress, in the boys' room. He had laid out his silk pajamas on the bottom bunk and hung his clothes in the closet that Ben and Avi shared before they went off to college. Ed feels as though he is the last adult left in the world.

When he comes home Friday evening, the kitchen is a disaster area. Rose sits at the table behind a pile of vegetables. Bags of them. Little yellow cherry tomatoes, radishes, curly red-fringed lettuce dripping in the colander. "Henry and Sarah are collaborating on dinner," she tells Ed. She is positively glowing among those vegetables. She looks happier than she has in years. There are grocery bags all over the counters, flecks of carrot peel on the floor. Henry has worked himself into one of his cooking frenzies. Flushed with exertion, he stands over a tray of hollowed-out oranges. He is piping sweet potato into each one with a pastry tube. Rose is beaming, and Ed can't help smiling to see it. "There's nothing like sitting in the kitchen with the family," she says. "If you had to cook in what they give us for kitchens at Venice Vista! It's a disgrace."

"You never liked cooking," Ed points out, kissing her on the cheek.

"No, I never did like cooking, myself," Rose admits. "But I like a kitchen with cooking going on in it. I like to be with the family. These kitchenettes at Venice Vista aren't built for cooking. Not at all. And outdated! Decorated in green! The Frigidaire is green."

Henry looks up from his orange shells. "I think the gaskets are going on yours, Ed." He points to Ed's refrigerator.

"Yeah, I know. The house needs work," Ed says.

"It's a lovely house," Henry rushes to add. "These row houses are charming. You could plant a little ivy by the door. Repaint. You could make it look like Georgetown.

"Ed!" he bursts out, suddenly. "What's the time? My challahs! Hold this." He hands Ed the pastry tube and rushes to check on the bread. Sarah stands at the stove dropping matzo balls into the chicken soup. Steam rises in her face. "It's such a pity you don't have a double oven," Henry sighs. "How will we get it all in? Susan says I'm terribly spoiled, and she won't let me get a convection oven." He wipes his hands on the ridiculous little checkered apron he has wrapped around his waist. "But the one implement I refuse to buy—absolutely *refuse*—is the microwave. I cannot reconcile cooking with radiation. It's unnatural. They say it doesn't brown the food. And, of course, you can't bake in a contraption that won't crisp. You don't get a crust. That's what I've been told, in any case. I won't touch them."

Ed comes up behind Sarah. "How are you?" he asks her. He kisses the back of her head.

"Stop that!" she snaps. She opens the oven door to check on her cake.

"Oh dear," Rose observes from the table. "Your cake has fallen."

"That's true," Sarah says, and she slams the oven door shut.

Henry whirls around, startled by the noise. "What will we do?" he cries. "Oh, I know what we should do. Make a fruit compote and cover it. Make a trifle. What fruit do we have?" He rummages in the grocery bags.

"I love trifle," Rose says. "We had trifle in England. I grew on trifle. I was such a little thing when they brought me out. Such a weak little thing. But when they gave me the trifle I blossomed out. How I blossomed out! With the cream on top. That heavy cream—"

"Oh," Henry gasps. "We didn't get cream. We'll have to run out and buy—"

"How I blossomed out," Rose says again. "My girth and my English grew equally. We weren't thin little things when we were Miriam's age."

"Would you get some cream, Ed?" asks Henry.

"No." Ed sinks into a chair.

"It's just that I can't leave the challahs," Henry says.

"Who would have thought," Rose muses, "that cream, which just melts on the tongue, can instantly turn into pounds."

"I don't think we can make trifle without cream," says Henry.

"Fine," says Ed. "Don't."

Rose looks over at Sarah. "I wasn't thin when I was Miriam's age. Is she still so thin? All my life I've had a passion for sweets. And for affection," she adds thoughtfully.

"Are you upset?" Henry asks Ed.

"No," Ed says. "I am not upset."

"Sarah," Rose says. "I would like to do just one thing."

"Yes?"

"Because I've really been at death's door."

"What do you want to do?"

"Go to the synagogue tomorrow. Together—with the whole family."

"You didn't tell me it was going to be Indian summer," Henry moans in the backseat of the car. He is sweating in his new fall suit, wondering if he should mop his brow with the blue silk handkerchief so beautifully folded in his breast pocket. "I don't think the air conditioner is reaching back here." Sarah looks back at him and feels some sympathy. He's gained weight since his wedding. His face is puffy in the heat, his brown eyes mournful. She and Ed haven't been to Congregation Shaarei Tzedek in months. It surprised her that Ed agreed to go.

"Why don't we ever come anymore?" Ed asks Sarah as he puts on a white satin yarmulke and steps into the sanctuary. "I forget. What was our excuse?"

During the service he remembers. Under the roar of the bellowing cantor comes a soft murmur of kibitzing. As the thin little rabbi delivers his sermon, the talking seems to grow louder. Ed tries to read some prayers to himself in the English. "How precious is your kindness, O God!" Ed reads. "The children of men and women take refuge in the shadow of your wings."

"New Haven," he hears on his left. "They're going to live in New Haven. I'm worried sick."

"The crime."

"It's terrible."

"We are divided within ourselves," the rabbi says from the bimah. "We are torn, and we *should* be torn. And yet —no, all the more—we love Israel."

"But that's where Yale Law School *is*," says the woman on Ed's left.

"The campus is beautiful."

"Beautiful."

"You give them drink of your stream of delights," Ed reads.

"Just eight-fifty a month," the concerned mother says. "But parking is going to be a problem." Ed shuts his book.

He is in a terrible mood by the time they get home. Sarah climbs upstairs and lies down with the air conditioner on high, but Ed paces around the house in his T-shirt and slacks. He looks into Miriam's room, where Rose lies on the bed, reading. Her short gray hair is brushed up from her forehead in a wave. He strides down to the living room, where Henry slouches on the couch.

"Let's go for a walk, Edward," Henry suggests.

"Too hot," Ed grunts.

"I was thinking this is an opportunity," Henry says. "We hardly ever see each other. I'd like to walk around the university. I saw the most marvelous stand there yesterday—selling ices."

They walk the narrow streets below Georgetown. Henry wears sunglasses and one of Ed's polo shirts pulled taut over his belly. He buys Ed a chocolate soda at the green Bella Italia wagon. He himself sips a wild strawberry, and they stride down the sidewalk together. Henry is appalled at the dearth of bookstores, intrigued by the cutwork parasols in a vintage-clothing store. "I wish Susan liked this sort of thing." He casts a critical eye at the Laura

Ashley window display. "Cluttered," he decides. "I would never allow my staff to clutter like that."

"What did you think of Congregation S.T.?" Ed asks.

"Not bad. Not bad at all. Except for that ghastly Holocaust sculpture. The air-conditioning was splendid."

"I meant—you know—spiritually," Ed says.

Henry looks at him, questioning.

"I don't know," Ed says. "Every once in a while I go there sort of expecting something. I mean, sometimes I feel like I'm in a crisis. Sometimes I want to go and hear some words of wisdom from the rabbi. But I just end up sitting with those ladies with the jewelry."

"What do you mean, 'crisis'?"

"It's not specific—"

"You can tell me," Henry says. "Believe me, this is something I know about."

Ed walks on, looking at the sidewalk. It's true, he thinks. Henry's been in analysis how many years? He's worked on his psyche laboriously. Stripped down and redecorated in layers. Draped himself with cultures and collections. Developed the most complicated persona possible—the expatriate Brooklyn Jew in Oxford. The unaffiliated scholar and aesthete as businessman. Henry has made himself at home in contradictions. Meanwhile, he, Ed, is completely at sea. At a loss.

"Is it Mother? You're worried about her?"

"Oh, partly, but it's not just that. It's the way the time is going. The way she's getting. The way the kids are getting. The generations are sort of flipping over. I think," Ed says slowly, "it would be very comforting to believe in God. Just for some sense of permanence. The stability. I think I would like to believe in God."

"You? Never!" Henry laughs.

"Why not?" Ed asks.

"Because you're a pragmatist and you always have been," Henry says.

"No, see, I know what it would take," Ed says. "I know what could convince me. If you showed me a miracle, for example."

"One miracle? Oh, Edward, if we saw a miracle you would either find some explanation or say it was a fluke."

"No. I could be convinced. Under the right conditions I could. Look at these analytic philosophers—these positivists—discovering God now that they're old and gray. I heard that A. J. Ayer on his deathbed actually lay there and said all his work was a lie and he actually did believe in the divine and in the immortality of the soul—and that it was possible to make ethical and aesthetic judgments. A few hours later he came out of it, though. Said he'd just panicked, and denied it all."

"Well, that's good," Henry says.

"Why?"

"Because it would have been so terribly sad for him to lose everything he believed in just like that. His life's work in sense perception. Everything he stood for as an atheist."

They walk along in silence. Ed pokes with his straw at the ice in the bottom of his cup. "The last two weeks have been bad," he says. "I'm not getting any work done. I'm not sleeping at night. I just lie awake thinking. Things will never be the same with Ma."

"She doesn't seem so different to me," Henry says. "Whenever I visit it strikes me how things are moving along so smoothly—in the same comforting old ways."

"What old ways? What are you talking about?" asks Ed. Can't Henry see that the house is splitting apart? "Miriam is getting married. Mother has decided to move in with us—"

"I've always looked to you and Sarah as constants,"

Henry says, "while I've gone through all the turmoil and changes in my life."

Ed just stands stock-still in the middle of the sidewalk, because Henry never ceases to amaze him. Constants! he wants to scream. The universe is expanding. The continents are sliding. The kids are shooting off from the house like comets, and he and Sarah are turning fifty-six in their wake. In the trails of dolls and old clothes they leave behind; in the dust of their mineral collections. "I just feel, when I'm talking to you and to Ma, that the time is getting bent," he says finally. "That things are bent out of proportion. All I want is for things to be normal. Where the kids are kids and Ma would be an adult, and the generations would be sort of in order. Henry, will you stop touching me!" He shakes off Henry's hand. "I hate it when you do that. The thing is, if Ma moves in with us I'll have a nervous breakdown. I know it makes her happy, living in that pink room, but it's too weird for me. I just can't take it if I'm supposed to be her father. And there is just no possible way to talk to her about it. How can you tell your mother something like that? There is no way in the world I can sit down and explain the situation to her." The brothers stand there blocking the sidewalk. Unconsciously, each rattles the melting ice in his cup.

Meanwhile, at home, Sarah is explaining the situation to Rose. "Mother," she says, "we all have very different personalities. Very different routines. You have your own life in Venice and your own network. Your doctor, your friends. Here in Washington you'd be completely isolated. You wouldn't have the support staff, the activities, the, uh, backup nurses."

Rose looks up desolately from the pink bed and Sarah shifts in Miriam's desk chair, knees knocking the underside of the desk.

"I don't have roots in Venice," Rose says.

"But you've lived there ten years," Sarah reminds her. "And we can't provide you with what you have there. Not without giving up our jobs. That's why I'm calling the travel agent."

Rose is crying softly on the bed, and Sarah comes over to her and puts her arms around her. "But you're coming back in June," she says. "Won't that be lovely, when you come back for Miriam's wedding?"

Rose thinks about it. "I could go on to England," she says.

Sarah hesitates a moment. Then she nods, feeling only slightly evil. "That's right," she tells Rose. "You can visit Henry and Susan in their cottage."

"The Cotswolds," Rose sighs. "Everything will be blooming."

"The heat never gets so bad there," Sarah says.

"That's true. They don't have that humidity. Your humidity is unbearable." She reminds Sarah of Ben's July bar mitzvah, when the air-conditioning failed in the social hall and she was nearly overcome by the heat. "I will never forget it. *Never.*" Her voice trembles with laughter, even though she is still crying.

Henry returns to England. Rose flies back to California. The Sunday after Rose leaves, Ed and Sarah drive to JCPenney to look for miniblinds for Miriam's room. "We'll get the toys into boxes," Ed says as they walk through the store.

"And we'll have to replace the carpet," adds Sarah.

"Why? What's wrong with it? We spent good money on that carpet."

"I thought the color—"

"I like the color. It's a very nice color for a guest room."

"Well, it's not going to go with miniblinds." Sarah trails her fingers down the plastic slats on display.

"So let's get some curtains. That's what I said in the first place."

"But they have to go with dusty rose."

"Fine."

A saleswoman finds them studying the white Battenberg curtains. "May I help you?"

"Well, Phyllis," Ed says, reading her name tag. "We're looking for something forty-five by fifty."

"That's the window size?" Phyllis asks.

"Yeah."

"And what kind of room would this be?"

"A bedroom," Sarah says. "Sort of a girl's room."

Phyllis nods. "How old is the girl?"

"Twenty-three," Ed says.

"She doesn't live at home." Sarah feels silly. "She's at Harvard Med."

"Actually, she's getting married in June."

"Congratulations."

"Thank you," Ed says. "We're turning it into a guest room, but we want it to sort of—go with what we have in there already."

"It's a dusty-rose room," Sarah explains.

"Let me show you what we have." Phyllis leads them to a window display.

"Mmm," Ed hums uncertainly.

"Then we have this with the eyelet . . ."

"No, no." Ed grimaces at Sarah. "What's that by the wall?" he asks. "That's not bad."

"This is new," Phyllis says.

"That's very pretty," says Sarah.

"It's called Fantasy Rose," Phyllis tells them. "It's got

the overall rose print in blush, gray, and cream in fifty-fifty cotton-poly. You've got the valance here, and the swag—" She fluffs out the material. "And then here's your basic tier. You use two curtain rods."

"That would look beautiful with the carpet," Sarah says as she and Ed talk it over by the water fountain. "If you're sure you don't want to replace the carpet."

"We're not replacing the carpet," Ed says. "I'm not spending a thousand dollars to replace a perfectly good carpet."

That evening after they hang the curtains, Sarah drags the telephone into Miriam's room, lies down on the bed, and calls Cambridge. "Hello, Miriam?" she says. "This is Mom. I'm calling from the shrine. We just put up the most beautiful curtains. They're pink with sort of gray and cream. I know. I know. Ed! You can pick up the phone. I got her."

"Ow, you're screaming in my ear," Ed says from the kitchen. "Hi, baby. Everyone's gone home. We got you these pink curtains. They're beautiful. They're ridiculous. It's going to be a guest room for when you and Jon come down. We're going to get a convertible sofa."

"You could have a baby girl," Sarah says, "and she could sleep here when you come visit."

"You could just come down by yourself when you finish Anatomy," Ed says, sticking to the near future.

The Persians

In memory of Marion Magid

Ed goes all the way to the campus mailroom to sign for his registered letter. He had complained about it over lunch, and said it was inconvenient, but as soon as he left the café, he went over to get the thing. He has been receiving a great deal of mail recently as well as phone calls: requests for comments on radio and television. In the wake of the bombing at the World Trade Center, Ed is in demand as a terrorism expert—and working at Georgetown makes him accessible, too. This very afternoon he is having a pre-interview with a radio producer from *Talk of the Times*. Over lunch he brushed off jokes that the letter was an invitation to the White House, but walking to the mailroom, he has no trouble believing it's from the Feds. He has received letters from the CIA in the past, although they were not particularly dramatic.

The letter is from Iran, on stationery with the letterhead in Persian. It is typed in English, and it reads:

In the Name of the Most High
Most Respectable Scholar,
Professor E. Markowitz:

Salaamon Alaikom—*With our wholehearted greeting:*

We acknowledge the estimable occasion to inform your highness that the "Celebration Congress of the Great and Glorified Divine Mystic Mullah Sadra" will be held in the City of Isfahan from 1st to 6th Zelqadan.

Hereby, we find it most timely to request to know when we may enjoy your high presence. Most pleasurably we will be informed that your excellency are leaving for Iran at the soonest possible convenience. As such, we may make preparations regarding the provision of tickets and rooms in the ancient city of Isfahan, of which it is said: Isfahan nisf Jahan—*Isfahan is half the world.*

With greatest respect for your graciousness,
Dr. V. P. Jamil

The Secretary
The Committee of the Celebration Congress

Ed has never seen a call for papers in quite this form. He stands there in the mailroom and reads it through twice. The glorified divine mystic Mullah Sadra is certainly not within his area of expertise, and he can't imagine where they got his name. It is a little frightening, although it is also proof that he is developing a truly international reputation. These are heady times for him; he is being sought on many levels. But it is the language of the letter that rings in his ears and puts a skip in his step as he walks back to his office. In this day and age, when one's graduate students call up and ask for "Ed"—the undergraduates waiting for only the slightest encouragement to follow suit—it is undeniably a delight to be referred to in the royal plural and to be called excellency. There is, perhaps, a courtier in every scholar; especially in those like Ed who study the modern world and do not have a chance to savor the past.

He paces around his office, waiting for his three o'clock phone call from the radio producer, Jill Bordles. He sorts the papers on his two desks, moving offprints from one pile to another. It's a large cluttered office with pictures on the wall of Sarah and the children. "This is my daughter who's getting married this summer," he will say to visitors, although the description does not match the picture of Miriam in her band uniform. The phone rings.

"Professor Markowitz," Jill Bordles says. "Hi. How are you?"

"Oh, fine," he says. "Busy. How are you?"

"I'm great. Let me tell you how we do this. It's really just a chance to find out about you and your work. To ask you some questions."

"Okay, shoot."

"I have a paper here you wrote in 1989, 'The Terrorist as Other.' You say here that our very attempts to understand the terrorist are already compromised by hidden assumptions that the terrorist is alien to us. That his morals and motives could never be shared by any of us in the civilized world."

"That's exactly right," Ed tells her. "And that's what puts us into a bind, because many of us have a double standard. In the Jewish community, for example, we refuse to see that the birth of Israel was facilitated by terrorist acts. The terrorist who acts against our own established political and social institutions is an alien and a renegade; we refuse to see him in our own history. In essence, we refuse to see the terrorist in ourselves."

"And so," Bordles says, "when we learn American history in school, we don't read about something like the Boston Tea Party as a terrorist act—because it has become part of our myth about ourselves."

"Yes. Absolutely. Although, of course, strictly speaking, terrorism as a concept was invented in the nineteenth century by Georges Sorel and put into practice by the Narodnaya Volya movement in Russia. But to speak about it in a more general way, then, absolutely. Something like the Boston Tea Party is a perfect example of my point. This is a heroic event for us from the third grade on. The destruction of English property never becomes an issue in the classroom. We don't think of it as a terrorist act at all. And yet, when we look at it closely, we find insurgency, secrecy, and sabotage—the three fundamentals of terrorist activity. And so what we are practicing in the classroom is a perfect case of sublimating the act to our iconography—or, in other words, what we are teaching is that the ends justify the means if the end is the United States."

"Professor Markowitz," Bordles asks, "do you then excuse something like the bombing of the World Trade Center in New York?"

"This is a question that we have to examine in its complexity," Ed says. "And so I prefer to use the word *understand* rather than the word *excuse.* This is what I think we all have to learn. We have to recognize our own contradictions. What have we allowed and excused in ourselves? What kind of rhetoric do we use to cloak our own rebellion, our own battles, our own invasions—the genocide and slavery in our own history? Then, with self-knowledge, we can look at the culture that produces the terrorist; we have to understand his—or her—mores and motivations."

" 'One country's terrorist is another's freedom fighter,' " Bordles quotes from Ed's book.

"You've really done your homework," Ed says.

"Oh, well, it's my job," she tells him modestly.

"I'm impressed."

"No, I was fascinated by your book. Particularly with one point—" He can hear her leafing through the pages. "There is a very subtle point you make here in chapter 6, where you say that, on the one hand, we have to understand that our own culture and history are rooted in violence, and not merely in the myth of pacifism and agrarian isolation that we promote. But, on the other hand, we have to avoid judging the terrorists of the Muslim world by the strictures of our own Judeo-Christian tradition as it is institutionalized in America."

"Yes, you are really getting to the heart of it there. You really put your finger on it." Ed is warming to his subject. "We have to look very carefully at the insurgents we call aliens. It is vital for us to examine the 'Other' in order to understand ourselves. But at the same time, we have to remember that the terrorist really is alien to us—his otherness is real, and his world is different from ours—and here's my point: if we can learn about ourselves from great, generous liberal minds like Tocqueville or Crèvecoeur, then we can learn from the terrorist as well. And if we have trouble with the parallel, then that says a great deal about us, and what we are willing to find in the mirror the Other presents to us. We have to be willing to broaden our reading of the responses to America, and move beyond the classics of democratic ideology to think about what these visceral reactions by terrorists tell us about America and its policies, its military might."

He has not quite finished, but Bordles interjects, "Professor Markowitz, I want to thank you for your time. I think you are going to be our perfect guest, because you have the kind of expertise and the kind of balance that we're looking for—not just in the political sense, but as a scholar."

"Listen, it's a pleasure," Ed says. "And feel free, if you want to ask any other questions; just give me a call."

"We'll be looking forward to seeing you on Friday."

⁓

Over dinner Ed tells his wife, Sarah, "She really read my book. It was very flattering. She was quoting me, chapter and verse."

"I like the letter," Sarah says, looking at it lying on the table next to her plate. "Are you going?"

"You want me to go to Iran?" Ed asks.

"Of course not. We still have to pick up that present for Katie Passachoff."

"I thought we said we weren't going to that bat mitzvah," Ed says.

"No, we're going."

"Oh, why?" he groans. "After a week like this, I have to get up on Saturday and drive out to Shaarei Tzedek for the whole day?"

"We discussed this a month ago," Sarah says unruffled. "We're supposed to look at their band for the wedding."

"Just look? Do they play any instruments or do they just stand there?"

"You know what I mean. They're having Phil's Harmonic, and they're supposed to be wonderful, according to Liz Passachoff."

"Oh, right, the Phil's Harmonic with what's-his-face."

"With Phil!"

"What a terrible name for a band. What's his last name?"

"Katz."

"Well, why didn't he do something with Katz? The Katzenjammer Kids or something."

"I thought we'd pick up a book for her tomorrow," Sarah says.

"All right." He sighs. "I'm just exhausted, and I've still got to prepare my lecture. But you know," he says as he gets up from the table, "I had a pretty high-level discussion with that woman from N.P.R. I formulated some things on the phone that I had never really articulated in quite that way before. This sort of interview situation really—it really gets the thought processes rolling."

"Well, good," Sarah says. "And hereby I find it most timely for you to unload the dishwasher."

Ed stays up until almost midnight preparing his lecture, and Sarah is sleeping by the time he gets to bed. He usually tosses and turns, but tonight he falls asleep almost at once, and he begins to dream. He is working in an Islamic scholar's garden, kneeling at a low desk. The arched windows are surrounded with intricate carvings, the garden itself exquisitely planted with flowers surrounding a fountain tiled in blue, purple, and green. The surface of his desk is like silk. However, on top of the desk he finds his familiar lecture notes, and he is sitting in Sarah's orthopedic chair with the knee rest, which is supposed to take the weight off your back.

He gets out of the chair with some difficulty and walks into a larger courtyard planted entirely with agapanthus in different shades of purple and lavender. There is a larger fountain here, the mosaic at the bottom flecked with gold. As he walks, he passes from one garden into another, each more splendid than the last. He is alone, except for a pair of peacocks who swish the gravel as they walk. The day passes, and he walks through a hundred gardens. He is lost and cannot find his way out. Then, to his horror, night falls. A velvet curtain literally covers the sky, the soft fabric embroidered with pearls.

At this point he stirs and realizes that Sarah has thrown the comforter over his head. He wrestles with it and heaves it onto the floor. When he settles down again, he is still in the maze of gardens. However, he has found the registration table for the Celebration Congress. The other participants are milling around with drinks, and they include Liz and Arnie Passachoff with their daughter, the bat-mitzvah girl. He looks for his name tag and finds that it is printed in gold in both Persian and English and reads: "His gracious Edward Markowitz, Table 15."

Then he realizes that he has left his lecture notes in the scholar's garden. Of course, he is not foolish enough to go back for them. He walks up to the conference chairman, who is sitting behind the registration table and wears black-rimmed glasses. "I want to give my lecture extemporaneously," he says.

"Everything will be as you desire," the chairman tells him. "Please accept your copy of the conference proceedings." He then gives Ed a book bound in gold cloth. Ed sees that it is an exhibition catalog, and that each plate depicts a miniature painting of one of the gardens he has walked through. There is the fountain flecked with gold. There is the courtyard of agapanthus. He reads in the catalog notes:

> *What can we say when we look at this consummate craftsmanship? These gemlike colors? We are con-*

> *founded by the miniaturist's artistry: he takes us into the garden itself, as if we were walking along its paths or listening to the play of a living fountain. This illumination, merely three inches high, is one of the loveliest landscapes on the face of God's earth.*

It's Henry, Ed realizes. It's his brother, Henry, in England, who put together this conference and wrote these notes. Only Henry habitually refers to "the face of God's earth," as if the world were a grandfather clock. He of the exquisite taste and the musty collections. Who has been nagging Ed for years to write a book about Islamic culture, despite the fact that, as Henry knows perfectly well, Ed's area is politics and modern history. It was his brother who arranged this invitation, not to modern Iran but to Persia.

Ed wakes up shivering. He does not remember any of the dream except for the thought that his brother has orchestrated the conference invitation. Could it be? Has Henry, living as he does on the fringes of academic Oxford, met someone at the Oriental Institute and given him Ed's name? Ed gets out of bed and washes his face. Henry probably had nothing to do with the letter from Iran. It was just that the letter reminded him of his brother. It was mannered; it was antique. Henry loves that sort of thing. He has always chosen the Old World, just as Ed has chosen the New. He likes to think of it that way, although, in fact, Henry is a businessman and it is Ed who works as a scholar. He goes downstairs to breakfast. He doesn't spend a great deal of time thinking about his brother. Or at least he tries not to. Henry's aesthetic transports exhaust him. The letter is still lying on the kitchen table where Sarah left it, and Ed folds it up and puts it on the stack of bills in the hall. He checks and sees that his lecture notes are in his briefcase where he left them.

After work that day, Sarah picks him up and insists that they go to the campus bookstore to get the present for Katie Passachoff. She reminds him: "You said tomorrow is out, and Friday you have that radio thing."

"Is it really necessary for both of us to get this present?"

"I'm tired of buying gifts and getting criticized later," she says.

"All I said was I thought it would be more appropriate to get a Jewish book for this kind of event." The two of them have been going to a lot of bar and bat mitzvahs in the past few months. Many of their friends are on their second set of children, and now Ed and Sarah have to go through these milestones again.

They go to the Judaica section of the bookstore and find several Haggadahs, *The Big Book of Jewish Humor*, and a coffee-table book called *Great Jews in Music*. "I was thinking more of a novel," Sarah says.

"All right, look through fiction. Find a few possibilities." Ed strides off and starts pulling books off the shelves. He prides himself on getting in and out of a store quickly. After a few minutes he has three books. "Okay, pick one of these," he says. "We've got *Goodbye, Columbus*—"

She shakes her head.

"This is a classic coming-of-age story!"

"No. I don't think it's the right thing."

"What are you talking about?"

"Ed, for you it's a coming-of-age story. She's a girl, and she's not living in the fifties."

"Well, excuse me!" Ed says. "Okay, we have the stories of Isaac Bashevis Singer."

"Oh, no."

"What?"

"Singer is not for a twelve-year-old."

"This is a nice hardback book," Ed protests.

"He's kinky," says Sarah.

"He's a great writer!"

"He's obsessed with defloration! That is not an appropriate gift."

"Fine. Then we've got *The Adventures of Augie March.* Now this is a great book."

"It's too hard for a twelve-year-old."

"Okay, either it's too hard or it's too kinky. So what do you have? Oh, very original. *The Diary of Anne Frank.* And what's this? I thought we said Jewish books. *Little Women*? Sarah! You're accusing me of living in the past. Talk about the fifties. You're dealing with the 1850s here."

"I was thinking about her age level," Sarah says.

"I thought we were looking for a great Jewish novel. I find classic Jewish literature and I get vetoed. Then you come up with *Little Women*?" He looks at her standing there with her big purse. He realizes that this is what she must have been reading when she was twelve, and he thinks it's sweet. "Let's try again," he says, and they turn back to the shelves.

"Oh—Chaim Grade," she exclaims. "He's wonderful. *My Mother's Sabbath Days.*"

"God, no," Ed says.

"Too sad?"

"It's only the saddest thing I've ever read. I couldn't even finish it. Tell me something, why do we have to get her a Holocaust book?"

"Who said anything about the Holocaust?"

"Everything you come up with is a Holocaust book. You're homing in on them."

Sarah looks up. "I am not! I'm just looking for the Jewish ones."

They spend half an hour combing the shelves and arguing. In the end, they buy *The Diary of Anne Frank* and *Surely You're Joking, Mr. Feynman.*

⁂

When they get home and drop their bags on the kitchen table, Ed says, "I'm absolutely sure Henry got those people to invite me to Iran."

"Who does he know in Iran?" Sarah asks.

"He knows everyone! He's a professional—"

"Raconteur?"

"Yenta. He probably met someone in an antique store, or at the Ashmolean, or the Radcliffe Camera, or at some society or other. He's a member of everything. And he got talking to some kind of Iranian and he volunteered me to give a paper. He told them all about me and my work, and now I'm in their records."

"In Iran?"

"Sure, they're reading up on me over there." Ed paces around the kitchen.

Sarah waves this away and makes herself a pot of coffee.

"How much do you want to bet he wangled this somehow?"

"You're going to call and ask him?"

"No, I'm not going to call him."

"Why not?" Sarah asks.

"Because whenever I call he gets hysterical because he thinks something has happened to Ma."

"Well, Ed, with you it's a reasonable assumption."

"So he could call me once in a while."

This conversation plays through his mind that night as he is falling asleep, and he dreams about his brother. He is in Henry's apartment in Oxford with its dark upholstery and clutter of books. "Henry," Ed says, "you gave my name to the Persians, and now they are sending for me."

"Dear Edward," Henry says. "How marvelous!" He is standing in a scarlet-and-green smoking jacket, with matching quilted slippers and a fez on his head, its gold tassel hanging down. "Did they send you letters? It's like something from Montesquieu's *Lettres Persanes*. Did I ever show you my edition? It's exquisite. Look at this engraving, with the Persians arriving at the French court, gazing at those Parisian clothes and those powdered headdresses. Here is one of them sitting at the table with her quill and her little travel desk, writing a letter back to Persia. This is the original eighteenth-century binding. Do you know how much this cost? Don't even ask."

"Okay, I won't."

Henry looks disappointed. "When are you leaving?"

"I'm not going to Persia," Ed tells him.

"But they're expecting you!"

"Don't you understand that it's dangerous?" Ed demands. "We're talking about a theocracy governed by Islamic absolutists!"

"But, Edward, how many people have this kind of opportunity? And think of the book you could write. Not just a book about them, but a book to them: *Lettres Persanes* in reverse, where *you* would be the exotic!"

"What do you think I am, an anthropologist?" Ed demands. "If anyone is going to be exotic, that would have to be you."

Henry reddens. "But I thought you would enjoy Persia. I wasn't going to say anything about it, but I went to a lot of trouble arranging that invitation. It was going to be a surprise for your birthday. Susan and I gave it a great deal of thought. We had planned to get you the new *OED* on disk, but I began to think about it—taking all that rich language and condensing it on that little disk like synthesized music. I thought since you wrote about understanding the Other, you could write your next book on becoming the Other."

"I'm not interested in becoming the Other," Ed says. "I'll leave that to you and your expatriate friends."

Henry pours Ed a cup of tea. "Edward, please don't be upset. I thought if you could go over there and sit down with them, then you could work out our problems, because you understand the Arab mind."

"I don't even understand you," Ed tells him. "I have no idea what's going on in the Arab mind."

"Isn't that what you should be finding out?"

"Not in person," Ed mumbles. "What is this, the hundredth time I'm telling you? Iranians are not Arabs; they're Persians."

He walks out of the room, and finds himself in his mother's apartment in Venice, California. Rose also pours him a cup of tea, and she offers him chocolate-covered chocolate Girl Scout cookies. "They came to the door, so I had to buy them," she says. "Have some, dear. But I want to tell you something about the Persians. They are no friends of Israel. Esther was a beautiful girl, and she did the best she could, but it was a mixed marriage. No one talks about King Ahasuerus converting. I think he did not. I got you a couple of things for the trip. Wilton frozen dinners. Very expensive, so eat them. And sucking candy for the plane. And also I clipped William Safire for you from the *Times*, about how the international terrorists are all operating out of New York because we have such civil liberties."

"Yeah, I saw that one already," Ed says.

"And what did you think?" Rose asks. "The Arab *mujahideen* from Lebanon are getting Egyptian passports in the Sudan and Iranian *meshugoyim* are infiltrating Paramus and Oklahoma City."

"Alarmist, as usual."

"He's a beautiful writer," Rose says, looking over the clipping. "I'd like to see you someday writing a column like that. Especially on Sundays, when he writes about the English language. It's just beautiful." Ed wakes with a start. The dream flashes before him and then vanishes.

⁂

Ed drives to the studio for the *Talk of the Times* interview. Jill Bordles ushers him in and introduces him to the other guest, Georges Zaghlul, a Lebanese Christian Ed has met several times before. The two of them sit on either side of the moderator, Bob Kennedy. At exactly three o'clock, Kennedy announces to the radio audience: "Hello, it's foreign-affairs Friday on *Talk of the Times.* We'll be discussing the quagmire in the Middle East today, and we'll focus on what Israel, the Arab states, and the U.S. can do to get the peace process rolling. We have with us today Professor Edward Markowitz from Georgetown University, a noted expert on terrorism and past fellow at the Oxford Center for Peace. And Georges Zaghlul, of the Committee for Peace and Justice in the Middle East. Welcome. Professor Markowitz, let's start with you. Just where do you see us in the process today? And how do you think the bombing here, the shootings and stabbings in Israel, the Muslim militants in Egypt, are going to impact whatever progress we have made so far?"

"Well, Bob, I'm an optimist," Ed says. "I see a move toward resolution and moderation on all sides. We've had the Israelis sitting down with their neighbors—"

"You're referring to the peace talks begun in the last administration," Bob says.

"Yes. And we have a climate in Israel where it's no longer sacrilegious to consider land for peace—"

"You mean the idea of Israel giving up land for peace," Bob glosses for the audience.

"That's right." Ed is starting to get annoyed by these interruptions.

"But what about the increase in terrorist activity? You're an expert on terrorism; does it concern you?"

"Well," Ed says, "terrorism is a complex phenomenon with many facets—"

"How about you, Georges Zaghlul?" Bob asks. "Do you see a distancing of the Islamic world from some of the tactics of these terrorists?"

"Certainly," Zaghlul replies. "Islam is a religion of peace and historically one of moderation and tolerance for minorities. But when we consider terrorism, we have to look beyond the headlines to the causes behind it. When young boys throwing stones are gunned down with automatic weapons, the situation becomes inflammatory."

"We have a long line of callers," Bob says. "Let's go to Carol in San José. Hello, you're on *Talk of the Times*."

"Hi, Bob. I love your show," says Carol.

"Thank you," he says.

"This is a question for Professor Markowitz," Carol continues. "During the Gulf War there was a travel advisory that suggested that we not fly unless it was necessary. I've been hearing a lot about airport security, and I was wondering if they are still advising people not to fly."

Ed blinks. "Not that I know of," he says. "I don't really follow airport security."

"All right, thanks for calling, Carol," says Bob. "Let's go to Joyce in Silver Spring."

"Hi. This is a question for both guests," says Joyce. "When you're talking about the Islamic world, I wanted to know—have either of you seen the movie *Not Without My Daughter*? It was based on the autobiography of an American woman who is trying to get her daughter out of Iran?"

"Yes, actually, I have," Ed says.

"I just wanted to know—is it really like that for women in the Arab world?"

"Of course, Iranians are not Arabs," Ed says.

Joyce qualifies herself. "I guess I mean the Muslim world."

"Well, I can say this," Ed tells her. "I thought the movie accurately showed the lack of freedom for women. There were a few scenes, of course, that must have been fictionalized. The scene where the woman gets in touch with an underground escape movement at the bazaar—obviously the details there were changed to protect the actual people who helped her."

"Oh, no, that wasn't fictionalized," Joyce says. "That was in the book."

At which point Bob Kennedy booms out, "Hasan in Oklahoma City, you're on the air."

"Hello, this is Hasan. I am listening to the two guests, and I want to know who they represent when they talk about moving to moderation. These men are both American people hired by Israel in a propaganda campaign—"

"Is this a question or a comment?" Bob Kennedy breaks in.

"First a comment, then a question."

"Well, all right. Let's keep it brief."

Georges Zaghlul adds, "I am not American and I am not funded by Israel."

But Hasan continues. "You must understand the propaganda of land for peace. This is lip-service by the Israelis. This is a cover-up of Israel's abuses of human rights, its nuclear arsenal, and its terrorist destruction of lives and property."

"Let me explain something," Ed says. "There is a plurality of opinions in Israel, as in every democratic state, and there is a history in which policy has shifted and changed just as it does in every country. But to say that every move toward moderation is compromised—"

"In other words, give peace a chance," Bob sums up for him.

"No," Ed says testily, "let me finish my point."

"You see," Hasan announces, "he is not interested in peace. He is interested in public opinion, and the reason for that is financial, because—"

"Listen, Hasan," Ed interrupts, "before we single out Israel, which is the only democracy in the Middle East, let's remember—"

Hasan talks over Ed's words. "Israel is a U.S. colony dedicated to a racist ideology. It is occupying land and holding indigenous peoples in concentration camps and building up weapons arsenals."

"Hold it," Ed says. "Let's look at this in context. Let's consider what Israel is reacting to. Israel is surrounded by absolutist, radical, anti-Western theocracies. Look at the Iraqis. Look at the Per—Iranians. All this aside, we have to recognize and applaud the movement in Israel to recognize the plight of the Palestinians."

Hasan says, "This is only Israeli propaganda."

"Where do you get your information?" Ed asks Hasan.

"All right, we have to move on," Bob Kennedy says.

"Have you researched this issue?" Ed presses on. "Or, let's hear what organization you belong to—"

Bob Kennedy is waving his hands at Ed and shaking his head.

"Let's hear the name of your organization," Ed says.

"All right," Kennedy says, "we have a lot to cover today."

"Just hold on a minute," Ed snaps, forgetting his professorial manner and his radio manners. "Let's hear who's paying you, Hasan."

"Georges Zaghlul," Kennedy interrupts, "what do you think of the issues Hasan raises. Are these legitimate concerns?"

"The concerns are very real," Zaghlul begins. As he speaks, Kennedy passes Ed a note: "Do not antagonize callers, please!"

Ed has a roaring headache by the time the two-hour show is over. He can barely see straight and almost hits a biker driving home. There is no point in going back to school. He gets a dusty bottle of Scotch from the cabinet over the refrigerator and pours himself a drink. They got him comfortable with their bright, intellectual-sounding producer—the one who could read—and then they just threw him out there and he couldn't hear himself think, let alone formulate his argument. And he had flattered himself that he would have a chance to make a real statement there on national radio, not just about tolerance and coexistence in the Middle East but about the way we examine other cultures, about examining our assumptions and moving beyond stereotypes into a more enlightened, more cosmopolitan view of the world. His temper had flared up again, shot to hell the balance Bordles had so admired in his book. He couldn't help himself, sitting there with that simplifying, bowdlerizing radio moderator, and those callers, by turns ignorant and vituperative. Of course, Georges Zaghlul had kept his cool; he is a lobbyist, a hired gun. But Ed made a perfect fool of himself. This is why, despite his dreams when he was young, he is an academic and not a diplomat. He has studied and written

—"brilliantly," according to the *Near East Review*—on diplomatic theory, but he doesn't have the personality for diplomacy.

The next day Ed and Sarah stand in the social hall of Congregation Shaarei Tzedek. Ed is wearing a peach satin yarmulke with "Bat Mitzvah of Katie Passachoff" printed on the inside in gold.

"Ed, I heard you on *Talk of the Times* yesterday," slim, snowy-haired Ida Brown tells him. They are all standing in the buffet line. "He was wonderful, wasn't he, Sidney?"

Sidney nods and says, "You took out that Arab from Oklahoma City. You really had his number. I said to Ida, 'I'm glad we had someone on there to defend Israel.' "

"Well, I didn't go on the show to defend Israel." Ed is feeling grumpy. "I was trying to talk about terrorism and its impact on the peace process."

"It all goes together hand in hand," Sidney Brown tells him.

The videographers are walking along the other side of the buffet tables, panning over the food. At the midpoint of the buffet table one of the chefs is carving up the prime rib.

The Greenbergs wave at them from the other end of the line, and Jeanne Greenberg seems to be calling out, "Loved you on *Talk of the Times*," while Art Greenberg gives Ed the thumbs-up sign.

Ed looks at Sarah. "You see," she says, "everyone loved it."

"Of course they did." Ed groans. "I gave them the Arab-baiting performance they were looking for."

"Relax. You made them happy!"

"Meanwhile, I'm a laughingstock at the department."

"Oh, stop. You're the man of the hour."

Several people come over and congratulate Ed at table 11. A few of them are old-timers in their eighties, and they congratulate Sarah, too, and tell her she must be very proud of her husband's accomplishments. She thanks them all.

A drumroll signals the arrival of the bat-mitzvah cake, which the caterer rolls in on a white table for everyone to see. It is magnificent—adorned with a marzipan book and a gilt ribbon bookmark. The pages of the open book are inscribed to Katie. There are holders on the table for the birthday candles. Katie Passachoff comes to stand by the cake, to be photographed. She is thin and long-legged in her floral dress, and she wears large round glasses. With the video cameras running, she takes the microphone.

"Another speech?" Ed asks Sarah.

"No," Sarah whispers back, "I think she's going to do the candle-lighting thing."

Sure enough, the keyboardist from Phil's Harmonic begins playing softly, and Katie reads:

Friends and family, I have got.
I love you all an awful lot.
With joy I ask you each to take
A candle on my birthday cake.

Three friends I have,
So great and jolly,
Darcy, Brittany, and Molly.

Ed and Sarah watch as the three friends get up to light candles. "I can't believe this with the rhymes and the piano," Ed says. "Have we seen that before?"

"She's very poised," Sarah comments, watching Katie read.

"You say that at every bat mitzvah," Ed reminds her. Then, a few minutes later, "How many candles does she get? There are seventeen people up there already."

"A lot of them are sharing candles," Sarah explains.

A woman Ed doesn't know leans over from the next table and whispers, "You don't know me. I'm Katie's aunt. I just wanted to say I heard you on Public Radio. I only heard the end, but did they say you wrote a book?"

Just at that moment Katie Passachoff is reading:

> *Much loved, and too seldom seen,*
> *Light a candle, Aunt Irene.*

"I think you're on," Ed tells Katie's aunt.

"Oh, you're right. Thanks," she says.

When the cake is finally rolled off for cutting, the band starts playing again and Sarah wants to dance. "All right, come on, we have to check out the band for the wedding. Listen, what's that they're playing?" Sarah hums a bit. " 'More'? I think they've hit our decade!"

They go out onto the dance floor, where a few couples are sham-dancing around the zest-filled Millers, who have had dance lessons and take to the floor whenever they can.

"Maybe we should take some lessons," Sarah says, looking over Ed's shoulder.

"Why?" Ed asks. "You know, I can't believe how many people were listening to me on the radio."

"That's what I've been telling you," Sarah says.

"But they'll never invite me back."

"So what? They want you in Iran. Do you think we should hire them?" She gestures with her head toward Phil's Harmonic.

"Yeah. They're good. I liked the guy who did keyboard for Katie's candle-lighting."

Sarah gives him a look.

"Oh, God, Fran and Stephen are working their way over here," Ed says. He steels himself for another battery of compliments on his performance.

"How are you, Sarah? Ed?" Fran asks them. "Isn't this lovely? Can you believe Katie is twelve years old already? I feel so old! I remember when she was born."

"You know," Stephen Miller says, "as the time passes you don't remember the years anymore, just the decades."

"And now your oldest is getting married?" Fran shakes her frosted head at Sarah. Fran chatters away, and Ed looks around for some means of escape. It's clear to him that as far as the talk show went—she and Stephen hadn't even been listening.

The Four Questions

Ed is sitting in his mother-in-law Estelle's gleaming kitchen. "Is it coming in on time?" Estelle asks him. He is calling to check on Yehudit's flight from San Francisco.

"It's still ringing," Ed says. He sits on one of the swivel chairs and twists the telephone cord through his fingers. One wall of the kitchen is papered in a yellow-and-brown daisy pattern, the daisies as big as Ed's hand. The window shade has the same pattern on it. Ed's in-laws live in a 1954 ranch house with all the original period details. Nearly every year since their wedding, he and Sarah have come out to Long Island for Passover, and the house has stayed the same. The front bathroom is papered, even on the ceiling, in brown with white and yellow flowers, and there is a double shower curtain over the tub, the outer curtain held back with brass chains. The front bedroom, Sarah's old room, has a blue carpet, organdy curtains, and white furniture, including a kidney-shaped vanity table.

There is a creaky trundle bed to wheel out from under Sarah's bed, and Ed always sleeps there, a step below Sarah.

In the old days, Sarah and Ed would fly up from Washington with the children, but now the kids come in on their own. Miriam and Ben take the shuttle down from Boston, Avi is driving in from Wesleyan, and Yehudit, the youngest, is flying in from Stanford. She usually can't come at all, but this year the holiday coincides with her spring break. Ed is going to pick her up at Kennedy tonight. "It's coming in on time," Ed tells Estelle.

"Good," she says, and she takes away his empty glass. Automatically, instinctively, Estelle puts things away. She folds up the newspaper before Ed gets to the business section. She'll clear the table while the slower eaters are contemplating seconds. And, when Ed and Sarah come to visit and sleep in the room Sarah and her sister used to share, Ed will come in and find that his things have inexorably been straightened. On the white-and-gold dresser, Ed's tangle of coins, keys, watch, and comb is untangled. The shirt and socks on the bed have been washed and folded. It's the kind of service you might expect in a fine hotel. In West Hempstead it makes Ed uneasy. His mother-in-law is in constant motion—sponging, sweeping, snapping open and shut the refrigerator door. Flicking off lights after him as he leaves the room. Now she is checking the oven. "This is a beautiful bird. Sarah," she calls into the den. "I want you to tell Miriam when she gets here that this turkey is kosher. Is she going to eat it?"

"I don't know," Sarah says. Her daughter the medical student (Harvard Medical School) has been getting more observant every year. In college she started bringing paper plates and plastic utensils to her grandparents' house because Estelle and Sol don't keep kosher. Then she began eating off paper plates even at home in Washington. Although Ed and Sarah have a kosher kitchen, they wash their milk and meat dishes together in the dishwasher.

"I never would have predicted it," Estelle says. "She used to eat everything on her plate. Yehudit was always finicky. I could have predicted she would be a vegetarian. But Miriam used to come and have more of everything. She used to love my turkey."

"It's not that, Mommy," Sarah says.

"I know. It's this orthodoxy of hers. I have no idea where she gets it from. From Jonathan, I guess." Jonathan is Miriam's fiancé.

"No," Ed says, "she started in with it before she even met Jon."

"It wasn't from anyone in this family. Are they still talking about having that Orthodox rabbi marry them?"

"Well—" Sarah begins.

"We met with him," Ed says.

"What was his name, Lowenthal?"

"Lewitsky," Ed says.

"Black coat and hat?"

"No, no, he's a young guy—"

"That doesn't mean anything," Estelle says.

"He was very nice, actually," Sarah says. "The problem is that he won't perform a ceremony at Congregation S.T."

"Why not? It's not Orthodox enough for him?"

"Well, it's a Conservative synagogue. Of course, our rabbi wouldn't let him use S.T. anyway. Rabbi Landis performs all the ceremonies there. They don't want the sanctuary to be treated like a hall to be rented out. Miriam is talking about getting married outside."

"Outside!" Estelle says. "In June! In Washington, D.C? When I think of your poor mother, Ed, in that heat!" Estelle is eleven years younger than Ed's mother, and always solicitous about Rose's health. "What are they thinking of? Where could they possibly get married outside?"

"I don't know," Ed says. "Dumbarton Oaks. The Rose Garden. They're a couple of silly kids."

"This is not a barbecue," Estelle says.

"What can we do?" Sarah asks. "If they insist on this rabbi."

"And it's March already," Estelle says grimly. "Here, Ed"—she takes a pink bakery box from the refrigerator—"you'd better finish these eclairs before she gets here."

"I'd better not." Ed is trying to watch his weight.

"It's a long time till dinner," Estelle warns as she puts the box back.

"That's okay. I'll live off the fat of the land," says Ed, patting his stomach.

"I got her sealed matzos, sealed macaroons, vacuum-packed gefilte fish." Estelle displays the packages on the scalloped wood shelves of her pantry.

"Don't worry. Whatever else happens, the boys are going to be ravenous. They're going to eat," Sarah assures her mother. They bring the tablecloth out to the dining room. "Remember Avi's friend Noam?"

"The gum chewer. He sat at this table and ate four pieces of cake!"

"And now Noam is an actuary," says Sarah.

"And Avi is bringing a girl to dinner."

"She's a lovely girl," Sarah says.

"Beautiful," Estelle agrees with a worried look.

In the kitchen Ed is thinking he might have an eclair after all. Estelle always has superb pastry in the house. Sol had started out as a baker, and still has a few friends in the business. "Are these from Leonard's?" Ed asks when Sol comes in.

"Leonard's was bought out," Sol says, easing himself

into a chair. "These are from Magic Oven. How is the teaching?"

"Well, I have a heavy load. Two of my colleagues went on sabbatical this year—"

"Left you shorthanded."

"Yeah," Ed says. "I've been teaching seven hours a week."

"That's all?" Sol is surprised.

"I mean, on top of my research."

"It doesn't sound that bad."

Ed starts to answer. Instead, he goes to the refrigerator and gets out the eclairs.

"Leonard's were better," Sol muses. "He used a better custard."

"But these are pretty good. What was that? Was that the kids?" Ed runs out to meet the cab in the driveway, pastry in hand. He pays the driver as his two oldest tumble out of the cab with their luggage—Ben's backpack and duffel, Miriam's canvas tote and the suitcase she has inherited, bright pink, patched with silver metallic tape, dating from Ed and Sarah's honeymoon in Paris.

"Daddy!" Miriam says. "What are you eating?"

Ed looks at his eclair. Technically all this sort of thing should be out of the house by now—all bread, cake, pastry, candy, soda, ice cream—anything even sweetened with corn syrup. And, of course, Miriam takes the technicalities seriously. He knows she must have stayed up late last night in her tiny apartment in Cambridge, vacuuming the crevices in the couch, packing away her toaster oven. He finishes off the eclair under her disapproving eyes. He doesn't need the calories, either, she is thinking. She has become very puritanical, his daughter, and it baffles him. They had raised the children in a liberal, rational, joyous way—raised them to enjoy the Jewish tradition, and Ed can't understand why Miriam would choose austerity and obscure ritualism. She is only twenty-three—even if she *is* getting married in June. How can a young girl be attracted to this kind of legalism? It disturbs him. On the other hand, he knows she is right about his weight and blood pressure. He hadn't really been hungry. He'll take it easy on dinner.

Meanwhile, Ben carries in the bags and dumps them in the den. "Hi, Grandma! Hi, Grandpa! Hi, Mom!" He grabs the TV remote and starts flipping channels. No one is worried about Ben becoming too intense. He is a senior at Brandeis, six feet tall with overgrown ash-brown hair. He has no thoughts about the future. No ideas about life after graduation. No plan. He is studying psychology in a distracted sort of way. When he flops down on the couch he looks like a big, amiable golden retriever.

"Get me the extra chairs from the basement, dear," Estelle tells him. "We've been waiting for you to get here. Then, Sarah, you can get the wineglasses. You can reach up there." Estelle is in her element. Her charm bracelet jingles as she talks. She directs Ben to go down under the Ping-Pong table without knocking over the boxes stacked there; she points Sarah to the cabinet above the refrigerator. Estelle is smaller than Sarah—five feet two and a quarter—and her features are sharper. She had been a brunette when she was younger, but now her hair is auburn. Her eyes are lighter brown as well, and her skin dotted with sun spots from the winters in Florida. "Oh—" she sighs suddenly as Miriam brings a box of paper plates from the kitchen. "Why do you have to—?"

"Because these dishes aren't Pesach dishes."

Estelle looks at the table, set with her white-and-gold Noritake china. "This is the good china," she says. "These are the Pesach dishes."

"But you use them for the other holidays, too," Miriam

tells her. "They've had bread on them and cake and pumpkin pie and all kinds of stuff."

"Ooo, you are sooo stubborn!" Estelle puts her hands on her tall granddaughter's shoulders and gives her a shake. The height difference makes it look as though she is pleading with her as she looks up into Miriam's face. Then the oven timer goes off and she rushes into the kitchen. Sarah is washing lettuce at the sink. "I'll do the salads last," Estelle tells her. "After Ed goes to the airport." Miriam is still on her mind. What kind of seder will Miriam have next year after she is married? Estelle has met Miriam's fiancé, who is just as observant as she is. "Did you see?" she asks Sarah. "I left you my list, for Miriam's wedding."

"What list?"

"On the table. Here." Estelle gives Sarah the typed list. "These are the names and addresses you asked for—the people I need to invite."

Sarah looks at the list. She turns the page and scans the names, doing some calculations in her head. "Mommy!" she says. "There are forty-two people on this list!"

"Not all of them will be able to come, of course," Estelle reassures her.

"We're having one hundred people at this wedding, remember? Including Ed's family, and the kids' friends—"

"Well, this is our family. These are your cousins, Sarah."

Sarah looks again at the list. "When was the last time I saw these people?" she asks. "Miriam wouldn't even recognize some of them. And what's this? The Seligs? The Magids? Robert and Trudy Rothman? These aren't cousins."

"Sarah! Robert and Trudy are my dearest friends.

We've known the Seligs and the Magids for thirty years."

"This is a small family wedding," Sarah tells her mother. "I'm sure they'll understand—"

Estelle knows that they wouldn't understand.

"I think we have to cut down this list," Sarah says.

Estelle doesn't get a chance to reply. Avi has arrived, and he's standing in the living room with Ed, Miriam, and Ben. She stands next to him: Amy, his friend from Wesleyan. Estelle still holds back from calling her his girlfriend. Nevertheless, there she is. She has gorgeous strawberry-blond hair, and she has brought Estelle flowers—mauve and rose tulips with fancy curling petals. No one else brought Estelle flowers.

"They're beautiful. Look, Sol, aren't they beautiful?" Estelle says. "Avi, you can take your bag to the den. The boys are sleeping in the den; the girls are sleeping in the sun room."

"I don't want to sleep in the den," Avi says.

"Why not?" asks Estelle.

"Because he snores." Avi points at his brother. "Seriously, he's so loud. I'd rather sleep in the basement."

Everyone looks at him. It's a finished basement and it's got carpeting, but it is cold down there.

"You've shared a room with Ben for years," Sarah says.

"You'll freeze down there," Estelle tells him.

"I have a down sleeping bag."

"You never complained at home," Sarah says.

"Oh, give me a break," Ben mutters under his breath. "You aren't going to have wild sex in a sleeping bag in the basement."

"What?" Ed asks. "Did you say something, Ben?"

"No," Ben says, and ambles back into the den.

"I don't want you in the basement," Estelle tells her grandson.

"Can I help you in the kitchen, Mrs. Kirshenbaum?" asks Amy.

Estelle and Amy make the chopped liver. The boys are watching TV in the den, and Ed and Sarah are lying down in the back. Miriam is on the phone with Jon.

"Did you want me to chop the onions, too?" Amy asks Estelle.

"Oh no. Just put them there and I'll take out the liver, and then we attach the grinder—" She snaps the grinder onto the KitchenAid and starts feeding in the broiled liver. "And then you add the onions and the eggs." Estelle pushes in the hard-boiled eggs. "And the schmaltz." She is explaining to Amy all about chopped liver, but her mind is full of questions. How serious is it with Avi? What do Amy's parents think? They are Methodist, Estelle knows that. And Amy's uncle is a Methodist minister! They can't approve of all this. But, then, of course, how much do they know about it? Avi barely talks about Amy. Estelle and Sol have only met her once before, when they came up for Avi's jazz band concert. And then, suddenly, Avi said he wanted to bring her with him to the seder. But he's never really dated anyone before, and kids shy away from anything serious at this age. Avi's cousin Jeffrey had maybe five different girlfriends in college, and he's still unmarried.

Amy's family goes to church every Sunday. They're quite religious. Amy had explained that to Estelle on the phone when she called up about the book. She wanted Estelle to recommend a book for her to read about Passover. Estelle didn't know what to say. She had never dreamed something like this would happen. If only Amy weren't Methodist. She is everything Estelle could ever want. An absolute doll. The tulips stand in the big barrel-cut crystal vase on the counter. The most beautiful colors.

By the time Ed goes off to the airport, everything is ready except the salad. They dress for dinner while he is gone.

"Do you have a decent shirt?" Sarah asks Ben, who is still watching television. "Or is that as good as it gets?"

"I didn't have a chance to do my laundry before I got here, so I have hardly any clothes," Ben explains.

"Ben!" Estelle looks at him in his red-and-green-plaid hunting shirt. Avi is wearing a nice starched Oxford.

"Maybe he could borrow one of Grandpa's," Miriam suggests.

"He's broader in the shoulders than I am," says Sol. "Come on, Ben, let's see if we can stuff you into something."

They wait for Ed and Yehudit in the living room, almost as if they were expecting guests. Ben sits stiffly on the couch in his small, stiff shirt. He stares at the silver coffee service carefully wrapped in clear plastic. He cracks his knuckles, and then he twists his neck to crack his neck joints. Everyone screams at him. Then, finally, they hear the car in the driveway.

"You're sick as a dog!" Sarah says when Yehudit gets inside.

Yehudit blows her nose and looks at them with feverish, jet-lagged eyes. "Yeah, I think I have mono," she says.

"Oh, my God," says Estelle. "She has to get into bed. That cot in the sun room isn't very comfortable."

"How about a hot drink?" suggests Sarah.

"I'll get her some soup," Estelle says.

"Does it have a vegetable base?" Yehudit asks.

"What she needs is a decongestant," says Ed.

They bundle her up in the La-Z-Boy chair in the den

and tuck her in with an afghan and a mug of hot chocolate.

"That's not kosher for Pesach," says Miriam, worried.

"Cool it," Ed says. Then they sit down at the seder table.

Ed always leads the seder. Sol and Estelle love the way he does it because he is so knowledgeable. Ed's area of expertise is the Middle East, so he ties Passover to the present day. And he is eloquent. They are very proud of their son-in-law.

"This is our festival of freedom," Ed says, "commemorating our liberation from slavery." He picks up a piece of matzo and reads from his New Revised Haggadah: " 'This is the bread which our fathers and mothers ate in Mitzrayim when they were slaves.' " He adds from the translator's note: " 'We use the Hebrew word *Mitzrayim* to denote the ancient land of Egypt—' "

"As opposed to modern-day Mitzrayim," Miriam says dryly.

" 'To differentiate it from modern Egypt,' " Ed reads. Then he puts down the matzo and extemporizes. "We eat this matzo so we will never forget what slavery is, and so that we continue to empathize with afflicted peoples throughout the world: those torn apart by civil wars, those starving or homeless, those crippled by poverty and disease. We think of the people oppressed for their religious or political beliefs. In particular, we meditate on the people in our own country who have not yet achieved full freedom; those discriminated against because of their race, gender, or sexual preference. We think of the subtle forms of slavery as well as the obvious ones—the gray areas that are now coming to light: sexual harassment, verbal abuse —" He can't help noticing Miriam as he says this. It's obvious that she is ignoring him. She is sitting there chanting to herself out of her Orthodox Birnbaum Haggadah, and it offends him. "Finally, we turn to the world's hot spot—the Middle East," Ed says. "We think of war-torn Israel and pray for compromises. We consider the Palestinians, who have no land to call their own, and we call for moderation and perspective. As we sit around the seder table, we look to the past to give us insight into the present."

"Beautiful," murmurs Estelle. But Ed looks down unhappily to where the kids are sitting. Ben has his feet up on Yehudit's empty chair, and Avi is playing with Amy's hair. Miriam is still poring over her Haggadah.

"It's time for the four questions," he says sharply. "The youngest child will chant the four questions," he adds for Amy's benefit.

Sarah checks on Yehudit in the den. "She's asleep. Avi will have to do it."

"Amy is two months younger than I am," Avi says.

"Why don't we all say it together?" Estelle suggests. "She shouldn't have to read it all alone."

"I don't mind," Amy says. She reads: " 'Why is this night different from all other nights? On other nights we eat leavened bread; why on this night do we eat matzo? On other nights we eat all kinds of herbs; why on this night do we eat bitter herbs? On other nights we do not dip even once; why on this night do we dip twice? On other nights we eat either sitting up or reclining; why on this night do we all recline?' "

"Now, Avi, read it in Hebrew," Ed says, determined that Avi should take part—feeling, as well, that the questions sound strange in English. Anthropological.

"What was that part about dipping twice?" Amy asks when Avi is done.

"That's when you dip the parsley into the salt water," Ben tells her.

"It doesn't have to be parsley," Sarah says. "Just greens."

"We're not up to that yet," Ed tells them. "Now I'm going to answer the questions." He reads: " 'We do these things to commemorate our slavery in Mitzrayim. For if God had not brought us out of slavery, we and all future generations would still be enslaved. We eat matzo because our ancestors did not have time to let their bread rise when they left E—Mitzrayim. We eat bitter herbs to remind us of the bitterness of slavery. We dip greens in salt water to remind us of our tears, and we recline at the table because we are free men and women.' Okay." Ed flips a few pages. "The second theme of Passover is about transmitting tradition to future generations. And we have here in the Haggadah examples of four kinds of children—each with his or her own needs and problems. What we have here is instructions on how to tailor the message of Passover to each one. So we read about four hypothetical cases. Traditionally, they were described as four sons: the wise son, the wicked son, the simple son, and the one who does not know how to ask. We refer to these children in modern terms as: committed, uncommitted, unaffiliated, and assimilated. Let's go around the table now. Estelle, would you like to read about the committed child?"

" 'What does the committed child say?' " Estelle reads. " 'What are the practices of Passover which God has commanded us? Tell him or her precisely what the practices are.' "

" 'What does the uncommitted child say?' " Sol continues. " 'What use to you are the practices of Passover? To you, and not to himself. The child excludes him- or herself from the community. Answer him/her: This is on account of what God did for me when I went out of Mitzrayim.

For *me*, and not for us. This child can only appreciate personal gain.' "

" 'What does the unaffiliated child say?' " asks Sarah. " 'What is all this about? Answer him or her simply: We were slaves and now we are free.' "

" 'But for the assimilated child,' " Ben reads, " 'it is up to us to open the discussion.' "

"We can meditate for a minute," Ed says, "on a fifth child who died in the Holocaust." They sit silently and look at their plates.

"It's interesting," says Miriam, "that so many things come in fours on Passover. There are four questions, four sons; you drink four cups of wine—"

"It's probably just coincidence," Ben says.

"Thanks," Miriam tells him. "I feel much better. So much for discussion at the seder." She glares at her brother. Couldn't he even shave before he came to the table? She pushes his feet off the chair. "Can't you sit normally?" she hisses at him.

"Don't be such a pain in the butt," Ben mutters.

Ed speeds on, plowing through the Haggadah. " 'The ten plagues that befell the Egyptians: Blood, frogs, vermin, wild beasts, murrain, boils, hail, locusts, darkness, death of the firstborn.' " He looks up from his book and says, "We think of the suffering of the Egyptians as they faced these calamities. We are grateful for our deliverance, but we remember that the oppressor was also oppressed." He pauses there, struck by his own phrase. It's very good. "We cannot celebrate at the expense of others, nor can we say that we are truly free until the other oppressed peoples of the world are also free. We make common cause with all peoples and all minorities. Our struggle is their struggle, and their struggle is our struggle. We turn now to the blessing over the wine and the matzo. Then"—he nods to Estelle—"we'll be ready to eat."

"Daddy," Miriam says.

"Yes."

"This is ridiculous. This seder is getting shorter every year."

"We're doing it the same way we always do it," Ed tells her.

"No, you're not. It's getting shorter and shorter. It was short enough to begin with! You always skip the most important parts."

"Miriam!" Sarah hushes her.

"Why do we have to spend the whole time talking about minorities?" she asks. "Why are you always talking about civil rights?"

"Because that's what Passover is about," Sol tells her.

"Oh, okay, fine," Miriam says.

"Time for the gefilte fish," Estelle announces. Amy gets up to help her, and the two of them bring in the salad plates. Each person has a piece of fish on a bed of lettuce with two cherry tomatoes and a dab of magenta horseradish sauce.

Sarah stands up, debating whether to wake Yehudit for dinner. She ends up walking over to Miriam and sitting next to her for a minute. "Miriam," she whispers, "I think you could try a little harder—"

"To do what?" Miriam asks.

"To be pleasant!" Sarah says. "You've been snapping at everyone all evening. There's no reason for that. There's no reason for you to talk that way to Daddy."

Miriam looks down at her book and continues reading to herself in Hebrew.

"Miriam?"

"What? I'm reading all the stuff Daddy skipped."

"Did you hear what I said? You're upsetting your father."

"It doesn't say a single word about minorities in here," Miriam says stubbornly.

"He's talking about the modern context—"

Miriam looks up at Sarah. "What about the original context?" she asks. "As in the Jewish people? As in God?"

Yehudit toddles in from the den with the afghan trailing behind her. "Can I have some plain salad?" she asks.

"This fish is wonderful," Sol says.

"Outstanding," Ed agrees.

"More," says Ben, with his mouth full.

"Ben! Gross! Can't you eat like a human being?" Avi asks him.

"It's Manishevitz Gold Label," Estelle says. "Yehudit, how did you catch this? Did they say it was definitely mono?"

"No—I don't know what it is," Yehudit says. "I started getting sick on the weekend when we went to sing at the Jewish Community Center for the seniors."

"It's nice that you do that," Estelle says. "Very nice. They're always so appreciative."

"Yeah, I guess so. There was this old guy there and he asked me, 'Do you know "Oyfn Pripitchik"?' I said, 'Yes, we do,' and he said, 'Then please, can I ask you, don't sing "Oyfn Pripitchik." They always come here and sing it for us, and it's so depressing.' Then, when we left, this little old lady beckoned to me and she said, 'What's your name?' I told her, and she said, 'You're very plain, dear, but you're very nice.' "

"That's terrible!" Estelle says. "Did she really say that?"

"Yup."

"It's not true!" Estelle says. "You should hear what everyone says about my granddaughters when they see your pictures. Wait till they see you—maid of honor at the wedding! What color did you pick for the wedding?" she asks Miriam.

"What?" Miriam asks, looking up from her Haggadah.

Ed is looking at Miriam and feeling that she is trying to undermine his whole seder. What is she doing accusing him of shortening the service every year? He does it the same way every year. She is the one who has changed—becoming more and more critical. More literal-minded. Who is she to criticize the way he leads the service? What does she think she is doing? He can remember seders when she couldn't stay awake until dinner. He remembers when she couldn't even sit up. When he could hold her head in the palm of his hand.

"I think peach is a hard color," Estelle is saying. "It's a hard color to find. You know, a pink is one thing. A pink looks lovely on just about everyone. Peach is a hard color to wear. When Mommy and Daddy got married, we had a terrible time with the color because the temple was maroon. There was a terrible maroon carpet in the sanctuary, and the social hall was maroon as well. There was maroon-flocked wallpaper. Remember, honey?" she asks Sol. He nods. "Now it's a rust color. Why it's rust, I don't know. But we ended up having the maids in pink because that was about all we could do. And in the pictures it looked beautiful."

"It photographed very well," Sol says.

"I'll have to show you the pictures," Estelle tells Miriam. "The whole family was there and such dear, dear friends. God willing, they'll be at your wedding, too."

"No, I don't think so," says Ed. "We're just having the immediate family. We're only having one hundred people."

Estelle smiles. "I don't think you can keep a wedding to one hundred people."

"Why not?" Ed asks.

Sarah clears the fish plates nervously. She hates it when Ed takes this tone of voice with her parents.

"Well, I mean, not without excluding," Estelle says. "And at a wedding you don't want to exclude—"

"I don't think it's incumbent on us to invite everyone we know to Miriam's wedding," Ed says crisply. Sarah puts her hand on his shoulder. "It's not even necessary to invite everyone *you* know."

Estelle raises her eyebrows, and Sarah hopes silently that her mother will not whip out the invitation list she's written up. The list with forty-two names that, mercifully, Ed has not yet seen.

"I'm not inviting everyone I know," Estelle says.

"Grandma," Miriam says, looking up. "Are you inviting people to my wedding?"

"Of course not," says Estelle. "But I've told my cousins about it and my dear friends. You know, some of them were at your parents' wedding. The Magids. The Rothmans."

"Whoa, whoa, wait a second," says Ed. "We aren't going to revive the guest list from our wedding thirty years ago. I think we need to define our terms here and straighten out what we mean by immediate family."

"I'll define for you," Estelle says, "what I mean by the family. These are the people who knew us when we lived above the bakery. It wasn't just at your wedding. They were at *our* wedding before the war. We grew up with them. We've got them in the home movies, and you can see them all forty-five years ago—fifty years ago! You can go in the den and watch—we've got all the movies on videotape now. You can see them at Sarah's first birthday party. We lived within blocks; and when we moved out to the Island and left the bakery, they moved too. I still talk to Trudy Rothman every day. Who has friends like that?

We used to walk over. Years ago in the basement we hired a dancing teacher, and we used to take dancing lessons together. Fox trot, cha-cha, tango. We went to temple with them. We celebrated such times! I think you don't see the bonds, because you kids are scattered. We left Bensonhurst together and we came out to the Island together. We've lived here since fifty-four in this house. We saw this house go up, and their houses were going up, too. We went through it together, coming into the wide-open spaces, having a garden, trees, and parks. We see them all the time. In the winters we meet them down in Florida; we go to their grandchildren's weddings—"

"But I'm paying for this wedding," Ed says.

At that Estelle leaves the table and goes into the kitchen. Sarah glares at Ed.

"Dad," Avi groans. "Now look what you did." He whispers to Amy, "I warned you my family is weird."

"I'm really hungry," Ben says. "Can we have the turkey, Grandma? Seriously, all I've had to eat today was a Snickers bar."

In silence Estelle returns from the kitchen carrying the turkey. In silence she hands it to Sol to carve up. She passes the platter around the table. Only slowly does the conversation sputter to life. Estelle talks along with the rest, but she doesn't speak to Ed. She won't even look at him.

~

Ed lies on his back in the trundle bed next to Sarah. She is lying on the other bed staring at the ceiling. Every time either of them moves an inch, the bed creaks. Ed has never heard such loud creaking; the beds seem to moan and cry out in the night.

"The point? The point is this," Sarah tells him, "it

was neither the time nor the place to go over the guest list."

"Your mother was the one who brought it up!" Ed exclaims.

"And you were the one who started in on her."

"Sarah, what was I supposed to say—Thank you for completely disregarding what we explicitly told you. Yes, you can invite everyone you know to your granddaughter's wedding. I'm not going to get steamrollered into this—that's what she was trying to do, manipulate this seder into an opportunity to get exactly who she wants, how many she wants, with no discussion whatsoever."

"The discussion does not have to dominate this holiday," Sarah says.

"You let these things go and she'll get out of control. She'll go from giving us a few addresses to inviting twenty, thirty people. Fifty people."

"She's not going to do that."

"She knows hundreds of people. How many people were at our wedding? Two hundred? Three hundred?"

"Oh, stop. We're mailing all the invitations ourselves from D.C."

"Fine."

"So don't be pigheaded about it," Sarah says.

"Pigheaded? Is that what you said?"

"Yes."

"That's not fair. You don't want these people at the wedding any more than I do—"

"Ed, there are ways to explain that, there are tactful ways. You have absolutely no concept—"

"I am tactful. I am a very tactful person. But there are times when I'm provoked."

"What you said about paying for the wedding was completely uncalled for."

"But it was true!" Ed cries out, and his bed moans under him as if it feels the weight of his aggravation.

"Sh," Sarah hisses.

"I don't know what you want from me."

"I want you to apologize to my mother and try to salvage this holiday for the rest of us," she says tersely.

"I'm not going to apologize to that woman," Ed mutters. Sarah doesn't answer him. "What?" he asks into the night. His voice sounds to his ears not just defensive but wronged, deserving of sympathy. "Sarah?"

"I have nothing more to say to you," she says.

"Sarah, she is being completely unreasonable."

"Oh, stop it."

"I'm not going to grovel in front of someone intent on sabotaging this wedding."

Sarah doesn't answer.

⁂

The next day Ed wakes up with a sharp pain in his left shoulder. It is five-nineteen in the morning, and everyone else is sleeping—except Estelle. He can hear her moving around in the house adjusting things, flipping light switches, twitching lamp shades, tweaking pillows. He lies in bed and doesn't know which is worse, his shoulder or those fussy little noises. They grate on him like the rattling of cellophane paper. When at last he struggles out of the sagging trundle bed, he runs to the shower and blasts hot water on his head. He takes an inordinately long shower. He is probably using up all the hot water. He imagines Estelle pacing around outside wondering how in the world anyone can stand in the shower an hour, an hour and fifteen minutes. She is worried about wasting water, frustrated that the door is locked, and she cannot get in to straighten the toothbrushes. The fantasy warms him. It soothes his muscles. But minutes after he gets out, it wears off.

By the time the children are up, it has become a muggy, sodden spring day. Yehudit sleeps off her cold medicine, Ben watches television in the den with Sol, and Miriam shuts herself up in her room in disgust because watching TV violates the holiday. Avi goes out with Amy for a walk. They leave right after lunch and are gone for hours. Where could they be for three hours in West Hempstead? Are they stopping at every duck pond? Browsing in every strip mall? It's a long, empty day. The one good thing is that Sarah isn't angry at him anymore. She massages his stiff shoulder. "These beds have to go," she says. "They're thirty years old."

"It would probably be more comfortable to lie on the floor," Ed says. He watches Estelle as she darts in and out of the kitchen setting the table for the second seder. "You notice she still isn't speaking to me."

"Well," Sarah says, "what do you expect?" But she says it sympathetically. "We have to call your mother," she reminds him.

"Yeah, I suppose so." Ed heaves a sigh. "Get the kids. Make them talk to her."

"Hey, Grandma," says Ben when they get him on the phone. "What's up? Oh yeah? It's dull here, too. No, we aren't doing anything. Just sitting around. No, Avi's got his girlfriend here, so they went out. Yeah, Amy. I don't know. Don't ask me. Miriam's here, too. Yup. What? Everybody's like dealing with who's going to come to her wedding. Who, Grandma E? Oh, she's fine. I think she's kind of pissed at Dad, though."

Ed takes the phone out of Ben's hands.

"Kind of what?" Rose is asking.

"Hello, Ma?" Ed carries the cordless phone into the

bedroom and sits at the vanity table. As he talks, he can see himself from three angles in the triptych mirror, each one worse than the next. He sees the dome of his forehead with just a few strands of hair, his eyes tired, a little bloodshot even, the pink of his ears soft and fleshy. He looks terrible.

"Ed," his mother says, "Sarah told me you are excluding Estelle's family from the wedding."

"Family? What family? These are Estelle's friends."

"And what about Henny and Pauline? Should I disinvite them, too?"

"Ma! You invited your neighbors?"

"Of course! To my own granddaughter's wedding? Of course I did."

"Ma," Ed snaps. "As far as I'm concerned, the only invitations to this wedding are going to be the ones printed up and issued by me, from my house. This is Miriam's wedding. For her. Not for you, not for Estelle. Not for anyone but the kids."

"You are wrong," Rose says simply. Throughout the day these words ring in Ed's ears. It is he who feels wronged. It's not as if his mother or Sarah's mother were contributing to the wedding in any way. They just make their demands. They aren't doing anything.

Miriam is sitting in the kitchen spreading whipped butter on a piece of matzo. Ed sits down next to her. "Where's Grandma?" he asks.

"She went out to get milk," says Miriam, and then she bursts out, "Daddy, I don't want all those people at the wedding."

"I know, sweetie." It's wonderful to hear Miriam appeal to him, to be able to sympathize with her as if she weren't almost a doctor with severe theological opinions.

"I don't even know them," Miriam says.

"We don't have to invite anyone you don't want to invite," Ed says firmly.

"But I don't want Grandma all mad at me at the wedding." Her voice wavers. "I don't know what to do."

"You don't have to do anything," Ed says. "You just relax."

"I think maybe we should just invite them," Miriam says in a small voice.

"*Oy,*" says Ed.

"Or some of them," she says.

Someone rattles the back door, and they both jump. It's just Sarah. "Let me give you some advice," she says. "Invite these people, invite your mother's people, and let that be an end to it. We don't need this kind of *tsuris.*"

"No!" Ed says.

"I think she's right," says Miriam.

He looks at her. "Would that make you feel better?" She nods, and he gets to give her a hug. "I don't get to hug my Miriam anymore," he tells Sarah.

"I know," she says. "That's Grandma's car. I'm going to tell her she can have the Magids."

"But you make it clear to her," Ed starts.

"Ed," she says, "I'm not making *any*thing clear to her."

⁓

At the second seder, Estelle looks at everyone benignly from where she stands between the kitchen and the dining room. Sol makes jokes about weddings, and Avi gets carried away by the good feeling, puts his arm around Methodist Amy, and says, "Mom and Dad, I promise when I get married I'll elope." No one laughs at this.

When it's time for the four questions, Ed reads them himself. " 'Why is this night different from all other nights? On other nights we eat leavened bread. Why on this night do we eat matzo?' Ben, could you put your feet on the floor?" When Ed is done with the four questions, he says, "So, essentially, each generation has an obligation to explain our exodus to the next generation—whether they like it or not."

That night in the moaning trundle bed, Ed thinks about the question Miriam raised at the first seder. Why are there four of everything on Passover? Four children. Four questions. Four cups of wine. Lying there with his eyes closed, Ed sees these foursomes dancing in the air. He sees them as in the naive illustrations of his 1960s Haggadah. Four gold cups, the words of the four questions outlined in teal blue, four children's faces. The faces of his own children, not as they are now but as they were nine, ten years ago. And then, as he falls asleep, a vivid dream flashes before him. Not the children, but Sarah's parents, along with the Rothmans, the Seligs, the Magids, and all their friends, perhaps one thousand of them walking en masse like marathoners over the Verrazano Bridge. They are carrying suitcases and ironing boards, bridge tables, tennis rackets, and lawn chairs. They are driving their poodles before them as they march together. It is a procession both majestic and frightening. At Estelle's feet, at the feet of her one thousand friends, the steel bridge trembles. Its long cables sway above the water. And as Ed watches, he feels the trembling, the pounding footsteps. It's like an earthquake rattling, pounding, vibrating through his whole body. He wants to turn away; he wants to dismiss it, but still he feels it, unmistakable, not to be denied. The thundering of history.

Sarah

Sarah parks at the Jewish Community Center of Greater Washington, her large purse on the seat next to her, along with a bunch of marked assignments. She has written copiously on each one, making her comments in green because the students find red threatening. Sarah took a series of pedagogy workshops years ago, and she scrupulously applies the techniques she learned. Her students, all adults, always comment on her warmth and motherliness. They don't realize that these are aspects of Sarah's professionalism. They do not see the teacher within, by turns despairing and chortling.

She takes out her compact and applies fresh lipstick, gathers all the papers and her purse, and strides into the building. She walks quickly, with a firm step; she has short gray hair, and eyes that had been blue when she was younger but are now hazel flecked with gold. The class is called Creative Midrash, and it combines creative writing with Bible study. Like the commentators in the compendium the Midrash, the students write their own interpretations, variations, and fantasies on Biblical themes. Sarah developed the concept herself, and she is happy with it because it solves so many problems at once. It forces the students to allude to subjects other than themselves, while at the same time they find it serves their need for therapy—because they quickly see in Scripture archetypes of their own problems. Above all, Creative Midrash forces the students to read, so they realize they aren't the first to feel, think, or write anything down, for God's sake. She always begins on the first day by playing a tape of Vaughan Williams's *Fantasia on a Theme by Thomas Tallis*.

It is five-thirty in the afternoon, and they are waiting for her, all ready to go, their notebooks out and turned to a fresh page, their pens poised. They love pens: fountain pens and three-color ballpoints, even elaborate, hollow pens that store twelve different ink cartridges inside. "Fifteen minutes of free writing," Sarah says, and they begin, covering their white notebook pages. She watches them. They range in age from thirty to somewhere near sixty, three women and one man. They are, in their own words, a mom, a retired homemaker, an actress, and a landscape-maintenance specialist. Sarah watches them all and thinks about dinner. She has a chicken thawed and the leftover sweet potatoes, but they need a vegetable. She'll have to stop and pick up something on the way home. She has to get something else, too. They are out of something, but she can't remember what. Something small, perishable. "All right," she says. "Why don't you finish up your thought." She waits. "Then let's begin. Debbie." She turns to the actress. Debbie has long hair and pale-blue eyes. You could call her nose large. It is a strong nose, beautifully straight. Everyone, including Sarah, takes out a copy of the poem Debbie wrote last week, and Debbie shakes back her hair and intones:

Eve

flesh of your flesh
bone of your bone
wo man
womb an
I am Eve
you are my day and night
I am Eve the twilight
in between
sweet soft neither dark nor bright
and how did I feel when
I was born from your dream?
no one was interested

Tomatoes! The thought comes to Sarah unbidden. That's what she has to pick up, because the ones in the fridge spoiled.

from my birth I belonged to you
you had named the beasts
already you had named me
you are the sun and I the moon
you burn
but I pull the waters after me
I slip from your garden to consort
with the enemy
because I would rather be wild
than beget your patriarchy
I would rather cover you with shame
you can have the cattle the foul of the air
and all the beasts of the field
the night will glow with the eyes of my cats

"Comments?" Sarah asks. No one says a word, so she begins. "Debbie, that was very strong. I like the way it flows and builds momentum. There was almost a rhythmic expression in your tide image. Were you playing with the word *foul* intentionally?"

"Where?" asks Debbie.

"Where you wrote 'foul of the air.' "

"Oh, that wasn't on purpose," Debbie says.

"You might want to change it, then," Sarah suggests. "Other comments?"

Michelle, who is the mom, says, "I noticed you didn't use any capital letters, except for 'I' and 'Eve.' "

"Yeah, I did that because I feel that capital letters and punctuation interrupt the flow of the poem and I associate them with male discourse and hierarchy, sort of dichotomous and either-or oriented, night-day, yes-no, and I see Eve as more of a mediator figure. But I didn't want to use a lower-case *i* or write *eve* without a capital, because I feel that in a way E. E. Cummings appropriated that idea, and what I was trying to do was take back the *I* for the female voice."

"It's about subversion," says Brian, the landscaper, once a graduate student, then sidelined for ten years by drugs, but now making up for lost time. He is an unnaturally thin man, sunburned, with a scant beard.

"Yeah, and it's very close to what I'm going through right now," Debbie says. "I'm having a conflict with my boyfriend about my cats right now."

Then Brian begins to read his "Dialogue Between Jacob and the Angels on the Ladder."

Scene: Desert at midnight, countless stars shining. On the rungs of Jacob's ladder, the spirits of THOREAU *and* WALT WHITMAN, *sitting with* JACOB.

WHITMAN (to Jacob, with a look of ecstasy): *You shall be as many as the stars in the sky*
You will multiply into millions
and every last one of your children will be million heirs because this is the night of your birth
this is your birth-night
and every grass blade, every insect and tiniest being in the world knows it
every animal, bird, fish, and locomotive knows it
THOREAU: *Given a choice, I think any man would rather sit by a warm fire than become a nation.*

"Wait, wait," Debbie says. "You're talking about grass blades? I thought this was supposed to be a desert."

"Maybe you should say grains of sand," Michelle suggests.

"Well, I think that's already in the Bible." Ida, the retired homemaker, is wearing her reading glasses and flipping through Genesis.

"There's nothing wrong with using images that are already in the Bible," Sarah says.

Ida pulls off her reading glasses and looks over at her. She has snowy-white hair. "Then I want to change mine," she says. "Can I change mine?"

"All right," Sarah says. "Brian, what do you think about using grains of sand?"

"But I was trying to sort of allude to *Leaves of Grass*."

"I don't know, this is really heavy. Really—abstract." Debbie is staring at the play. "Have you thought about getting some more action into it? I mean, I don't think you want to end up with just all these talking heads!"

Brian looks dismayed.

"I see it more as a Platonic dialogue," Sarah says.

This seems to cheer Brian. "I want it to be like *Under Milk Wood*," he confides to the class. "That's my dream."

~

Sarah picks up the groceries and then the dry cleaning on her way home. "Four shirt, two dress, one skirt, pleated, one blouse. This could not come out," the cashier tells her. She looks around wearily as the cashier rings everything up. As always, hanging in the window is a wedding dress, freshly cleaned, in clear plastic, the dry cleaner's tour de force.

When Sarah gets home, Ed comes out of the house to help her carry everything, so they are both outside when the phone rings, and Ed runs up the steps in front of her with his keys jingling in his pocket and his shirt coming untucked. "Who is it? Your mother?" Sarah calls out as she comes in.

He waves his hand at her impatiently. "Ma? What is it? What? You're in the hospital? What happened?"

Sarah picks up the phone in the kitchen and hears her eighty-seven-year-old mother-in-law crying. "Yes, yes, I'm in the hospital," Rose sobs from California. "They took me here. I didn't even know what was happening to me. I was unconscious. I could have been dead."

"Mother, wait, slow down. Start from the beginning. What happened?"

"What hospital are you in?" Sarah breaks in.

"St. Elysius? Or Egregious?"

"No, no, that can't be it. That's a TV show. Try to think, Ma."

"Maybe St. Elizabeth's," Rose says. "How should I know? I was unconscious."

"Ed, I think we should talk to Dr. Klein," Sarah says.

"Sarah, I'm trying to hear what happened. Start from the beginning, Ma."

"I told Klein I needed a new prescription. My refills ran out. I went to three different pharmacies, and they wouldn't fill the prescription for my pills. I went to Longs, Rexall, and Pay Less, and they all said I needed a new prescription from my doctor. But when I told Klein I needed him to write a new one he wouldn't do it, and so I told him that if he didn't write me one I would tell the state medical board he drugged Gladys and Eileen when they passed away, and he just said he didn't know what I was talking about. I said, 'You damn well know what I'm talking about. You killed them with morphine.' Then he just walked out and left me alone in his office. So I had to go all the way home, on the bus, by myself. I was exhausted, I was ill. I went straight to bed. I put on my videotape of *Pride and Prejudice*, and I took some of the pills I had saved, because I felt so ill. Then, when I woke up, I was in a hospital bed in a hospital gown."

"Oh, Christ," Ed groans. "Ma, now I want you to give me the telephone number by your bed. I'm going to call the doctor."

This is not the first time Rose has overdosed and collapsed, but that doesn't make it any easier. Sarah remembers Rose's second husband, Maury, who passed away in 1980. He was a cheerful man ten years older than Rose, and as the years went by he only seemed to become more jovial. He whistled happily, walking with his cane through the increasingly grim streets of Washington Heights. He became ever smaller and more spry, his clothes hung on him, and his face was shrunken behind his black-framed glasses; he had almost turned into Jiminy Cricket, but every day he and Rose went out to lunch at the deli, and every week he brought home stacks of large-print books from the library. The two of them traveled, and he used to collapse in dramatic places. On the observation deck of the World Trade Center. In the botanical gardens in Montreal. In Hollywood, on Hollywood Boulevard. He would sit in the hospital and talk about the service in different cities. Sarah had always marveled at him because he was such an extraordinarily cheerful man. When he died, she found out that he had been taking Percodan, among other things. It wasn't just good nature. He'd got Rose started on pills. After the funeral, they also found out that he hadn't paid taxes for years, and that he had squirreled away his money in small sums in over a hundred different bank accounts around the country. It was then that Rose drafted her amazing handwritten will, a document she never tires of showing the family. Ed was the one who took care of all Maury's deferred aggravations. He closed up the Washington Heights apartment, collected the money from all the accounts, and moved Rose to Venice, California, where she could be near her other son, Henry, who was managing a gallery there. But Henry left for England—years ago—to start one of his new lives, and taking care of Rose is again Ed's responsibility.

Ed is pacing in the living room with the phone, talking to Dr. Klein, and Sarah picks up her extension in time to hear Klein say, "Well, it seems that she was stashing the pills away. She wasn't taking the prescribed dose. Unfortunately, she took them for her moods."

"Well, why didn't you check on her before?" Ed says.

"Well, Ed, I cannot control everything that she does in the privacy of her own apartment. I cannot take total responsibility for her actions. Of course, I asked her whether she was complying with the prescription, but I'm afraid she didn't tell me the truth."

"No, no, I'm sorry, my mother is not a liar."

"She has a severe dependency on her medication and—"

"Well, that's the point. I thought that was what we were trying to work on, to wean her away with the limited doses."

"Yes, that is what we were trying to do, Ed," Klein says. "But it wasn't working. I think we've had this discussion before. It's really a question of patient management. Now, Rose has decided to enter a residential treatment program at Santa Rosa."

"Why weren't we consulted about this?"

"It was her decision."

"No, I think it was *your* decision," Ed snaps. "You told her she had to do this."

"I advised her to do it, because she has got to start understanding her dependency. She has to find other ways to deal with her boredom and loneliness."

"Oh, so this is really all my fault," Ed says. "Because I'm trying to take care of her long distance. It all comes down to me. I should be there twenty-four hours a day. It's not your fault and it's not her fault, so it's got to be my fault."

Sarah is up half the night because Ed is so upset. He lies on his left side and then rolls over, punching his pillow with his fist. He kicks at the blankets, then flops onto his back. Sarah lies on her stomach and thinks about Rose. Boredom and loneliness. It's a real question: Can an elderly woman subsist on *Masterpiece Theatre* alone? Rose is, as Sarah's student Ida calls it, a retired homemaker—except that she was never so professional about being a homemaker, or about being retired. What she really wants, Sarah thinks, is to return to the houses of her childhood. She is nostalgic for them; they are still the backdrops of the romance she has developed about her life. Her parents' house in Bukovina, her foster parents' grand house in England, where she was sent during the First World War—a place with servants and vast drawing rooms. Rose did not suffer in the wars directly, but she imagines she did, and in her mind's eye sees them sweeping away the world she loved. She has often told Sarah that *Gone with the Wind* is the most beautiful novel ever written, and urged her to try to write one like it, threatened to write it herself, although she says she has never had the strength. But it is hard to sustain a life with memories, especially when the best memories come from novels.

~

"I call these Identity Haiku," Michelle tells the Creative Midrash class the following week. She pauses, then adds, "I was going to do traditional haiku, but it was really cramping what I wanted to say, so I didn't do the syllable thing."

1.
generations
stars in sky
yellow stars
holocaust

2.
sun rise
moon rise
tower
sun down
moon down
babel

3.
cut
cry
covenant

"These are really beautiful," Debbie says.

"Why didn't you use titles?" asks Ida.

"Um, I just thought it would be overkill. I felt like it would be almost stating the obvious if, say, I titled Number 3 'Circumcision.' "

"I love the way you stripped down your images to the essentials," Sarah says. "Tell us more about why you called them Identity Haiku." As she learned in her pedagogy class, Sarah shows with her body language that she is listening to Michelle. She leans forward and nods her head, but she is thinking about Rose, who has been calling each night. The residential treatment center is a prison! It's Sing Sing. Auschwitz. No one can leave. What do they do there? They sit in a circle; they have to talk about their past with a facilitator. She can't bear it. To listen to them talk. This one was raped when she was seven years old! That one was assaulted by her own father and brother. This one was a prostitute! "Such horrible things! Things we would *never* talk about. Now they put all of it on TV, but I would never watch!" Sarah can only imagine Rose sitting in that circle of chairs with these other patients, some the age of Rose's children, some the age of her grandchildren. And then Rose herself, half dead from shock, asked to tell about her own abuse. And even to begin, to talk about her childhood after what she has heard! To speak of her own treasured past, the elegant life that she has always treated as something to fold and fold again in tissue paper. No one listening to her, no one interested except the facilitator, probing with long needles, trying to draw blood. Naturally, she wants to go home, but she cannot just check out. "This is a clinic," the doctor told her, "not a hotel." Ed took a flight out to L.A. last night to talk to the doctors or straighten out the Medicare insurance claims or save Rose, depending on how you want to look at it.

It is Ida's turn to read. She is a beautiful woman. A woman who goes to the hairdresser every week and comes to class with her white hair curled and shaped. And she dresses up for the class. She comes in suits and gold jewelry—quite a contrast to Debbie in her rumpled shirts or Brian, who sometimes forgets to take off his bike helmet. She is the oldest in the group, just as Rose is. Her voice is tense as she reads; it chokes up on her and she is embarrassed.

Naomi and Ruth

My daughter and I are like Ruth and Naomi, but with a twist. When my husband passed away, may he rest in peace, and we went on the way, as it says in the Bible, I said to Ellen, "Don't stay with me, go on and live your life."

"I want to stay with you and take care of you," she said.

"No, you need to live your own life," I said.

"Okay," she said. So she went back to New York where she was attending NYU film school.

I stayed here alone in the house. She wants to make films, and if that is what she wants, so be it, but I tell her, "Ellen, I wish you would meet someone. You are almost thirty."

She tells me, "Mother, I have met someone, and we have been living together for five years." But this is something that is breaking my heart. This man, a broker, is eleven years older than Ellen and not Jewish.

This is what I want to ask her—"How do you think you can live in New York like a Ruth gleaning in the alien corn? How do you think you can come to him and lie at his feet in the night so that one morning he will marry you? How can you go on like this living in his apartment for five years? If I had known this would happen when we went on the way, I would not have told you to go. I would have said, 'Stay.' "

Something about this pricks at Sarah. Tears start in her eyes.

Debbie rakes back her long hair and says to Ida, "Well, she's got to make her own choices."

"I have a question about the genre of this," Michelle says. "Is this like an essay or a short story?"

"Ida," Sarah says, "this is—" She wants to say that it moved her, but she cannot. The words would sound cheap in the context of the class with its formalized intimacy. "It's very simple and beautiful," she says.

Debbie is looking over her copy, pondering Ida's work. "I guess it's an age thing," she says.

Sarah's desk stands at the window of her bedroom. She has always wanted a study, and she and Ed are hoping to redo one of the other bedrooms in the next few years. The kids are away at college—one at medical school—so they don't have the money to do anything with the house. Sarah and Ed went to a local one-woman performance of "A Room of One's Own," and it occurred to Sarah as she left the theater that Virginia Woolf never had any children. Her own desk is piled with papers, some hers, some Ed's, also bank statements she has not yet filed, bills marked paid, issues of *Writer's Digest* and *Poets & Writers Magazine*, and copy for the Shaarei Tzedek newsletter, which she edits. Sarah is the Washington stringer for several national Jewish periodicals, and she writes frequent book reviews. She sits at her desk and thinks about what insufficient time she has for her own work. She has written one novel, published in 1979 by Three Penny Opera, a book about a woman—a painter—growing up in Brooklyn and Long Island, but she didn't move fast enough after that publication, didn't follow it quickly enough with a second novel, and she regrets this, the loss of momentum. She writes poetry as well, poetry that is perhaps too old-fashioned for a contemporary audience. With its wordplay and complicated rhymes it is closer to the seventeenth century than to John Ashbery. It has been difficult for her as a poet, to be influenced by Donne, Marvell, and Herbert, but to write about giving birth, a son's bar mitzvah, Yom Kippur. Several years ago she sent a collection of her poems to her brother-in-law, Henry, who runs a small press of his own in Oxford. But Henry felt that Sarah's work, while "extraordinary," was not moving in quite the direction that Equinox was trying to move in with its current series. She still finds it strange that even Henry, who loves Victorian furniture, eighteenth-century books and bindings, antique china, and plush novels—he who, as a person, is almost baroque—nevertheless admires poems that are sleek, smooth, minimalist, functioning like state-of-the-art appliances. As she boots up her computer, the phone rings.

"Sarah?" Ed says. "Hi. Listen, we've got a mess here. She's already racked up twenty thousand dollars for hospitalization. That and the treatment program are covered, but there is another sixteen hundred for consultations with Klein, which they aren't covering."

"What do you mean?"

"They say they aren't covering it. We're disputing the bill, so—"

"How is she?" Sarah asks.

"Not so hot. Disoriented, exhausted. She's lost

weight." He sighs. "Sarah, I got here and I realized this is it. We can't kid ourselves about this any longer—she can't stay out here alone. We've got to bring her home."

"You mean bring her here?"

"Yeah, we've got to bring her back to Washington."

She thinks for a moment. "I can cancel my Thursday class," she says. "I'll try to get a flight out tomorrow."

Sarah and Ed sit in a pair of chairs in Dr. Stephen Klein's office. For Sarah, the scene is vaguely reminiscent of certain meetings with the assistant principal of Woodrow Wilson Junior High School concerning their son, Ben, and his academic progress.

"Well, I have spent at least an hour with her in private consultations each day of her stay here," Klein is telling them.

"And these were the sessions where you . . . ? What did you do exactly?"

"I listened to her. I talked to her about dependency, addictive behavior—"

Ed interrupts. "All I know is that my mother looks terrible, she's lost weight, you've run her ragged."

Dr. Klein shakes his head. "Remember, you haven't seen her for at least six months. And she is recovering from a massive overdose."

"Massive overdose!" Ed's face reddens. "Is that the way you like to dramatize it to your patients? Look, my mother is eighty-seven years old. Spare her the shock therapy. You've got her out at Santa Rosa in a program with a bunch of teenage junkies. I thought this was the age of multiculturalism, mutual respect, universal access, emancipation of the elderly. You're sitting here rubber-stamping an elderly woman, putting her onto the therapeutic conveyor belt with no regard to her age, her cultural background—"

"Can I show you something?" Klein asks. He puts a videotape in the VCR and turns on the television. "Rose?" a woman's voice asks. "May we have your permission to videotape this conversation for you and/or your family to look at later?"

"All right," Rose replies. She is sitting up in a hospital bed looking small and gray, an I.V. in her arm.

"Now, Rose, tell me, how are you feeling—on a scale of one to ten, with one being the worst and ten the best."

"I feel lousy," Rose says.

"But on a scale of ten, how do you feel?"

"One is the best?"

"One is the worst, ten is the best."

"Ten is the best?"

"That's right."

"And what's the worst?"

"One. Rose?"

"I have a one."

Sarah smiles in spite of herself, but Ed bursts out, "Can—can you turn that off?"

"Why?" Klein asks.

"Because we are having a conversation here!"

"I understand that, Ed, but I thought the tape was relevant."

"It may be relevant. However, I am not going to watch my mother being interrogated, okay? It's ugly."

"Addiction is ugly. It's also complicated, and really I think this is something you should consider—not now, when you're upset, but later on. I think counseling as a family would be very valuable for Rose—and for you."

"Oh, my God," Ed snaps.

"I see a lot of anger here," Klein points out gently.

"Damn right."

"No, I don't mean the anger at me. The conflict is between you and your mother. This isn't about me at all."

"Oh, yes it is," Ed fires back. "This is all about you and your indiscriminate diagnoses, your mismanagement of an elderly patient's prescriptions, and the fact that you railroaded her into entering a totally inappropriate treatment program."

"That's—that's a serious charge," Klein says. "I repeat that it was her decision to enter the program. I have her signature on all the paperwork."

"You can give me the paperwork, because you are no longer her doctor," Ed snaps.

"I'll be happy to release the records to you as soon as her account is clear. I know that you're worried, I see that you're upset, but I can assure you I have given Rose the best treatment I knew how to give, and I have been generous with my time. I'm not even charging you for our session here today."

At this, Ed stands up, turns on his heel, and strides out of Klein's office through the reception area and out the door.

Sarah turns and walks out after him, but she stops at the desk of Klein's receptionist. "Do you take Visa?" she asks.

For the next three days, Ed and Sarah pack up Rose's apartment in Venice. They phone Goodwill and several of the Jewish agencies to try to give away the washer, the dryer, and some of the big furniture. "You know, it's telling," Ed says to Sarah. "Now you have to pay a collection fee to give things away."

"Well, sure," Sarah says. "They have to come with a

truck. They have to sort the stuff." She imagines the warehouses with piles for everything that comes in: REHABILITATE, SCRAP, SMITHSONIAN. A triage system, something like the Santa Rosa treatment center? Now that Rose is home, she looks much better. She is frail, of course—thin—but her color is back, her eyes bright. The apartment is bustling. She is going home with her dear son and daughter-in-law, and she will not be alone anymore. She is supervising the movers as they pack up her china and her little cut-crystal liqueur glasses. She is being swept away to a new place, beginning a new chapter, and this is something she enjoys. But Ed and Sarah look terrible. Disheveled, exhausted from packing, paperwork, and schlepping. Each night they drag themselves back to the Sea Breeze Motel and collapse with muscles aching. The motel has bars on the windows and, in the bathroom, tiny white towels that seem to have been put there mostly for symbolic value. They picked the place because of its location near Rose, and it turns out to have one other advantage. For fifty cents they can get the bed to vibrate, and this soothes their aching backs. At the end of the day they try to unwind, lying on their backs, feeding quarters to the bed, and watching C-SPAN on television.

On the third night, they are lying there on their backs watching the *Prime Minister's Question Time*, the bed vibrating beneath them, and Ed is talking on the phone to his brother, Henry. "Well, of course we're giving away the secretary," Ed says. "We're giving all the big furniture to Hadassah. That's what Ma wants. What? What?" He turns toward Sarah. "He says he wants the secretary."

"So let him ship it to England," Sarah says.

"It's a very fine piece? No, okay. No, I would call it a —nice piece, not a very fine piece . . . You want to ship it to England, you go ahead . . . What—are you crazy? Where are we going to put it in D.C.?" He looks over at Sarah.

"If he really wants it, he can ship it to England," Sarah says.

"What? I can't hear you," Ed talks over her into the phone. He turns to Sarah again. "Henry says Ma will want the secretary in Washington. She may not want it now, but she will later. And she'll want the lamps with the silk-shantung lampshades."

"He may be right," Sarah says. "She'll want them later."

"Henry, have you *seen* those lampshades in the last five years?"

"Ed, maybe we should get a container and ship everything to D.C."

"What did you say?" Ed asks her. She repeats what she said. "All right, fine." He hands her the telephone. "You and Henry work it out, I'm getting an Excedrin." He takes another couple of quarters off the Formica nightstand and feeds them expertly into the meter on the headboard.

Henry is still talking, unaware that the phone has changed hands. "Now, the carpets are simply not worth shipping. They aren't really Chinese carpets, you know. We could very well give those away, but the lamps could be considered antiques in a few years, and silk-shantung lampshades are almost impossible to find anymore. They just don't make—"

⸺

Sarah teaches the first class after her return home in a haze of jet lag. She had given the students an assignment to do while she was gone: "Write a midrash about the crossing of the Red Sea in a genre you have not yet used in this course." Now, as she listens to the students, she finds that the results are mixed. Michelle has written a short story about a young Jewish girl who is in love with an Egyptian and has to watch her lover fall with his horse and chariot into the sea. Naturally, she refuses to join Miriam and the other women as they sing and dance in triumph after they have crossed to safety. Instead, she writes her own song to sing by herself to the desert air. Brian has written an essay of questions, hypotheses, and test cases in true Midrashic fashion. It begins:

> *It is a mystery why it says in the Torah that after all Moses' pleas, God hardened Pharaoh's heart. Why would God want to make it harder for the Israelites if he was on their side? Was it a test? Or is this some kind of mystical metaphor? I, being of philosophical inclination, take it as such. I think these phrases in the ancient scriptures are invitations to us to ask questions about the nature of human agency and its interactions (reactions?) to God as a historical agent in the world.*

After hearing only seven pages of this, Debbie looks at Sarah and asks, in her blunt way, "Is this creative writing?"

Sarah is annoyed. "Let's let Brian finish," she says.

"Sorry," Debbie mutters.

When it's Ida's turn, she shakes her head. "I apologize," she says. "I wasn't able to complete the assignment. I'm still waiting for an idea."

"Don't censor yourself," Michelle advises her.

"Yeah, I used to be really bad about that," Debbie says. "Do you ever try brainstorming?" For her part, Debbie has written an autobiography of Pharaoh's sacred cat:

> *I with my green eyes have seen three hundred generations. My dam was the Upper Nile and my father*

the Lower Nile; my older sister the Great Sphinx, who taught me the riddles of man.

When Debbie finishes, Sarah nods her head. "That's very—strange and compelling," she says. She hates it. Rose is staying in their daughter Miriam's old room. Sarah has been taking her to look at residences. Every day she drives her out to see them, and every day Rose insists she could not possibly live in one, and that the only times she was ever happy were when she was in the midst of the family.

"I was wondering," Michelle says to Sarah, "would it be possible for us to do an assignment that isn't a midrash? Because, for me, it's hard to connect my feelings to the Bible all the time."

"It's *really* hard," Debbie agrees.

"Could we just try to write a story set in modern times?" Michelle asks.

Ida adds to this, "I'd like it if you would bring in a midrash of your own that we could look at."

"Have you ever written one?" Brian asks.

"Yes, I think I did one years ago," Sarah says. "I could look for it. But I want to remind all of you that creating art is hard work, and that the artist sees restrictions as opportunities. Now, for your next project, your first restriction is that you cannot use the word *I*."

"Oh, jeez," Debbie groans.

"What about using *me*?" Michelle asks.

"But we can use all the other pronouns?" Brian asks.

⁓

Sarah makes hamburgers that night, and the three of them sit down for dinner—Sarah, Ed, and Rose, who eats her burger plain on her plate with a knife and fork. "I heard you didn't like the Helena," Ed says to his mother.

"The facilities were gorgeous," Sarah says.

"Were they gorgeous, Ma?" Ed asks.

"Cold," Rose says.

"What? You said the air-conditioning was wonderful!" Sarah says.

"I mean the atmosphere was cold. It was institutional."

"Well, it's an institution," Ed says.

"Yes, it was no home for me."

"They had a lovely swimming pool."

"I don't swim," Rose points out.

"And they have buses to the Kennedy Center for all the performances."

"You could go to the symphony and the ballet, Ma. And the theater."

"I didn't like it," Rose says.

"What's not to like?" Ed demands.

"The people." Rose taps her head. "Not all there."

Sarah shakes her head. "They were lovely people. Cultured people!"

"You see what you want to see," Rose tells her.

Ed takes another burger under Sarah's disapproving eyes. "Your furniture is coming, Ma. We have to settle you in."

"You know, they have chamber music there every week," Sarah tells Ed.

"Look, I'll tell you what, Ma," he says. "Sarah and I are going to move to the Helena, and you can stay here. How would that be?"

⁂

Sarah sits down at her desk after dinner. She tries to work on one of her overdue book reviews, but her heart isn't in it. She is too tired, her mind full of too many other things: the knowledge that in order to get any work done, she and Ed need to settle Rose in a residence. They hate pushing her into it, but Rose is not going to leave their house happily. They are going to have a fight about it. Ed will be miserable. The knowledge that her class is not going well. These particular students do not work well together as a group. Discussion is fractured. All sniping and defensiveness. The chemistry is wrong. She told them today she once wrote a midrash of her own, but she does not know where it is. It was a little piece about the Biblical Sarah and about her own feelings about becoming a mother. She picks up the King James Bible that she had assigned as a class text along with Robert Alter's *The Art of Biblical Poetry*, and Peter Elbow's *Writing Without Teachers*, and she turns to Genesis 21. She reads: "And the Lord visited Sarah as he had said, and the Lord did unto Sarah as he had spoken. For Sarah conceived, and bare Abraham a son in his old age." And her eye skips down to where it says that Sarah said the child's name is Isaac because "God hath made me to laugh, so that all that hear will laugh with me." As she looks at these verses, she sees them differently now from the way she saw them in the past. She is fifty-six years old, and she has four grown children, and it occurs to her that she is not much like the Biblical Sarah in that respect. She did not have a child in her old age. She has certainly never had any problems with fertility. She has pined, but not for children. She has pined to have a literary career, to have her work discovered by the world. This has been her dream since her school days, when she discovered John Donne and felt suddenly and secretly clever, as if, like a safecracker, she could find the puns and hidden springs in his poetry. And when she wrote her essays in college about this image and that metaphor, what she was really wondering was how to become like Shakespeare—without seeming to imitate him, of course. When would she be called into that shining multitude of poets and playwrights, mainly Elizabethan, who rose in shimmering waves before her at Queens College? She wrote her M.A. thesis in English Literature about Emma Lazarus—not about the poem on the Statue of Liberty but about her major and forgotten works, the verse plays and poems.

But she did not have enough time to be poetic. She had her small children, and she had Ed's career to think about. Her professors warned her of the time and the sacrifices she would have to make if she pursued a Ph.D. One old codger had even suggested that if she got a Ph.D. and an academic position, she would be blocking the career of some talented man with a family to support. Of course, that idea never went far with her. But she did have the idea that a Ph.D. would be hard to get. And a job harder. She decided against it. The truth is, it was easier for her to worry about Ed's career. She did not have to face the possibility of failure.

She had wanted fame, not classes at the Jewish Community Center; she had wanted to write dazzling poems, not just for her friends and relatives, but for the world. She was thirteen when she lay in bed in her parents' house, read *Hamlet*, and wanted to be as good as Shakespeare. And now that she is over fifty, if the Lord came to her in a dream and said, "You will achieve what you desired," she would laugh, certainly. If an angel or an agent came down from New York and said, "You, Sarah, will write a great novel, a best-seller. Not a pulp romance, but a good book, wise and luminous, with a future movie bursting from its pages," then she would laugh for all to hear—although she would take down the phone number of the agent just in case. In the meantime, she has her book reviews, her class, her children, her mother-in-law. She gets up from her desk. She has written none of this down, and so she will have no model for her students when she comes in to the next class. She can tell them that she looked in her files and couldn't find the midrash she wrote. Or she could tell them she thinks it is important for them to find their own voice, and that she doesn't want them to look at her work, because it might cramp their style.

"Knock, knock," Rose says at the door.

"Yes. Come in," Sarah calls back.

Rose opens the door. She is wearing a pink quilted robe and matching slippers. "Sarah, dear, do you have any books? They packed all my books, and I can't find any."

"Oh. Of course we have books. Downstairs." Sarah adds absentmindedly, "What kind of book do you want?"

Rose considers the question. "I like trilogies," she says.

"You know, I think the only trilogy in the house is Ed's Gulag Archipelago."

"Nonfiction?"

"I'm afraid so."

"Ed never read fiction. Do you have a novel? I like any kind of novel, not too sad. About a family—with some romance. But well written. It must be well written."

On a whim, Sarah opens the closet and hunts around on the floor for the box where she keeps copies of her own novel. "Here, Rose, why don't you read this?"

"*Irises, Irises.*" Rose ponders. "Oh, that's your book. Sarah Markowitz. I've read that already. Of course. Years ago. Do you have a sequel?"

"No, I don't."

"You must write a sequel."

"Well, I have to come up with an idea."

"The next generation," Rose says immediately.

"Well, maybe you could reread it and give me some advice."

Rose takes the book, and the two of them walk down the hall to Miriam's old room. Sarah mentions that there is a literary discussion group at the Helena.

Rose shakes her head. "I could never live there."

"But all your things are going to arrive, you know. We couldn't fit the secretary in here."

Rose looks around the little bedroom, considering the problem. "It could fit," she says. "But it wouldn't look very elegant, one thing on top of another."

Sarah hardly expected this. She feels a rush of hope. Her house to herself, and Rose at the Helena. Of course, she doesn't know that in the next three weeks she will be looking for new silk-shantung lampshades and spending hours at House of Foam, out near the airport, as workmen pump new, high-density stuffing into Rose's sofa. For a moment, she sees free evenings unfolding before her, the empty rooms expanding. What are wistful literary dreams compared to that?

One Down

On a background of blue velvet stand two baby pictures in silver frames. Then letters in silver script scroll up the screen:

Miriam Elizabeth and Jonathan Daniel
produced by
Edward and Sarah Markowitz
Zaev and Marjorie Schwartz
supported by
Ben, Avi, and Yehudit Markowitz
and Dina Schwartz
and also starring
Ilse Schwartz
Estelle and Sol Kirshenbaum
and
Rose Markowitz
as themselves

This is the opening Miriam and Jon have chosen for their wedding video. Bill, the videographer, has it all mocked up for Ed and Sarah in his studio. When the monitor darkens again, the two of them sit there in silence. Then Sarah says, "That wasn't my daughter, by the way."

"Oh, I know," Bill reassures her. "Those baby pictures are just samples. Miriam and Jon are going to bring in their own."

"Well, they'd better take care of that—" Ed says.

"Not to worry," Bill tells them. "We won't be putting all of this together until after the wedding. You've got plenty of time to think about length, too. I've already gone over this with Miriam and Jon. You have the option in addition to the two-hour version of going for" —Bill reaches behind him and deftly swipes a black binder from his desk—"four hours, or the deluxe, which would be six hours. That would cover the whole wedding."

"Gavel to gavel," Ed says.

"Exactly. From hors d'oeuvres through to the getaway car."

"Yeah, I don't think we need that," Ed says.

"It's pricey. But truthfully, for the money, I think your best choice could very well be the four-hour version."

"What's wrong with two hours?" Sarah asks.

"That would come with it, of course. The four hours comes with the two-hour cut. And what's wonderful is you have your options in terms of viewing time. Believe me, I know that right now two hours seems long to you, but when you're looking at a wedding, you're looking at some brutal cuts, and inevitably what happens is a lot of memories end up on the cutting-room floor."

⁂

"I'm going to sit down and get some reading done," Ed says when they get home to Foggy Bottom. He sits down on the couch where he's been working on the stack of books he has to review. Just a few of the many new books on the prospects for peace in the Middle East. There they lie on the coffee table in their slick dust jackets, gaudy reproaches to Ed, who has not finished his scholarly book on peace and the changing role of terrorism. He opens the morning's *New York Times*.

Sarah puts her purse on the kitchen table and starts making phone calls. "Hello, this is Sarah Markowitz. I want to add to our order—yes, I'll hold."

"Sarah," Ed calls from the living room, "listen to this. 'The Palestinian will hate Israel no matter what Israel does. Give land for peace and you will give up all the security Israel has won in previous wars. A Palestinian state will be a launching pad and a suicide, mandated by America, which I compare to Dr. Kevorkian helping the patient go under to put him out of his misery.' Sarah, are you listening?"

"You know those books aren't very well written," she says.

"No, no, this is a letter in the *Times*. Oh, this is choice: 'The solution to the problem was simple, but it was not followed in the past. Give the Palestinians a one-way ticket out of Israel. Now that time has passed, and the opportunity is gone. The cold war is over, the Soviet Union is gone. Israel ends up paying the peace dividend in the Middle East.' " Ed shakes his head. Then his eye catches the name at the bottom. "Sarah!"

"Yes," Sarah says into the phone. "This is for the Markowitz wedding. We need to add another tux, same style, 44 long, yes, the double-breasted."

"Sarah!"

She stretches the telephone cord so that she can stick her head out the kitchen door and glare at Ed. She waves her hand at him. "Could you hold the line a second?" She claps her hand over the mouthpiece of the phone and hisses, "Ed, stop bellowing at me. I am trying to place an order—for your brother—"

"Sarah, look who wrote this thing."

"I don't know, and I don't care."

He thrusts the paper in her face. "Just look at this. What does this say? *Zaev Schwartz*, Scarsdale, New York!"

"I'm very happy for him. Could you add the deposit for that onto our bill? Did I say that the neck is seventeen? Inseam? I don't know the inseam. Damn, I can't find his measurements. Look, I'm going to have to send him in. Would tomorrow be all right? He's flying in from England tonight." She sighs. "Thank you. Goodbye."

"Zaev Schwartz!" Ed exclaims and coughs as if the name were a frog in his throat. "As in—our groom-to-be—his father!"

"It could be a different Schwartz."

"How many Zaev Schwartzes in Scarsdale do you think there are?"

"Could be two or three," Sarah says.

"And spelled that way? I'm telling you, this is the one. Of all the people in the entire country, he's the one who wrote this crap. Can you believe it?"

"You said it was choice."

Ed closes his eyes. "Sarah, this is going to be part of our family! Zaev Schwartz and I are going to be—uh—"

"You're going to be nothing," Sarah says. "You're going to be in-laws."

"Co-grandparents." Ed looks again at the newspaper. He feels depressed. "Doesn't he know my work? Doesn't he have the slightest consideration for my position?"

"How could he know your work?"

"He could read! He could have talked to me about it!"

"You've met the man twice. And, Ed, people don't just pick up scholarly journals and browse through them."

"Scholarly! He could have read me in the *Post*."

"Well, I guess he doesn't get the *Washington Post* in Scarsdale. Look, I've got too much to do right now. I have to call the florist, the band—"

"Sarah, he's a reactionary, a maniac," Ed says helplessly.

"You knew that before." Sarah is brisk. "You've spoken to the man."

"I didn't know he goes around *publishing* this garbage! You know, there are people who make a whole career out of letters to the paper. This is a hobby for people, getting their prejudices published. This is what they do with their time—"

"Well, Ed, they have a right to express their opinions."

"Sure."

"So, enough. You don't have to deal with the man on a professional basis. You're overreacting."

"See, your father and I, for example. We've had our differences," Ed says, "but not *philosophical* differences. Your father and I have always been completely harmonious."

"Right, and you and your brother—"

"Henry and I have always been in complete agreement about the Middle East."

"Do you think we should tell Miriam you're getting cold feet?" Sarah asks Ed as they stand at the gate waiting for their daughter's plane to start unloading.

"I've got cold feet? Am I the one getting married?"

"That was going to be my point," says Sarah. She looks through the plate-glass wall out into the night, where the long covered jetway extends and clamps onto Miriam's plane. When Miriam was little, she used to call the process biting the apple. "Let's not mention all this to Miriam, okay?"

"I had no intention of mentioning it." Ed feels put upon. Isn't it his right as a father to mention it? But Sarah insists he take the high moral ground. Then the passengers start trickling out, a few aggressive business types surging forward in the crowd, the servicemen, the kids with backpacks, the families brushing off crumbs, and in the midst of them their daughter, the medical student, sinking under all her bags.

"Ooh, a poodle *kopf*!" Sarah pulls Miriam's hair out of her face. "You need a haircut! We've got the tuxes and the flowers under control, but Uncle Henry needs to go in to try his on. They'll never fit him if he doesn't."

Ed says nothing. A whole conversation is whirling through his head as he imagines Sarah poohpoohing him:

—What does it matter? Why do you have to dramatize this?

—Oh, nothing's the matter. It's just that I have devoted my whole professional life to studying this issue and trying to get people to appreciate its complexity.

—Now, Ed, did he do this just to insult you?

—Look, I don't care why he did it.

"Daddy?" Miriam asks him. "What's wrong?"

"Nothing," Ed says with great precision.

"You look kind of—disgruntled."

"Yeah, well, I guess I'm not feeling very gruntled at the moment."

"We still have to finalize with the band," Sarah tells Miriam in the car on the way home.

"I thought we did that already," Miriam replies from the backseat.

"No, we still have to finalize the songs for the first dance."

"What first dance?" Miriam asks, alarmed. "Mommy, we aren't having mixed dancing at the wedding."

"What are we, Puritans?" Ed mutters. Miriam and Jon in their young-blood traditionalism are having an Orthodox wedding with *glatt* kosher food, a *very* young and baleful Orthodox rabbi, and separate dancing circles for men and women.

"You mean you and Jon aren't going to have a first dance?" Sarah asks.

"Nope. There is going to be no mixed dancing, remember? We had that big discussion and everything—"

"Well, yeah," Ed says. "But there's gotta be a first dance. First you and Jon dance together and then you dance with me, and Jon dances with his mother—and that's how it's gotta be. Gotta be."

"Daddy, do we have to have another fight about this?" The voice is plaintive from the backseat.

Ed ignores this. "Look, Miriam, I'm not going to say another word about it."

"Good," says Miriam.

"Except for this. I'm paying that band, and when the time comes, they will play the first dance and we will dance it. That's all there is to it. End of discussion. This is a wedding, not a wake."

"Sweetie," Sarah ventures to Miriam as they pull up to the house, "if there isn't any social dancing, Grandma and Grandpa won't understand."

Ed tries to put his arm around Miriam as they walk in, but she shakes him off and runs in.

"Hey, don't be mean." Ed is hurt. He slides her duffel

bag off his shoulder and glides unencumbered into the kitchen. Religion hasn't come to his daughter gracefully; it's made her fierce and punctilious. She has burst out of their household with its pleasant suburban Judaism and become a little refusenik. She refuses to eat in restaurants unless they have rabbinic supervision, refuses to drive anywhere on the Sabbath, refuses to attend services at her family's own synagogue because it has mixed seating and the rabbi uses a microphone. Jonathan is just like her, but more nonchalant. He wears a yarmulke wherever he is. She and Jon have printed up a long explanation of the arcane rituals they have chosen for their nuptials—this to be distributed by the ushers for all relatives and guests who are confused or curious.

The answering machine is blinking. Ed pushes the play button. "Edward? Hello? Am I on the air, as it were? This is your brother, Henry. We just got in. Our room was double-booked, and they've given us the most extraordinary suite. We had hoped to come by tonight, but the thing is, we're completely exhausted—I don't suppose Sarah had the time to see about my morning coat? If she hasn't, please, please tell her not to worry. Susan and I are going to rummage something up by ourselves. Believe me, I have a very good idea the sort of bewildering haze that must be descending. Do you—" The message cuts off with a series of beeps, although Henry seems to have continued talking in happy ignorance.

Sarah wakes early the next morning, and her first thought as she lies in bed is Henry's morning coat. He has to be stopped. All the ushers are wearing tuxedos! She and Ed tried to call the hotel last night, but it seemed that Henry and Susan had disconnected their phone. She left several messages for Henry, and particularly for Susan. If she can only reach Susan, her gray-haired English sister-in-law, fearlessly sane. She feels instinctively that Susan will understand. In the meantime, there is the rib-eye roast to worry about—and, of course, the kids are coming in, and the Schwartzes. She is having them all for Friday-night dinner. Except for Jonathan and his sister, who won't drive on *Shabbes* from the hotel. She looks over at Ed, deep in sleep, face crushed into his pillow. Then she jumps out of bed.

Several hours later Ed opens his eyes. He has slept long, but he is exhausted. He struggles into his robe and hunts downstairs for the paper. An eerie quiet has descended over the house. Sarah has not left him a note. Now the question is how to use the time. Which is worse, to give up on the day, or to start something and feel that every minute some new crisis will break? He knows that the phone is going to ring. It will be one of his colleagues calling to tell him he saw the letter by Zaev Schwartz. Who is really going to make that connection? Ed likes to torture himself; he realizes that. But the knowledge does not cheer him up. It only adds an edge of self-loathing to his worrying. Then the phone does ring, and Ed nearly jumps out of his skin.

"Hello, Ed?" It is his mother, Rose, calling from the Helena, with her *Vienna Waltzes* CD on in the background. When he visits her, his ears ache with the music and its incessant carousel gaiety.

"Hi, Ma. How are you?"

"Have they arrived?"

"Who? Miriam is here. I guess she went out with Sarah. And Henry and Susan got in last night."

"Oh, I knew that. They called me. I meant the Schwartzes. When are they coming in?"

"Sometime this afternoon, I think."

"And you're going to meet them?"

"No, they're renting a car."

"You're not going to meet them?" She is shocked.

"No, Ma—"

"Why not?"

"Because this is a very complex day!" He feels awkward with this defense, because apparently he has been somewhat left out of the complexity. Somewhere Sarah has left him behind.

"And how is she going to walk all the way through Dulles?" Rose asks, referring to the grandmother, Ilse Schwartz. Rose uses pronouns instead of names and expects everyone to understand her completely. This is not a function of her eighty-seven years. She has always done this.

"I'm sure they'll have a wheelchair for her at the airport," Ed says.

"Yes, I've been in those chairs, and, I can tell you, they don't clean them."

"Ma, what do you want from me? If I were there, would the chairs be cleaner? They will take care of it, okay? They don't need me there with one more car. And, in fact, I don't think I even *have* a car here."

"They went to the beauty parlor?"

"Look! Sarah didn't leave me a note. She could be at the hotel for all I know."

"Well, it's not very gracious," Rose says.

⁓

Ed is just sitting down to eat a sandwich of herring in cream sauce when Sarah bursts into the kitchen with Miriam, who looks much smaller after her haircut. His brother, Henry, follows, a taller, heavier man than Ed, and Henry's wife, Susan, brings up the rear, bearing a black garment bag from Mr. Tux.

"Oh, Edward!" Henry exclaims and takes his hand. "It is hot, hot, hot out there. Merciless." He mops his forehead with his handkerchief. "And that tuxedo franchise. Good heavens. The boy there pinched me!"

"Inadvertently," Susan says. "Don't exaggerate, darling. Where should I put this?"

"I was standing in front of the mirror—"

"He was checking the fit in the seat of the pants," Sarah explains.

"—his trousers," says Susan.

Henry cuts them off with a wave of his hand. "*Basta!* I don't think we need to recreate the experience here. Suffice it to say, everything was not as it should be." He turns to Ed. "I hope you're wearing your own.

"It was extraordinary," Henry confides once he is seated at the table with his tall glass before him. "The shirt felt exactly like a hotel sheet; the fabric was absolutely impregnated with chemicals. And do you know, the pockets had Velcro in them!" He turns around and sees that Miriam has gone upstairs with Sarah. "Far be it from me to question the bride," he whispers to Ed. "But where did she get these ideas about the wedding?"

"It's all part of the Orthodox shtick," Ed says gloomily.

"Really! I had no idea this was a religious ritual—tuxedos for eleven a.m. Sunday morning! I could have *brought* my tuxedo. I only suggested renting because Moss Bros. wouldn't let their morning coats out of the country. But tuxedos? Is the dark color significant? Does it have some connection to the frock coat?"

"No, no, it's not a religious ritual, Henry. It's just what people do. I'm talking about—wait a second." Ed interrupts himself and snatches yesterday's *Times* from the recycling bin. "Did you see this?"

Henry puts on his glasses and reads. He sits stock-still for a moment and then folds his glasses up again. He gasps. "Edward! Can this be?" Ed feels a sudden affection for his brother, a real warmth. Henry, with all his scholar-in-exile Anglophiliac affectations, can truly respond to the letter, really understand what it means to Ed. "Good God!" Henry cries. "Tell me this isn't the father of the groom."

" 'Fraid so," Ed says with grim satisfaction.

"But it's so—badly written!"

"Not to mention the point of view."

"The point of view, of course. And the way it's expressed. 'A Palestinian state will be a launching pad and a suicide.' This is really—just too much. You know, it's almost anti-Semitic to print something like this unedited. No, really, Edward. This is an attempt to publicize the Jewish redneck element in the national press."

"But apparently these rednecks exist."

"Not—"

"Not anybody you know? The man is coming down here to become part of our family. And what can you possibly do about it?" Ed demands.

Henry spreads his hands. "What can anyone do? I suppose you'll have to be civil. Where do people learn English like that?"

"Of course I'll be civil." Ed folds the newspaper into quarters. "In fact, I am only mentioning this to you now so we don't have to go through this, you know—"

"Later," Henry says.

"Right. This is going to be Miriam's day, for God's sake, not Zaev Schwartz's."

⁓

Sarah opens the door to Miriam's room that evening to tell her to get ready for dinner. Miriam is asleep on the bed. Wedding presents cover the floor and the desk; foam peanuts squeak under Sarah's shoes. There is a KitchenAid mixer trailing ribbons, a cut-crystal bowl, a sterling candy dish that looks like a large tomato. Then, on the desk, the boxes from the shower, nightgowns, and salad bowls. And glimmering from its open box, in the shadowy light, Henry's shower gift, an enormous topaz ring, perhaps an inch in diameter, smoky gold, almost gauche like a stage ring, almost medieval.

"Miriam, you'd better get dressed. They'll be here in fifteen minutes," Sarah says.

Miriam groans. "I'm so tired." She has taken off the past month from her clinical rotations. It's been weeks since she's stayed up all night every Monday, Wednesday, and Saturday, held cameras for the microsurgeries, checked on the demented patients who throw their feces at the nurses. But she seems to be suffering retroactive sleep deprivation nonetheless. "Where is everybody?" Miriam asks.

"Your sister is setting the table."

"She's here already?"

"Yes, she's here. Your brothers are out getting Grandma."

"Oh, okay."

"So get dressed," Sarah says. "And put on something presentable."

"Like what?"

"I don't know. Like a dress."

"They're all wrinkled."

"Well, you should have thought of that before." Sarah is losing patience. "You'd better iron something."

"Mommy?" the plaintive voice again.

"What?"

"I don't know. I feel kind of—small."

"Well," Sarah pauses at the door, her mind full of cooking times and the fact that there is a crack in the top of the jellyroll. She hears a sort of snuffle from Miriam. Something between sniffling and sighing.

"I just feel like everyone's ordering everyone else around and, and being really clinical about everything." This is Miriam's nightmare, to find that the ugly light and brisk indignities of the hospital follow you into real life as well. Some medical students find symptoms of every disease they study in themselves, but Miriam sees hospital sterility everywhere she looks, a lack of feeling. She has become more religious in the past two years. What else could she be in those white corridors?

"Miriam, I'm not being clinical. I'm trying to make dinner," Sarah says. "Wear the pink dress. The fuchsia one."

The Markowitzes array themselves in the living room, waiting for the Schwartzes. Rose sits in a straight-backed chair; Miriam's brothers sit politely with their feet on the floor but seem too big for the furniture. Susan is upstairs with Sarah, who is ironing Miriam's fuchsia dress, and Ed and Henry pace around together talking about Oxford, almost as if they thought they were being filmed. When the doorbell finally rings and everyone comes in, Miriam is still upstairs, running through the Friday-night service by herself in the dark. Ed holds the door open for Zaev Schwartz.

Zaev is a small, somewhat jowly-looking man with dark shadows under his eyes. He seems to be in an expansive mood now, as he gives Ed a white Xerox copy of a newspaper clipping. "Ed, I don't know if you saw my editorial."

"Mm, mm hmm." Ed places the page with saintly delicacy on the coffee table. Zaev looks disappointed.

In the meantime, the groom's grandmother Ilse Schwartz asks, before she and Rose are even introduced, "Zaev, where is the bride?" Ilse is older and smaller than Rose. She lived in Germany and Israel before following her son to the United States, and her accent is German, with Israeli overtones. Rose looks at Ilse's small, quick eyes and high cheekbones and thinks that she is an imperious woman. Ilse is just a few years Rose's senior. It is Rose who is the grandmother of the bride. Shouldn't she be treated with a little courtesy?

They all sit in the living room before dinner and try to make conversation. "Ed," Zaev says. He has a deep voice, and his accent is the inverse of his mother's, Israeli with German undertones. He is an engineer, which may or may not account for the fact that as he speaks he seems to be giving instructions. "I have never seen heat like you have here in this city. I said to Marjorie, I cannot imagine living with this every summer. I see you have air-conditioning," Zaev continues. "We are talking about putting it in this summer."

"We have the window units," Zaev's wife, Marjorie, explains. She is a moon-faced woman, who seems to Sarah almost aggressively gentle and unassuming.

"But we are thinking about installing central air. Do you know something about this?" Zaev asks Ed.

"No," Ed says.

"Putting central air into a house like ours, built when ours was built, is a major project. A major job. The house has to be raised from its foundation to install the vents."

Henry interjects, "But there are those garden units, are there not?"

"The Japanese ones. That is another option. But you know what the problem is with those? There is just one circuit running the whole system. If anything happens to that circuit, okay?, the whole system goes down. And then you've got a major problem."

Miriam comes down, and Ilse goes to her immediately, gives her a kiss, and ushers her to a seat next to her. "Miriam," she says confidingly in her heavy German accent. "Why have I not heard from you?"

"Heard what?" Miriam asks.

"I have heard nothing from you since you announced your engagement! I've had no letters."

"Oh. I guess I've been so busy I didn't have time," Miriam says.

Ilse shakes her head. "Miriam, do you know that when you marry, you are not just marrying a young man, you are marrying a family."

"It will be interesting to see," Zaev tells Ed and Sarah, "how Miriam and Jon are going to manage when they are homeowners. Jon has never shown any interest in learning about buildings."

"Are you planning to buy them a house?" Susan asks with her very polite, very dry English accent. Sarah cheers her silently.

"No, no, no. I wish I could." Zaev is completely unscathed. "But those guys—" He shakes his head in the direction of the kids.

"Oh, the kids work hard," Sarah says.

"They think they are working hard. Jon doesn't know the meaning of the word *work.* He has no idea. Do you know what Palestine was when I grew up? It was dust. I had my own business, okay?, raising chickens at thirteen. I was doing yard work after school every day—Jon has only had chores in the house to do; he has always had clothes, books, whatever he wanted. This is all he knows. If anything ever happens in this country, is he going to survive? I hope so. But I don't think so. People laugh when I say this, but my mother"—he nods in Ilse's direction—"she came from a very wealthy family, and they lost everything. They were completely unprepared—"

"But she survived," Sarah says.

"Our grandfather Ludwig had seven children," Ilse is explaining to Miriam. "My father was Walter. There were five children, four daughters, Grete, Annette, Otalie, and I, and one son, Frederick. For my parents, he, Frederick, was the only one. My brother was a great mind, he followed the family footprints. You see, he was a biologist like our grandfather and our father, and our two uncles. You have heard of the Krebs cycle?"

"You were related to Krebs?" Miriam asks.

"My uncle knew him. He prepared work on the Krebs cycle before Hans Krebs came to England. He was a great man."

"No kidding," Miriam says, thinking Ilse is still talking about Krebs.

"And my brother inherited his mind."

Rose is sitting in disbelief. This woman is reciting her entire genealogy without acknowledging anyone else in the room! And it seems an intrusion to Rose to hear Ilse carry on about her family: her brother, their house in Breslau, Ilse's three sisters, "one to England, one to New York, I to Palestine escaping, and one perishing in Dachau." The story is not so different from that of Rose's family, and that makes Rose feel odd. She can't help feeling that this is her tale to tell, or that at least she should be telling hers first. She has come to believe in the singularity of her own experience as a refugee in England during World War I, and an immigrant in America. In her mind's eye, with her background as a reader of historical romances, she can't help believing that if there is a greater trend or larger story to be told, then it would have to be her story writ large. It isn't polite the way Ilse is talking; it's nearly plagiarism. "Sarah," Rose says.

"Yes, Rose. You know, I think we should all come to the table. Kids, would you help me carry out the food?"

Rose follows Sarah into the kitchen. Sarah is directing her sons, both taller than she is—"Carry that out first. Both hands"—and she is trying to cut the meat with her electric knife while fending off Miriam with her pained disapproval at the use of electricity on the Sabbath.

Rose takes her pocketbook, climbs the stairs, and hunts around in the small powder-blue bathroom for some hand lotion. She takes the orange bottle of pills out of her purse, swallows one pill, and sits down at the edge of the bed in Sarah and Ed's room. She feels a little dizzy. Below she hears the whir of the electric knife, the family moving into the dining room. Something in all this brings back a memory, real or imagined. She is a small foster child in England, lying in bed listening to the clink of a dinner party below. She has been feeling rather neglected lately, during the preparations for this wedding, but she has not said anything. She is also weaker. She is sure of it. The stairs in this house seem taller and harder to climb. The bookcases higher. Perhaps she will sit on this bed all evening and no one will think of looking for her. She will disappear like Alice down the rabbit hole. She will find a small medicine bottle with a label on it: "Drink this."

Miriam comes in. "Grandma, it's time for dinner. Are you okay?"

"I feel weak," Rose says.

Miriam looks at her concerned. Rose remembers with a rush of pleasure that Miriam will be a doctor. "What kind of doctor are you going to be, dear?" she asks as Miriam helps her down the stairs.

"I don't know," Miriam says.

"I think a psychiatrist might be a good profession," Rose tells her. "Is it a psychiatrist or a psychologist? I can never remember. What's the difference between them?"

"Psychiatrists can write prescriptions and psychologists can't."

"Psychiatrist. That's what I said, isn't it?"

"So you read my article?" Zaev asks Ed at the table. He is too proud of it to let it sit there on the coffee table in the other room without comment.

"You mean your letter to the editor," Ed says. He looks at Zaev and tells himself again that now is the time to act with restraint. It's going to be Miriam's day.

"So what did you think?" Zaev asks.

"I thought it was completely off the mark," Ed tells his future co-grandparent. "To be perfectly frank, it was a complete misreading of the political situation—a very promising, hopeful situation."

Zaev stares at Ed. Then he smiles slightly. "A misreading? No, this is not a misreading. I have some experience—"

"So do I," Ed says.

"You are an academic."

"That's right."

"Yes, that's my point," Zaev says. "With all due respect, you have readings and misreadings, but let me tell you, I have some experience with this area—"

In this area, Ed thinks.

"Listen," Zaev begins.

Ed's inner voice replies, Don't take that patronizing tone with me. Don't start making your global pronouncements about life, the work ethic, and the peace talks to me.

Zaev says, "You have to live in *Eretz Yisrael*—on the land—"

I know what *Eretz Yisrael* means, Ed thinks. You think I don't know a word of Hebrew.

"You have to walk through the hills and valleys. Then you see how small it is and you have a better idea what this land-for-peace means. The country is a splinter, a—what do you call it?"—he turns to his wife.

"A sliver," Marjorie says.

"Really, sliver? Okay, a sliver between the deserts and the enemies. The American government has never been interested in the borders, only in keeping it quiet. This is what I mean when I talk about Kevorkian. This is why I always say that Americans are more interested in painting over the problem than getting to the bottom and solving it. They don't like to get to the root of the matter. This is how they want to get the job done. Do you know, when I wanted to repaint windowsills, three painters told me it would be easier to paint over than strip down to the wood? I spoke to Marjorie's sister. She said, Look, just get someone to schmear it for you; it will look fine. I said, Not a chance. Not a chance. That's not how I do things. This is what I'm talking about when I referred to foreign policy."

"Spare us the metaphors," Ed whispers under his breath.

"What was that?" Zaev asks.

"Nothing," Ed says.

"Sarah," Marjorie says, "this roast is delicious."

"Thank you," Sarah tells her. "Would you like some more?"

"I don't think I could eat any more," Marjorie confesses. She smiles and says, "It's exciting, isn't it? I was talking to a friend of mine in New York whose son got married last summer, and she said something interesting to me. She realized when Ethan got married that it wasn't just a milestone for him—it was a big milestone for *her* as well!"

"Yes, I think that's true," Sarah says. "How about dessert?"

"Can I help you clear?" Marjorie asks.

"No, thanks, stay where you are."

"But I'd like to help." Marjorie rises in her seat and is surprised to find that Sarah puts her hand on her shoulder to keep her there.

"Ed, I need you for the tea," Sarah says.

When he gets into the kitchen and the door swings behind him, Sarah folds her arms across her chest and glares at him.

"What?" he asks, whispering urgently. "I have been perfectly restrained."

"Go," she says.

"That's it. You brought me in here just so you could glare?" He whispers in her ear. "Can I help it if the man is a silly, self-righteous ass?"

"Shah!"

⁓

The dinner is over. Sarah lies on the couch exhausted. Her muscles ache.

"Well, I think that went quite well," Susan says.

"Except for the political interlude," Henry adds.

"Daddy, why did you have to be so grouchy?" Miriam accuses Ed.

"*I* was grouchy?" Ed tries to be good-humored. "I beg your *pedeshka*. Your father-in-law—fine, future father-in-law—was the grouchy one."

"You don't have to have a scene with him every time you see him."

"I didn't have a scene with him."

"Just because you don't like him," Miriam starts.

"It is completely irrelevant whether I like him or not," Ed says. "But I wish you would stop criticizing me."

"I am not criticizing you!" Miriam is getting weepy

again. "You've been acting completely weird ever since I got home." She pauses and then says with sudden insight, "And this isn't even about Jon's father. It's about me getting married!"

"*My* getting married," Ed roars.

"That's what I just said."

"You know, Miriam, I've said in the past, someday you and I are going to sit down and get this straightened out, and I think today is the day we are going to do it! How old are you, twenty-four? You're going to be married in what, two days? Come over here and I'll tell you about gerunds."

"He doesn't listen to me," Miriam says to her mother. "Didn't he hear what I just said?"

"I have news for you," Sarah tells Miriam. "This is not about your getting married. It really is about Jon's father."

Rose decides to give Ed and Sarah a piece of advice. "I've always followed one rule," she tells them from her chair in the corner. "I've never said anything about my in-laws, and I think this is the best thing to do, to avoid trouble in the family. No matter what you think, you should keep it to yourself."

"Come over here, sweetie." Ed puts his arm around Miriam on the couch. "Gerunds are very simple." Miriam closes her eyes and puts her head on his shoulder. She is exhausted. She is not listening. As far as she can tell, he is saying: When you're in reverse, use your common sense and turn the wheel in the direction you want the car to go! "You see? It's dead simple," Ed says.

> *Welcome to our wedding, and thank you for sharing our* simcha, *joy! Our wedding begins with a* kabbalat panim, *literally meeting of faces. Miriam and Jon will hold separate courts, where you can greet*

them. Miriam will be in the social hall, and Jon will hold his groom's tisch, or special groom's party, in the lounge. There he will give a brief d'var Torah, *say a few words of Torah learning.*

Susan is reading the wedding program in the social hall, where Miriam is sitting in her gown, two hundred eighty guests milling around her. "Mm," Susan says. She is wearing a floral dress and a broad-brimmed hat, which she feels does not sit quite right on her head. She has a large head.

"They're marvelous, aren't they?" Henry is standing next to her, stout in his tuxedo, savoring his teriyaki and pineapple on a stick. "I'll have to go get some more."

"No, Henry," Susan says. "It's time for the ceremonial veiling of the bride."

"Veiling? What veiling?"

"You aren't reading the program," Susan reproves him.

Henry peers over at hers. "We haven't been to the groom's court."

"No, I don't think there's time," Susan protests, but Henry guides her into the lounge.

The little room is full of dark-suited men crowding around a long table where Jonathan stands, tall and slim, giving a learned talk from notes and a stack of open volumes of the Talmud. "Good heavens," Henry whispers in Susan's ear.

"I'll meet you outside," she says.

"Wait, why are you leaving?" he clutches her arm.

"Henry," she whispers, "there aren't any women here."

Henry sees that Ed and Zaev are also standing near the door in their tuxedos, each with a white rosebud boutonniere. They are whispering together like ushers at the back of a theater. "Can you hear him?" Zaev asks Ed. "I can't hear one word."

"Can't hear a thing," Ed replies. "And, to be perfectly honest, that doesn't bother me."

"No? I thought you liked this kind of thing."

"What are you talking about?"

"I thought Jon caught this Orthodoxy from Miriam."

"From my daughter! Absolutely not."

"Where does it come from then? I send my son to a yeshiva so he'll learn some Hebrew. Now what have I got? A Talmud scholar! Where does it come from? This is what I want to know."

"Well," Ed says, "I'm just going to try to enjoy the wedding and not think about it."

Then Zaev claps Ed on the shoulder and tells him, "We think alike!"

The speech has ended, and suddenly wild singing begins. The men lock arms and dance around Jonathan. They dance him out the door and nearly flatten Henry against the wall. He escapes, clutching his drink and egg rolls.

"Henry, over here," Susan calls to him in the social hall. "Hurry, or you won't be able to see."

They cannot see Jonathan when he emerges from the huddle of men and stands before Miriam. He rocks back on his heels and pulls the net of Miriam's veil over her face. Then the singing starts up, and the dancing huddle dances him away again. The photographer wants to take more pictures of the family as they stand around Miriam —her brothers, shaven and smoothed down; her sister, who is telling Rose she feels like a sachet pillow in all this lace; Ed, who looks as though he's straining to remember something. But Sarah won't allow any more pictures, because they are running so late.

In the sanctuary a flute plays an Israeli version of a ditty from the Song of Songs, and Miriam walks down the aisle with Ed and Sarah on each side. The guests all rise from their seats as she passes. Henry watches his niece in her slow procession, her gown billowing over her parents' knees in the narrow aisle. He can't help it; he begins to cry. Susan opens her purse and gives him some tissues. "They're crushed, but they're quite clean," she whispers to him. Henry dabs his tears. "She's lovely, isn't she?" says Susan.

"No, it's not that," Henry says. "It's just that I was thinking about our wedding."

"Ours was rather different," Susan says.

"But it reminded me, just the same," Henry tells her.

Rose cannot hear a word, even though she is sitting in the front row. Her hearing aid is acting up, and she can't seem to adjust it properly. The ceremony, the celebration, it is all happening in registers too high or too low. The rabbi is murmuring his speech into the microphone and not enunciating at all. She isn't sure about this man. He couldn't be more than thirty years old, and to her that is not a rabbi. Rose saw earlier that he wasn't even wearing a wedding ring. He does not seem to be established in life, but just looks rather wistful. Perhaps he had a young lady friend who listened to his proposal and then declined! But that is neither here nor there. A proper rabbi wouldn't have such doleful eyes. Miriam, however, is every inch the bride. The dress is not what Rose would have chosen, but it suits her. Rose likes a simpler style. Not so much with the bows and ruffles. And she would have had a proper wedding march. Not Wagner, of course, but at least Mendelssohn.

The rabbi hands Jonathan the light bulb wrapped in a cloth napkin, and Jon stamps it to pieces under his new black Florsheim dress shoe. Rose's hearing aid shrieks as the band sings out its klezmer recessional. The family and the bride and groom are streaming back down the aisle, all the tension of the morning slipping from them.

> *It is a* mitzvah, *good deed, at a wedding to entertain the bride and groom, so as you dance and sing, feel free to let loose and do whatever!*

At the head table, Ed has finished his chicken breast stuffed with wild-rice pilaf. He stands up and surveys the twenty-seven round tables in the social hall, each covered with a peach tablecloth. He feels proud, tired, responsible. He is the ruler of this peach domain. Sarah stands next to him and dings her glass with her spoon, and the hall quiets. "As many of you know," Ed says, reading from his written text, "Sarah and I are Miriam's parents. We would like to say a few words about this young couple we are here to celebrate with. They are gifted with many things: intelligence, energy, determination, youth."

"And they have given us much as well," Sarah adds from her part of the speech. "They have given us joy and laughter. And, of course, they have given us Zaev and Marjorie. We look forward to sharing many happy occasions with you in the future."

Ed takes the microphone. "Jon and Miriam are deeply committed to the sciences, to Judaism, and they have a lot to offer—both to each other and to the world. This is a time of hope in more ways than one. It is a new beginning for Miriam and Jon, and for the Jewish people as a whole. A time of renewal and peace in Israel. There are always going to be skeptics in this world, pessimists and cynics, but at times like this we have a chance to rejoice and to build lasting relationships. I can only say that we wish you the best in love and in life. *L'chaim.*"

"You changed the speech," Sarah tells him when they sit down. "That wasn't in there."

"Yes it was," Ed says.

"In the old version! I specifically edited out that part."

"I know, Sarah, but the new version didn't say what I wanted to say!" He leans back in his chair happily. He doesn't even notice that Zaev has taken the microphone until Zaev starts talking.

"My name is Zaev Schwartz. Marjorie and I would like to thank Ed and Sarah for their hospitality and to say something as well to all of you. First of all, how happy we are that Jonathan found a girl like Miriam to marry. We always wondered what kind of a girl Jonathan would find and now we know. Our son, Jonathan, is very academic, and when he introduced us to Miriam we could see that she was, too. I was sure even then that on this level they would be compatible. As the New Yorkers here know, Jon was always with his head in a book when he was a child—"

"My God," Ed whispers to Sarah, "how long is he going to talk?"

"He would walk everywhere while he was reading and never look where he was going. Miriam, however, I have observed, is of a much more practical bent and she always keeps her eyes open. What we *hope* is that in the future she will keep Jonathan from bumping into the obstacles of life. Because one thing that we all know is that there is no such thing as a perfect world. The best intentions"—he asks Marjorie for a word off-mike—"don't always work out. And the academic theories *most* of the time when they go for a test run take a nosedive. We wish you much health and happiness," Zaev concludes. *"L'chaim."*

Ed has mixed feelings as he leads Miriam to the dance floor. Annoyance at Zaev's rebuttal to his toast, but also a sense of relief. So the man got up, acted like a complete jerk. He didn't come off well; he really wasn't well spoken. Ed took it all with complete equilibrium. This was a wedding reception, after all, not a debate. He and Miriam dance to "You Are the Sunshine of My Life." The videographer trails them with his extension cords. "How're you doing?" Ed asks Miriam.

"I can't believe it's going so fast," she says.

"What?"

"The time, the day."

It's not going so fast, Ed thinks.

⁓

"Is there any coffee?" Rose is asking Sarah at the table.

"Or some tea," Ilse says from her seat on the other side of Rose. "They have tea, do they not?" Ilse asks Rose conspiratorially. Rose looks at Ilse and thinks perhaps there is a bond between them.

"It's coming around," Sarah tells them.

"I am very tired," Ilse tells Rose.

"I am exhausted," Rose says.

"How did you like the rabbi's sermon?" Ilse asks Rose.

"I don't like to criticize," Rose says in German.

"I feel this way, too," says Ilse. "Better to keep silent." Ilse smiles down at the white orchid at her wrist. Rose tires of making conversation. After all, she and Ilse have little in common.

The circle dancing has begun again, fast and furious. The crowds hoist up the bride and groom in chairs. Miriam almost slides off her chair but catches herself just in time. The videographer and his assistant are standing on aluminum ladders to film aerial views of the crowd. Miriam and Jon ride around on their thrones. It is not like flying, more like riding horseback.

On the ground, Marjorie says to Sarah, "You know,

when Zaev and I got married, I think they forgot to lift us in chairs."

"Really?" Sarah asks.

"I think so. They just forgot about it."

Sarah looks at the sweaty mass of Jon and Miriam's friends, the ring of dark-suited boys around Jon, the lacy circle of girls surrounding Miriam. It is not at all like the wedding she and Ed had. When she and Ed entered the hall together, all the guests at the tables stood up and applauded them. Then there was dancing, the fox-trot, the cha-cha, the samba. It had been a very elegant wedding.

Ed comes up behind her. "The band wants to know—one more set?"

"Okay," Sarah says. Liz and Arnie Passachoff come up to tell Sarah they have to slip out early. They have another wedding. "It was beautiful." Liz kisses Sarah.

"One down, three to go," Arnie says, glancing over at Ben, Avi, and Yehudit, who stand near the band mugging for the cameras.

"It's a real milestone for you," Liz tells Sarah.

"And for Jon and Miriam, too," Sarah says.

After Liz and Arnie slip out, Sarah looks at the dancers rushing by hand in hand, some more, some less graceful. She catches sight of Jon in the men's and Miriam in the women's circle. Their flushed faces, Miriam's pinned-up bustle trailing a little. What are they thinking? There is no way to know. They didn't hear a thing their fathers said. They are surrounded by their relatives, yet they are completely oblivious. Yes, she thinks, this is love. The rest will be on video.